George James Atkinson Coulson

Harwood

A novel

George James Atkinson Coulson

Harwood
A novel

ISBN/EAN: 9783337028404

Printed in Europe, USA, Canada, Australia, Japan

Cover: Foto ©Andreas Hilbeck / pixelio.de

More available books at **www.hansebooks.com**

HARWOOD.

A NOVEL.

BY THE AUTHOR OF "THE ODD TRUMP."

New York:
E. J. HALE & SON, PUBLISHERS,
MURRAY STREET.
1875.

PREFACE.

Most Courteous Reader:

The Author has only endeavoured to indicate in these pages how Youth may pass into Manhood through the portals of Grief; how Manhood may grow into full maturity in the practice of self-abnegation, without the lapse of years. For the rest, the story is simply told, and appeals to nothing but your gentler sympathies. And if it shall happen that the characters herein rudely sketched shall assume shape and identity, and grow with you, as they have with him, into living realities, and so awaken your kindly interest, then the Author will have accomplished his purpose and won his reward.

CONTENTS.

HARWOOD.

CHAPTER I.

PRELIMINARY.

YE who listen with credulity to the whispers of fancy, and pursue with eagerness the phantoms of hope; who expect that age will perform the promises of youth, and that the deficiencies of the present day will be supplied by the morrow; attend to the story of "Harwood" and the publishers.

The foregoing is a slight improvement upon the opening sentence of "Rasselas." It has been quoted to many an unhappy student of rhetoric as the culmination of elegance in English composition. It is an undeniable fact that this history of the Abyssinian prince, admitted to the front rank among English classics, is almost unknown to the present enlightened age; and it may be that it has been ostracized, like Aristides the Just, because humanity cannot stand prolonged arrogant assumption, even if well founded. The courteous reader will, therefore, please note that the above sentence is a quotation. The last thing I should dream of doing would be to kill Harwood by writing too elegantly at the outset.

To descend to plain prose, then, I invoke the reader's patience while I relate the story of Harwood's birth. And I counsel the cultivation of this virtue the more earnestly, not only because of its inherent excellence, but also because patience is the very attribute that will be most exercised in getting through the following pages.

More than a dozen years ago I was an exile from home and kindred. It does not matter how this came about, and it is enough to say that the exile was endured in the way of known duty. The Sahara to which I banished myself was the City of New York, and the solitude of that desert was the more horrible from the density of its population. Some good writer, whose name has escaped me, has made a similar remark in different language, and the fact that two writers, who have never met to exchange opinions, should assert the same general proposition, is a strong argument in favour of its verity.

During the day I was constantly occupied, having charge of interests of considerable importance, and labouring under a consciousness of responsibility that was heavy enough to keep my thoughts employed. But.

" When night came o'er the plain,
And moonlight o'er the sea,"

I found myself longing for human companionship. I wandered about the corridors of the hotel, and looked, with all the curiosity I could muster, upon the various types of humanity that crowded them. In all seriousness, I was an object of pity, because in all the throngs I there encountered night after night, there was not a solitary being that awakened or experienced one thought of human sympathy within me or for me. The hotel life became intolerable within a week. To escape from it I wandered through scores of streets running from the Hudson to East River in search of lodgings. At last I found a house in a quiet neighbourhood, where I rented a room. The excitement of the change and the study of my new surroundings availed for two or three nights, and then the loneliness came back.

In all essentials my life was a vagrant one. I always got out of the house when dawn arrived, and wandered about the streets aimlessly until breakfast time. I not only wanted companionship but I also wanted good coffee. At the period to which I refer coffee in its virgin state was a very expensive article, but coffee that was made of chicory, baked beans, burnt sugar and sole leather was comparatively cheap. It is highly probable that tea of some sort of chop, unsophisticated, could be found in most of the eating places; but coffee, never! I read with a daily shudder about forty signs in shop windows, which mendaciously announced that the purest Mocha or Java (always roasted and ground, so as to defy analysis) could be obtained within at an absurdly low figure. My early education had been faulty in that I had never been taught to imbibe tea. In my mind's eye this fragrant beverage was evermore associated in some weird fashion with panada, senna and manna, quassia and chamomile flowers. I longed for coffee but I

found it not. Why, in the name of wonder, did not some enterprising Yankee open a coffee house on Broadway, and set a little
nigger in the window behind plate glass, and let him turn a coffee
roaster, fed with the genuine berry in sight of an admiring public?
He would have rivalled Astor in wealth by this time.

I got meals in this vagabond fashion at numberless eating places,
from Delmonico's down or up, as the reader chooses. I cannot
say that I ate breakfast or dinner. I fed just as a horse does, but
did not dine. You cannot dine in a civilized manner while your
jaws only masticate in grim silence. They were also intended to
be used in conversation; but in my dining places I heard no conversation—nothing but the clatter of dishes and the gnashing of
teeth. This was suggestive, and my loneliness increased. *I began
to pity myself.* And here I pause to warn the gentle reader to avoid
similar folly. It is the first step toward madness. It is the most
indigo-hued of Blue Devils!

One night I met the landlady as I entered my lodgings, and she
very politely invited me into the parlour, saying, " I would find it
more cheerful." In sheer desperation I followed her, and she introduced me formally to four men and four women. They were all
eight talking when I entered, but my glum countenance dampened
them for a little time. I sat by a young lady, and after due delib-
eration I startled her by announcing that it had rained that day.
It is possible that she had learned the fact before, but she was too
polite to say so. And then, the ice being broken, all eight began
to talk again. They talked at me, across me, under my arm, over
my head, and every way but *to* me. I cannot say what kept them
back, but they were somehow repelled. I was negatively magnet-
ized. They had but one topic, upon which they rung countless
changes. It was—well—let us say—the taking of Sebastopol.

My heart was sick of Sebastopol, of Inkermann and of Balaklava.
The Charge of the Six Hundred seemed to be a very foolish piece
of business, and I had a horrible suspicion that the account
was about three quarters lies. But the women—two of them were
deeply pious—made a kind of hideous religion out of the taking of
Sebastopol. The Rugged Russian Bear was the Vicar Apostolic of
the enemy of mankind. Those of the Six Hundred who rode, as
Tennyson says, into the mouth of some place, came out again and
were incontinently canonized. I don't believe they came out at
all. While the talk went on I sat apart and mused. I thought
of thousands of gentle women, and tens of thousands of little chil-

dren, who were widowed and orphaned by the glorious strife over which those four women gloated. There was nothing in their talk to indicate any personal interest in the savage contest, but it is certain that they feasted most ravenously where the carnage was greatest. One of the men was Reverend, and I said something to him about this strange appetite that possessed the women. His answer was a quotation from Holy Writ: "For wheresoever the carcase is there will the eagles be gathered together." He meant me to understand that the women were she eagles, and he thought the eagles were good birds. I did not tell him that those mentioned in his quotation fed on carrion. It was less lonely in my room, and I slipped out unnoticed, leaving them regaling.

It was too early for bed, so I lighted a cigar. Something that had been said in the parlour brought to my mind a family I had known in another city. There were some remarkable incidents in their history, and as the smoke gathered around my head I began to fill up intervals in their story, weaving a sort of plot. I found comfort here, and getting my portfolio I began to write. It was a total change in my habits of thought: It was the inception of a Purpose: I would write a Book!

And so, night after night, for months, the work proceeded. My loneliness was gone. The people who grew up into shape and individuality were living realities to me. Oh, reader! if they shall also grow into realities with thee!

Thus was "Harwood" born. During the day the calls upon my faculties were almost incessant, but I would catch myself or my thoughts at odd intervals slipping away from the unreal events of my daily life to the dear friends who were waiting for me in my portfolio. I always quitted them with regret and returned to them with delight. In them I found companionship and sympathy. I did not force them to keep within any set grooves. I had settled their destinies, it is true; yet I allowed them to reach their various goals in their own way. Ordinarily, they were tractable enough, but sometimes they took the bit in their teeth and bolted. The reader will please bear this in mind, and whenever these characters misbehave in any way, remember that the author was blameless.

One night—or rather one morning, for I remember hearing the clock strike two—I wrote "Finis." It was a great shock to me. For a week I was dispirited and nervous, and then I began a sequel: "The Lacy Diamonds." Have patience, gentle reader; it is progressing.

CHAPTER II.

BOOK MAKING.

WHEN "Harwood" was finished I was still a comparative stranger in New York. I had business acquaintances by the score, but I had no intimate friends. The good natured people whom I encountered in my daily occupation treated me well and kindly, but I knew none of them well enough to venture even a hint of authorship to them. Busy men, all of them, hunting dollars while the sun shone, and begrudging the minutes wasted in unremunerative conversation. There were certain topics of absorbing interest to me which would also interest them. But they all looked at these only on one side, and I soon discovered the profitless nature of any discussions.

It chanced one day that business brought me into contact with a publishing house that had not been long established in the metropolis. The accidental acquaintance thus begun ripened rapidly into friendship. The members of this firm knew something about Sebastopol and the Charge of the Six Hundred, and held my views about that notable conflict. It was very refreshing to me to spend occasional half hours in this pleasant company; and meeting always a cordial welcome, I gradually fell into the regular habit of smoking my after-lunch cigar in their establishment, discussing new books with reference both to their commercial value and their intrinsic merits. Very frequently I would find them engaged in reading and correcting proofs of their own publications, of which they already had a considerable list. I had forgotten "Harwood," which was packed away among sundry fragmentary manuscripts at home—after taking a journey which will be recounted in the succeeding chapter. I retained a somnolent sort of interest in the bantling, feeling a father's affection for it, mingled with a compassionate appreciation of its demerits. With Touchstone I thought, "An ill-favoured thing, sir, but mine own." So, while I gathered in many new facts, and became somewhat learned in the art of book making, the thought of getting "Harwood" dressed in type never occurred to me.

As a rule, my friends did not publish fictitious literature. Reams of this description of property were offered to them on the most flattering terms. Nearly all the authors who sent their precious manuscripts generously proposed that the firm should print the work at their own expense, and allow the usual royalty to the writer. I am convinced that none of the authors dreamed of anything less than ten editions, if the work could only be got into print and within reach of a hydra-headed public, waiting with bated breath for copies, hot from the press. As our intimacy progressed I learned the stereotyped form of rejection. "The present state of trade;" "would be pleased to print at the expense of the author, involving an outlay of so many dollars;" and other polite intimations that must have been eminently disgusting to the manuscript makers. There seemed to be an inexorable law that connected authorship with impecuniosity.

On one occasion I happened to be present when my friends were packing up one of these forlorn manuscripts to return "by express" to the rightful owner. I had heard of its arrival some days previously.

"Have you really read that great mass of papers ?" I inquired.

"Certainly," answered the junior.

"How much is there ?"

"Seven hundred and eight pages," he replied.

"What is it about ?"

"I don't know. The title is—" and he turned the parcel over and consulted the first page—"'The Remorse of the Victim.' There are some very good things in it. Some of the words are in five syllables."

"Did you understand them all ?" said I.

"Oh, no," he answered coolly. "I don't think the author understood them either, but that makes no difference. Did you ever read 'Talmanasia ?'"

"No."

"Nor 'Shanghi ?'"

"No, certainly not," I replied, with a shudder.

"My dear sir," said he, with a grisly compassion, "you are not abreast of the age! Haven't read 'Shanghi!' Don't you ever read *anything* ?"

"Yes," I faltered, "I read the *Herald* sometimes. Have *you* read 'Shanghi ?'"

"Not exactly *read* it, but I have sold five hundred copies. It is a great success. The publisher paid ten thousand dollars for the manuscript and copyright. Made money on his investment too."

This interview made a profound impression upon me. I knew a

man who was the happy owner of " Shanghi," and as my conscience forbade an investment in that direction, I borrowed the
book, from which I had read sundry extracts when it appeared.
That night I sat down resolutely and began the book. I read two
chapters at the beginning, two in the middle, and two at the end
of the story. I did *not* have a stroke of apoplexy, nor cerebro-
spinal meningitis; but I shall die in the belief that an additional
chapter would have given me both these ailments with a touch of
delirium tremens thrown in. The next day I took " Harwood "
with me at lunch time and left it with my friend.

"I have known you to read about forty bulkier manuscripts," I
said, "and I have brought this for you to read. I just want your
candid judgment, comparing this with the forty you have read and
rejected. Of course I have no expectation of printing it. Read it
at your leisure."

" What is it ?" said he.

" It is a novel which I wrote some years ago. It kept me from
going mad while I was making it. If you find, in attempting to
read it, any symptoms of delirium tremens creeping over you, I
hope you will stop in time. I have not read one line in it since
I finished it, and I do not expect ever to read a line of it in the
future."

" All right," he answered cheerfully, " I will read it with
pleasure."

It will only be when the gentle reader closes this book (with a
sigh of relief) that he can appreciate my amazement at my next
interview with my book making friend.

" ' Harwood ' is a first class story," said he, decidedly, " and we
will be glad to publish it if you desire us to do so."

" Are you serious ?" said I.

" Entirely serious," he answered. " We will print it whenever
you say the word, but I advise you first to try some one else—I
mean some other publishers."

" I do not understand you," I replied. " I have little or no
acquaintance with other publishers, and if I had I would select
your house out of the whole world of publishers. What do you
mean by such advice ?"

" Simply this: we are not much known to the trade as publishers, especially of fiction, and our customers are mainly among
houses that do not deal in novels. Now, it can do no harm to
take ' Harwood ' to these other firms which have a larger outlet

for just this sort of literature, and if they will print it, giving you a copyright, let them have it on any reasonable terms they may propose. Haven't you written another story?"

"Yes," I answered with a charming blush, "I have written a sequel to 'Harwood'—that is, I am writing it now."

"Well, suppose you get one of these firms who have a large list of novel-buying customers to issue 'Harwood,' and suppose they place it in the hands of five or ten thousand readers, don't you see that another novel by the author of 'Harwood' would have a large sale?"

The senior partner stood by, apparently endorsing this proposition. These gentlemen have had large experience in book making, I thought, and they must be right.

"Have you read 'Harwood?'" I asked.

"Not all of it," he replied, composedly. "I have looked over it. You know, if we print it I shall have the opportunity to read the proofs. Your penmanship is peculiar, *very* peculiar. I have read manuscript for forty years, and thought I was equal to anything, but yours is——very peculiar."

It did not seem politic to pursue this branch of the subject. I tucked "Harwood" under my arm and prepared to depart.

"Do not misunderstand us," said the junior, following me to the door. "We would be glad to publish your book at once, but, for your own sake, and for the sake of the larger circulation, you had better let Pippinville or Charlesburg have it. They have an outlet for ten thousand copies, and that is better than ten thousand separate advertisements. Go to Pippinville! I read the manuscript aloud, and all my auditors pronounced it a first rate story. If you are doubtful, you might submit it to some other critic, in whom you have confidence; but, remember, we are ready to print whenever you say the word. I don't like the title much; it indicates nothing."

"I'll call it 'The Remorse of the Victim,'" I said promptly.

"I don't think that would be an improvement. What do you call your other story?

"'The Lacy Diamonds.'"

"That is better. Good morning."

CHAPTER III.

THE FIRST ORDEAL.

I HAVE read somewhere of a young mother who waited with un-speakable anxiety for the verdict of society upon her baby. To her it was the loveliest infant that ever wore long clothes. It did not talk or walk, but that mother was entirely satisfied that it could do both if it pleased. She had always rather liked babies, and made full allowance for any little departures from the path of rectitude of which they were guilty; but the peculiarity in her baby's case was that it made no such departures. When it first said "Goo!"—which, by-the-bye, is a very common remark for in-fants to make—that mother translated the monosyllable into a long speech in English without the aid of lexicographers. If you had the temerity to suggest a possible error in her rendering of "Goo!" this young mother, if polite, would not pluralize the original and apply it to you in words, but she would do so in her inmost soul.

Some such experience was mine a few months ago when I dug "Harwood" out of a mass of fragmentary manuscripts. You see it was my first born. The horrible dread of a public verdict—the possible *bête noir* of all embryo authors—haunted me and kept the precious infant hidden a dozen years. I cannot tell what brought him to light at last, but am free to confess that I entertained a profound affection for him. I did not read the manuscript! There were one hundred and fifty-six closely written pages! It was written on foreign post paper, very thin and flimsy, and the ink had faded a little. I had selected this paper because I intended to mail the manuscript to *Parlours' London Journal,* which in fact I did. I do not call that the first ordeal, however, because nobody with a grain of sense could expect a journal that published such trash as *Parlours'* contained would appreciate "Harwood." In due time I got my manuscript back with a polite note (I don't believe the fellow read a page of it), and a gentle rebuke for not sending "postage stamps for return MS.," according to advertise-ment. It is only just to qualify the above remark about trash, which should be limited to the *serial* stories in *Parlours'.* All the rest is of good quality.

Between the date of "Harwood's" birth—or I should say his death, at the murderous hands of *Parlours'*—and the date of his resurrection, I had written sundry small squibs, waifs upon the broad sea of light literature, and these had met with a fair degree of success. They were printed in a monthly still living, and which I hope may live a thousand years. The editor (may he live a thousand years, too!) has been my true and constant friend, and one strong manifestation of his friendship was in his treatment of my fugitives. He would change objectionable words, and mend my lapses in taste or diction—never altering but to improve, never touching but to adorn. Sometimes he would wholly reject some carelessly written story, healing the bruise to my vanity by saying "it was not worthy of my reputation!" and he was always right in the rejection, if his salve *was* a flattering unction. I knew his taste was perfect, his judgment sound, and his scholarship beyond question. Had I been handled by a critic less acute or less friendly I should have been snubbed, and should have laid my pen aside. But he encouraged while he instructed me, and of all the helpers I have met in my literary working he has been most helpful. What can I render him in requital? I dedicate "Harwood" to him with the hand of my heart.

Having said this much in his praise, the melancholy duty remains to say a word *per contra*. He is an editor! To fill this office worthily it is necessary that a man should divest himself of ordinary human attributes. Of course, I refer to editors of magazines, whose chief writing is in the reviews or critical notices of new books. Your regular review writer is not necessarily truculent, as in most cases he does not read the books whose titles he places at the head of his articles, using them merely as mottoes, upon which he builds his essay. He need not read more than a sentence or two (in order to quote) and he scarifies or pats his author on the back without the slightest reference to the special deliverance under review, but with due regard to his previous record, his political or theological proclivities, or any other matter which the reviewer wishes to praise or blame. I know this is the system, for I, also, have written quarterly articles. But this does not apply to your magazine editor!

The busy bee sucks his sustenance from the opening flower, and it is honey. The gentle lamb that little Laura had, and the cross-grained old ram he became in later months, subsisted on grass. The giraffe that stalks over the arid African desert browses on the tree tops. The ostrich, his countryman, is said to feed on tenpenny nails. The fierce Rodent, whose story is so frequently repeated in "The House that Jack built," ate corn or malt, and was eaten in turn by Grimalkin. The larger feline beast that prowls in tropic jungles, with shaggy mane and hideous roar, eats antelopes and other small deer—and man eats meat and bread until he becomes an editorial critic. Then he changes his diet and subsists upon the gore of authors! He tomahawks them, he scalps them (unless they have failed to use the Balm of Columbia and have ceased to be hirsute), and he sucks their blood. He sits upon their carcases like a vampire and fans them with his wings while he drains their arteries!

As my kind friend belonged to this fraternity it would hardly be supposed that I would trust "Harwood" in his clutches. But I did. It was like sending a dear little infant to play in the lava beds with Captain Jack in the neighbourhood. But I did it, thus arguing:

If he grinds his bones into powder and gloats over my misery in bereavement, it will be in manuscript, and, therefore, more tolerable. It is far better to be crushed in this form than in print. And, besides, he has to crunch the bones, like Bulwer's Griffin, in solitude, and cannot appeal to an admiring public until the book is published. Then, he has praised my minor efforts once and again, and perhaps he may say, " it is no worse than the current trash of the day !" Or he may have recently gorged himself with the gore of some unlucky wretch who preceded me, and, with sated appetite, would glance complacently over part of the hundred and fifty-six pages. Or he may dismiss me with a graceful wave of his editorial hand, and with compassionate kindness say, "Burn it, my friend, burn it!" These are the various things I *expected*. I knew he would tell the truth; I knew he would pounce upon blemishes and root them out; and one morning I drank a cup of strong coffee and sent him my manuscript!

After the thing was done beyond recall I began to repent. I did not much care for the demolition of my book, but I suddenly remembered that my characters would also perish! "Oh, my gentle Ret!" I thought, "how could I be so cruel as to consign thee to such tender mercies! If I had sent thee to visit Scarfaced Charley it is true thy lovely tresses might dangle at the belt of the savage, but now! thou art exposed to a more hideous fate! In painting thee I have dealt so tenderly with thee from the very first that I have grown to love thee, my darling, and now, poof!

2

with one stroke of his pen this vampire will consign thee to blank annihilation." I was heartily miserable. *Parlours'* murder did not hurt me one whit, but this time, if killed, " Harwood " would be beyond the curative powers of burnt brandy.

And so passed two wretched days. On the third my manuscript came back, neatly wrapped up and sealed. You know when you bury a fellow you put him in a mahogany box and varnish it. My friend is neat and orderly in his habits, and I fancied I could see him smacking his lips as he wrapped up that corpse, and gleefully wrote my address in those plain round characters of his. I knew, when I should raise the lid—I mean, unwrap the parcel—I should find his " comments " among the bones, written in the same plain hand.

Brush away the tears from your eyes, dear sympathizing reader, and go on with me to the end. I untied the parcel, found the comments neatly folded reposing upon the first page of my manuscript, and, summoning all my manhood, I opened and read what follows :

" MY DEAR —— : You need not be afraid to send that story to any publisher; and as for the critics, you may snap your fingers at them. It is good—out and out. I had intended taking it by instalments of 30 or 40 pp., but I got so interested in the thing that I went clear through in two sittings. It is natural, affecting, powerful.

" But——"

The reader need not heed the " buts," though I did. A whole army of " buts " could not vanquish that elegant sentence which I have honestly quoted, every word. You cannot add to it. Oh, reader, be encouraged! If a blood-thirsty editor could say so much, what must thou not say, who art so kind and gentle? Oh, critic! let fall thy blade on vulnerable crests; " Harwood " bears a charmed life!

Here endeth ordeal the first.

CHAPTER IV.

THE SECOND ORDEAL.

THOSE "buts" of my friendly critic gave me occupation for several nights. I cannot point out all the amendments he suggested now. The reader will please give him credit for any passages that appear particularly brilliant. The needed emendation was a labour of love, and I was specially elated at the thought that I had "bagged" one of the gunners, whose business was to slaughter romances. As for the rest—Thomas, Richard and Henry —I have been snapping my fingers at them, in my mind's eye, ever since I emerged from the primal ordeal. The athlete who comes unscarred from his first arena enters the second with the calm confidence that presages victory.

It was necessary to make a selection. There are numerous publishers in this happy country, who give to its myriad readers all sorts of printed pabulum. I could not divide "Harwood" to oblige them, and I did not desire to stir up a contention among them by letting them all know the manuscript was open to propositions from type setters. Clearly, I was bound to move cautiously and see what "terms" would be proposed. One at a time.

The name that first occurred to me was

FIDLER & BROTHERS.

There were four reasons for giving this firm the precedence: first, they publish an unlimited quantity of novels. It is probable that they have some mode of classification unknown to the general public, but I arranged them in three classes in my own mind—as those I had read, those I had tried to read, and those from whose titles I had recoiled with unspeakable horror. Among the first class was a recent novel called "Biddy's Mistress". I read this while it was being printed serially in *Parlours' Journal,* and survived, because I took it in small doses as one takes castor oil in small, gelatinous capsules. The only impression left by the story is a feeling of thankfulness that it is over, and will not have to be taken again. I may as well say here, that "Biddy's Mistress" is by the author of about a dozen similar stories that have appeared serially in *Parlours' Journal,* and I am satisfied that they were all written by the editor of that periodical. Nothing but the fond blindness of paternity could ex-

cuse any editor for printing such astounding trash. And this
prolific gentleman is the writer of the polite note that accompanied
my returned manuscript, and that contained the complaint about
postage stamps! Yet, Fidler & Brothers have reproduced these
inane narratives, which, being capsuled, I place in the first class—
as those I have read. "Biddy's Mistress" was the last, and my resentment is still aglow against it.

. Now, I argued, if Fidler & Brothers can print and find circulation for "Biddy's Mistress," what may they not do with "Harwood?"

The other three reasons may be taken together: Messrs. Fidler
& Brothers also print three periodicals of their own, and I think
they give serials in all of them; one of these has a circulation that
is "unprecedented." If, therefore, they should appreciate my
work, and present it first—serially—in the unprecedentedly cir-
culating medium; and secondly, using the same type, print it in
book form, I should be sure of reaching the greatest possible number of readers. It was not precisely patriotism that inspired me
to make the offer to them; it was philanthropy. I wished to confer the greatest good upon the greatest number. That I failed
was not my fault; but it was the lasting misfortune of all Fidler
& Brothers' clients.

To recount the story of my failure with this enterprising firm,
let us begin at the beginning: I took my precious manuscript
and visited their colossal establishment one day about noon. I
climbed numberless steps in a spiral iron staircase, in search of
the authority who controlled the unprecedented periodical. I
found him occupied with a mass of manuscripts, and looking as
cool and collected as a blue bottle fly caught in a glue pot; or, if
you please, in a mass of amber.

"Sir," said I, with a polite bow, "I have brought you a manuscript."

"For the Unprecedented, sir?"

"Yes, sir; if it should be found suitable;" and I handed the
precious packet. He received it very graciously and placed it in a
pigeon hole.

"I will have to trouble you to call again, sir, in about a week,"
he said. "I have several manuscripts here that have precedence."

"Before I go, sir," said I, "allow me to show you a note I have
just received from another editor, who is also a very severe critic,"
and I produced my friend's epistle. "You need only read the
first sentence to see *his* estimate of the work."

He took that note, which ought to be printed in golden letters and placed in a gorgeous frame, glanced incuriously at it, and handed it back without comment. I thought I had "done" him, whereas I had only "done" Harwood.

Let me explain.

The forty unfortunate gentlemen who were smothered in boiling oil by Ali Baba's servant had, no doubt, an affection for each other. Indeed, there · is a proverb extant, applied to persons of their occupation, which gives them credit for honourable dealings among themselves. But editors are not troubled with similar amiable weaknesses. My opinion is, they would enjoy cutting each other's throats. · So, when I revealed to the editor of the Unprecedented the flattering opinion of the other, I might as well have committed "Harwood" to the flames. Love me, love my dog.

Punctually, at the end of the week I climbed the spiral stairs again. My editor was ready for me. Doubtless he was ready an hour after my first interview.

"I have read your book, sir," he began, with the benevolent smile that always precedes rejection. "I found it very interesting."

"I hope you will find room for it, then, in the 'Unprecedented.'"

"Well, no," he said, with gushing tenderness, "it does not exactly suit."

"Will you please favour me with your reason ?"

"It is quite readable," said he, gently, "but it is not quite up to the Mark !"

I began to get into a rage, not violent, but suppressed. "Harwood" was rejected, so I might indulge in a venomous remark or two.

"I believe you printed "Biddy's Mistress," not only in your periodical but afterwards in a book."

"Yes ; that is one of Snooks'. We always print Snooks' stories."

"If you will allow me to say so," I ventured to say, "I think my story is better reading than 'Biddy's Mistress.'"

"Yes, so do I; but Snooks has a reputation, and I think he writes more in modern style. Your story is a little old fashioned, but it is quite interesting."

"If you mean by 'old fashioned' that it does not contain any indecent allusions, to make it unfit to appear in any virtuous household, you are certainly right."

This only made him smile. It occurred to me, also, that there were several old fashioned stories that did not come under that category.

" If you choose to offer your manuscript to the other periodical," said the editor, " it may be they will take it."

" Thank you, no!" answered I. " I wished to print it in your Unprecedented for the sake of the circulation and consequent notoriety. I am writing a sequel—'The Lacy Diamonds'—and I depended a little upon the reputation 'Harwood' might gain to create a demand for that. Of course, I expected your house to print it in book form also."

" You might apply to them," said the editor politely, "but I don't think they would print it."

" Of course not," I said, as I rose to leave him; " I could hardly expect Messrs. Fidler & Brothers to do so. As there is no international copyright, they get food for their types without expense. I am sorry you have had to read so many pages of defective penmanship in vain."

" Oh, that is a mere matter of business," he replied wearily; " while I am reading one I do not have to read another."

As I revolved around the spiral staircase in descending, I thought I would count the steps. There were seventy-one. If he had rushed out after me and offered me for " Harwood" ten dollars a step for the two times I had surmounted them and the two times I had descended, he would have received a prompt denial— " Harwood" was no longer for sale. Twenty eight hundred and forty dollars would have been no temptation.

At the last step I found my good humour again. That wretched man up stairs has to sit there day after day, reading manuscripts! How could I harbour resentment against him? And then he has to cater to a depraved taste, and it was not his fault that " Harwood" did not reach the Mark. I wonder if " Biddy's Mistress" has made that attainment? Fidler & Brothers have published, it and sold ten thousand copies, no doubt. People have bought the book and read it, all over the country. Heaven forbid that the author of " Harwood" should ever write up to that Mark!

CHAPTER V.

THE THIRD ORDEAL.

ALMOST all modern novel writers have fallen into the pernicious habit of printing their works serially. The fraud was, doubtless, originally introduced by magazine proprietors, who secured a continuance of subscription by stringing out a long novel, by a popular author, through consecutive numbers of their periodicals. Dickens, Bulwer, Thackeray, Collins and others fell into the trap, which (in their cases) was probably well baited; but it is an abominable practice, and, so far as authors are concerned, it is suicidal. People have slidden naturally from books to magazines, and in another generation they will slide from magazines to newspapers; and then the last refuge of fiction writers will be the *New York Ledger* style of narrative, "To be continued." All of the "deathless" works of Fielding, Scott and others, who lived before serials were invented, will be dead as several door nails!

I must confess, however, that this choice bit of moralizing is an afterthought, which came to my mind at the end of the third ordeal, which remains to be recounted.

In addition to the slight stories which I wrote for the magazine edited by my friendly critic, I wrote a multitude that he could not find room for. These were published in various New York periodicals, the best of them in *Pippinville's Hebdomadal.*

Nothing could be more satisfactory than the treatment I received from the conductors of this periodical. Of all the papers I prepared for them none were ever rejected, excepting one, and I think that was crowded out, perhaps, by matter from other contributors. At all events, my relations with the *Hebdomadal* were always pleasant, and I felt certain that I had the inside track there when I concluded to offer my larger bantling to them. Messrs. Pippinville are very extensive publishers also, and have the reputation of liberality in their dealings with authors whom they immortalize with their types. For book printing my prospects were a hundredfold brighter with them than with Messrs. Fidler & Brothers. But I had the "serial" fever still raging, and the *Hebdomadal* was my next choice, failing the *Unprecedented.* The editor was a graceful writer, whose occasional contributions

I had always read with great pleasure, and it is quite possible that he had a fairish sort of opinion of my offerings, for which he has given me several small cheques.

When I presented myself and my manuscript to Mr. Bland, therefore, I felt confident that I should find this last ordeal a very smooth one. There might be reasons, such as far extended engagements with other writers, that would bar "Harwood," but I thought his merits would be recognized at least.

"Good morning, Mr. Bland," said I, as I entered his sanctum. "I have not been in the *Hebdomadal* for so long a time that you are in danger of forgetting me. The last time I was here you surprised me by returning my manuscript."

"We are still rejecting very freely," answered Mr. Bland. I don't know whether he intended this for a semi-apology, for a stopper upon further offerings, or for a warning. I was undaunted, however, and I drew out my hundred and fifty-six pages.

"Well, sir," I said, "I beg to offer you a novel——"

"Oh, you will have to see Mr. Chokemoff," he answered, hurriedly; he attends to the publication of books. You will find him——"

"Excuse me," said I, interrupting him. "I don't want Mr. Chokemoff. I wish you to print this serially in the *Hebdomadal*. Of course, Messrs. Pippinville will utilize the type already set up, and print it in book form after you have done with it."

"I don't see how I can do it," answered Mr. Bland, discontentedly. "I already have a serial running, and have no space to spare, unless," he added, after a pause, "it should be for something particularly attractive."

"Perhaps you can decide better after looking at my manuscript."

"Very well, leave it with me, then; I will try to look through it in a day or two."

A "day or two" always means three days at least. I waited three days and called again. Mr. Bland had not had time to examine "Harwood," but he opened the parcel and glanced at it with infinite disgust.

"Thin paper!" he muttered, wrathfully, "and pale ink! It seems to me that writers go out of their way to give trouble to manuscript readers!"

"I regret the thin paper very much," I said, "but I intended the story for an English journal, and——"

"To save a few cents postage you wrote on this abominable paper!" he answered, finishing the sentence for me. "Oh, dear! it is in the form of a journal!" and he turned over a dozen leaves rapidly, "and letters!!" and here his patience entirely forsook him, and he stuffed the thin leaves back into the portfolio with a groan.

"My dear sir," I began, humbly, "I could not help it. The form in which the story is told—and most of it is literally true——"

" That is no advantage!"

" Well, the most natural way to get the events narrated was as I have done it. Indeed, I do not see how I could do otherwise. If I could only persuade you to read a little way into the story——"

"Leave it until Saturday, then," he said, savagely. "I *will* read it, but I don't see how I can use it."

I waited until Monday.

Mr. Bland was quite composed when I appeared the next time. He had read enough to get humanized a little.

" I have read part of your story," said he. " It is interesting, but the title won't do. You ought to call it 'Adventures in the Southwest.' The name don't indicate anything. That description of the panther business is very readable ; but the title won't do."

" You have not read enough, sir." I was getting mad by this time. " If you had gone a little further you would have found that the title is very appropriate. Now, please understand the case. I have no difficulty to surmount to get 'Harwood' into type, but I am anxious to secure a large circulation. I am writing a sequel, 'The Lacy Diamonds,' and if I can make 'Harwood' a success the next book will make its own way. If you print it first in the *Hebdomadal,* and afterwards in a duodecimo book ——"

" Can't do it," said Mr. Bland, "it will have to be octavo. Could not use the type in duodecimo."

" Well, I don't care about the size, but I do care about getting the Pippinville imprint. If you would only break your leg, or something, so that you would have to lie about at home for a few days, you might get time to read the whole of the story."

"Leave it a few days longer," he answered, setting his teeth with desperate determination, " and I will get through it; but I don't see how I can possibly use it in the *Hebdomadal.* Perhaps the house will publish it, though."

It is possible that the reader has had some experience of battle-fields. If so, he will remember that the excitement that resembles trepidation passes away pretty soon after one gets positively under fire. At first, the guns make a great deal of noise, and the chance of getting hurt appears quite promising, especially if one can *see* the fellows that are shooting; but in a short time one ceases to notice the dust and smoke and the snappish rattle of the guns, and goes into the business with cold blooded ferocity. I began my series of ordeals with becoming modesty and humility; at the end of the third and last I was bloodthirsty. I knew perfectly well that the next interview with Mr. Bland would be the crisis. I postponed it ten days. He should not say I hurried him.

I am somewhat discomposed at revealing to the "general public" so many of the secrets of book making, but candour is one of my weaknesses. It may be that some would-be author will light upon these revelations, and, profiting by my experience, he may be led to abandon that Sisyphus-like occupation. It is the easiest thing in nature to write a book; it is somewhat more difficult to get type, as these adventures of mine will prove, and then there is something still to be encountered. Critics? Bah! who cares for critics? If any would-be author dreads them, let him try *himself* to cut up some other author. He will soon find what a harmless sort of amusement it is! But, rash man, know there is the PUBLIC! Ah, there is the only ordeal to be dreaded! You may get some kind friend (like the present writer, for example) to give you a word of encouragement; you may get through Fidler & Brothers and Pippinville and Co., but beware of that hydra-headed monster—The Public!

CHAPTER VI.

The Third Ordeal Concluded.

AT the expiration of the ten days I found Mr. Bland in his cosy sanctum. He was waiting for me and his mind was made up. But being a good natured man he intended to let me down gently.

"I have read your manuscript," he began, "and found it interesting."

" In spite of the journal and letters ——"

" Yes. Those are certainly faults, but not fatal faults. It would have been far better to have told the story in the third person, instead of the first. But there are more serious objections."

" What are they ?"

" Well, it is an American novel. Nobody wants an American novel. I hardly know how an American novel could be made a success.",

" I believe you have printed two or three in the *Hebdomadal*, and issued them afterwards as books, and you have had a good sale for them. Indeed, I have been told that the author had obtained a very handsome price from another publisher for her last copyright." This was intended for a shot between the eyes. I knew there must be more or less soreness on that subject, as there is more or less rivalry between publishers.

" We did print the books you refer to," said Mr. Bland, " but there was something *in* them. I mean in quantity. Now, yours —— Why, there's nothing of it !"

" One hundred and fifty-six pages——"

" Equal to less than a hundred of print! Have you counted the words ?"

" Yes. There are between four and five hundred words on a page."

" Well. The *Hebdomadal* has seventeen hundred nearly. If I were to print " Harwood " serially it would run through about three months and then it would make an octavo of eighty pages. There's nothing of it ! I tell you there's nothing of it !"

" I might enlarge it somewhat," said I, rather disconcerted. "There is hardly any descriptive writing in it ——"

" No use. It is too old-fashioned. And then the date !"—and he pulled " Harwood " out of his pigeon hole and viciously tore him open—" Eighteen hundred and thirty-six ! Do you know that was nearly forty years ago ? Why, nobody was born at that era ! You might as well have laid the scene on Mount Ararat and described the landing of Noah and his family. Oh, the date is totally out of the question."

" My dear sir, I think I have mentioned before that the sequel —'The Lacy Diamonds'—— "

" Oh, we have nothing to do with the sequel. The date must be obliterated. You need not have *any* date. What in the world

do you want with a date? Nobody cares about dates—that is,
nobody is going to grope in the darkness of remote antiquity when
he is reading a novel. Scratch out all the years, and leave the
months only."

"Well, that might be done, I suppose. Perhaps you are right.
Anyhow, I perceive the *Hebdomadal* rejects the story. Give me
the manuscript."

"There's Mr. Chokemoff. You might try him. The story is
interesting. I read a hundred and forty pages and then turned
over to see how it ended. But there's nothing of it! They might
perhaps print it and give you a copyright, if you could make it
three or four times as big. I don't see how you could enlarge it,
though. Look at this!" and he snatched a book from a shelf,
"here is one of those novels you spoke of—there are four hundred
pages of over eight hundred words! Three hundred and twenty
thousand words! Now, there is something of that!"

"I am ashamed to say that I have not read it. In fact, I did
not try. Good morning, Mr. Bland."

My portfolio felt very lank and light as I turned my back upon
Pippinville's establishment. I saw great rows of fat books,
quartos and octavos, and wondered how the writers had ever got
so many words together. Do words roll out of successful writers
as water bubbles up from a spring? I saw "Trench on Words,"
and had half a mind to buy it. I knew a man in New York who
could talk straight on for seven years without fatigue, and without
saying anything. I thought of getting him shut up somewhere
with a stenographer, and so making the requisite number of pages.
Words! I had been under the delusion that Ideas were the important things.

But the objections to "Harwood" looked formidable as I reflected upon them. "Old-fashioned and out of date!" If this is
well taken then Ivanhoe and The Talisman come under the same
condemnation. Perhaps these critics referred rather to the style
than to the matter? And here "Harwood" is possibly faulty. I
endeavoured to write plain, simple English, and modern light
literature is often made up of dictionaries and encyclopedias.
"Journal and letters!" Well, "Rob Roy" is all made up of letters,
and "Redgauntlet" is largely so composed, and these books have
been tolerably successful. As for the journalistic form, Wilkie
Collins has managed to invest it with considerable interest in
"The Woman in White." The "Date!" Mr. Bland was parti-

cularly savage in his assault upon the date. But I happened to remember a book, entitled "Waverley; or, 'Tis Sixty Years Since." If Sir Walter could go back sixty years I might venture on forty.

Supposing these disposed of, there remains the unanswerable "Nothing of it!" Poor, little "Harwood!" After my long incubation have I really only hatched out a mouse? Is it only on a par with one of those pious Sunday-school books, whose heroine gets to heaven by having a drunken father, and a mother dying of consumption? One hundred and fifty-six pages! Do you call that nothing? And besides, the story is all told, be it long or short. It seems to me that the time to stop writing is when you have completed your story. Something must be done, however, to enlarge my book, and I suddenly remembered that I could get valuable suggestions from Mr. Vampyre.

I became acquainted with Mr. Vampyre some years ago in this wise. I had been writing a series of articles for the *New York Blazer* and found it necessary to read proofs. To do this I was obliged to climb to the fifth story of the *Blazer* building about twice a week. The proofs were always brought to me in Mr. Vampyre's office—a little apartment with one window opening on the street—and I usually made my corrections at his desk. He was introduced to me as "the book editor," and he was and is the most curiously amiable man that I know. Six feet in his stockings, or out of them, weighing about two hundred, bearded like the pard, he is as gentle as an infant, and seemingly incapable of anger. Yet his "Book Notices" are perfectly terrific. The *Blazer* has only one mission among books, and that is to exterminate them. We became rather intimate while I was making my series (though since these were finished I had not seen him for two or three years), and he would sometimes read passages from *his* proofs. The contrast between his jolly good nature and the blood-thirsty stuff he wrote was positively ludicrous.

I found him at his desk on the last day of my third ordeal, and he brought the ordeal to its conclusion.

"What in the world is that parcel under your arm?" he asked, after we exchanged greetings.

"It is a manuscript."

"Too big for the *Blazer!*" he said; "what is it?"

"A novel! And I give you fair warning that I am not going to stand any of your slashing. You must speak well of it when it appears."

"Can't do it, my boy! I am sorry for you, but this shop don't deal in 'soft sawder!' If you dare to print that lot of stuff, I'll certainly skin it!"

"Have you no bowels of compassion ——"

"Not a bowel! But I can probably slash it in such a fashion as to attract attention to it, and that will make it sell. This is all you will care about, you know. Are you going to print it anonymously?"

"Certainly. But I'm in a quandary, and have climbed up your horrid staircase to ask you for help."

"What is the trouble? I am quite ready to help you in any way in my power, except by partial criticism. That is not in my line." Here a pallor overspread his handsome face, and he faltered out, "You won't want me to *read* your manuscript?"

"Not a word; never fear. But the trouble is that there's nothing of it!"

"Is that all? My dear fellow, that is precisely the trouble with all the books I review. I got through 'The Double Parricide' last week. It contained five hundred pages, and there was nothing of it, I assure you, especially after I had done with it!"

"My novel is nothing like 'The Double Parricide,' Mr. Vampyre. It is a very sensible story, and the only serious defect is want of bulk. It won't make enough pages of print!"

"Well, why can't you keep on writing until you get it long enough?"

"Because it is finished. How can I 'keep on' when my characters are all dead—or married, which is about as bad? One can't keep up interest beyond the *dénouement*."

"I suppose not," said Mr. Vampyre, reflectively. "How many words have you?"

"Seventy-five thousand."

"Great Methuselah! How many do you lack?"

"Seventy-five thousand."

Mr. Vampyre whistled softly, and meditated. He is a man of unlimited expedients, and I knew I should get some practical suggestion from him if I waited. His life was spent among books, and he would certainly know what was best to be done. He opened a drawer in his desk, got out two cigars and a match. We smoked five or ten minutes, while he looked over the pages of my manuscript. At last he closed the portfolio with a sigh of relief.

"Will you leave this bundle of stuff with me until to-morrow?"

" Certainly."

" Well, come up again to-morrow. I have an idea! In fact I have two ideas. But I must get through this proof now for to-morrow's paper. Keep a good heart. I see the way out of your trouble!"

————

CHAPTER VII.

EUREKA !

THE misgivings that had preyed upon my mind in the interval between my two interviews with my friend Vampyre were all dispelled by his cheerful greeting on the second morning. He was seated at his desk. There was in his *tout ensemble* that air of conscious power belonging to men weighing two hundred pounds avoirdupois and adorned with a big beard. He had an enormous roll of manuscript before him from which he appeared to be making selections, as he was busily taking a pile of sheets from the general mass and smoothing them out in a separate parcel.

" Now, my friend," he began, " sit down here, and heed my major proposition. If I understood you yesterday, your trouble is want of bulk ?"

" Yes, that is the main difficulty."

" You have no doubt about the quality of the stuff you have scratched down here in these hundred and fifty-six pages ? By-the-bye, you write an atrocious hand! Do you know that the printers get paid by the quantity of matter they set up ? Well, every minute that you compel a printer to waste in deciphering your abominable hieroglyphics is so much of a fraud. There is no excuse for it in your case, because your manuscript is really legible in spots !"

" I did my best, Vampyre. The *Blazer* printers used to say my copy was good."

" They lied, then. But to my question. Does the matter suit you, as far as it goes ?"

" Yes. Very good judges have complimented——"

" Pooh ! Don't be misled by praises. Wait until I get my knife at work on you ! I have made a memorandum of a dozen passages I intend to skin when it gets to print ! Ha! ha! Listen to this:

'As the red gleam of the lightning illuminated the plain Lord Fitzgerald spurred his steed in his mad career. He held the bridle in his teeth, and with petronel in one hand and sword in the other——' "

"What in the world are you reading, Vampyre?" said I, aghast, "there is no such passage as that in my book!"

"Not yet, my boy, but there will be! Now just lay aside your vanity and listen to what I propose. This manuscript," and he laid his hand impressively upon the roll, "was sent to me by a schoolmate of mine. Poor Tom! he was always a little shaky in his upper story, and now all of his lunacy has been collected in this mass of precious stuff! He writes me to 'read it, and to do what I please with it.' Well, now I can serve two friends at once. You can take as many pages of this as you need, and incorporate them in your immortal work—what d'ye call it? Oh! yes—"Harwood." You can change the names, you know, and as many sheets as you take will reduce the lot that I have to burn! For my friendship for Tom demands the bonfire! Just think of it! six hundred and odd pages, of five hundred words each! and all of it very similar to the passage I read to you. I ask you, on your conscience, can I do less than burn them?"

"All, except what you have selected for me," I answered, with suppressed rage. "You think I can make up the required bulk with such matter as you read?"

"Exactly! I have picked out the most stirring passages, and I think you might send Tom a cheque for a moderate sum if you use his stuff. Don't say anything uncomplimentary though, for he is as short tempered as the Double Parricide man. But I have not told you about him?"

"No."

"Well, you ought to know the story. Probably you can utilize that also. He came up here two hours ago, and was completely out of breath when he came in. I gave him the chair you occupy, and he sat there and fanned himself with his hat about fifteen minutes, while his lungs resumed their normal action. He is a little fellow, about your size, though scarcely so heavy, but as plucky as a dog."

"Are you Mr. Vampyre?" he said at length.

"At your service, sir."

"Did you write the review of the 'Double Parricide' in last week's *Blazer?*"

"I did, sir."

"Well, sir," he said, rising, and stretching himself out as long as he could. "I am the author of that work!"

"Ah, indeed," I answered politely, "resume your seat, sir. I am glad to meet you."

"And I am glad to meet you, sir! I have climbed up these infernal steps of yours to tell you my opinion of you."

"Quite unnecessary, my dear sir. I dealt as lightly with your work as possible. There were many things I intended to say about it, but want of space forbade. For instance, the title is absurd !"

"What do you mean, sir ?"

"Why no man can be a double parricide unless he is a double fellow, like the Siamese twins. How the deuce can a fellow kill his father twice ?"

"I cannot tell you what his answer was. He talks two or three languages, and being very much excited, he went from English to French and from French to German, and he cursed me roundly in all three. At last, the little whelp made a dive at me. I think he intended to elongate my nose. I caught his arm, then took him by the waistband and dropped him out the window."

"Vampyre !"

"Oh, it did not hurt him much. He fell on a wheelbarrow and knocked it into splinters. The owner of the wheelbarrow made no allowance for the altitude from which the author had descended, but collared him incontinently, as he rose from among the fragments. There was a crowd in a minute, and some policemen came up and took them all off."

"You don't expect me to believe that, Vampyre ?"

"No. But I do expect your readers to believe it, if you present it properly. But that was my second plan. What do you say to my first ?"

"I have to decline. I can't make Lord Fitzgerald assimilate with ' Harwood.' "

"Well. It would save a good lot of writing. I thought you would probably decline, for, all authors think their own productions better than any other's. You could easily mix in these scenes. Why, Tom has a real earthquake in this selection. Listen ! 'As the roar of the tempest increased, Lord Fitzgerald was startled to feel the solid rock, upon which he stood, vibrating in the throes of an earthquake——' "

"My dear Vampyre, such a shocking affair would knock the life out of 'Harwood!' I must positively decline. Let me hear your second plan."

"It is very simple. How many people have seen your manuscript? I infer that you have been the round of the publishers, or you would not have discovered your attenuated condition."

In answer to this question, I told Mr. Vampyre all that I have told the reader in the first five chapters. When my narrative was finished, Mr. Vampyre, who seemed to enjoy the story amazingly, clapped me on the back triumphantly.

"Go in and win, my boy! Write down all you have told me, word for word, and let it be the introduction to Harwood. You will accomplish two or three things at once.

"First, you will get that much matter in addition, and make your bulk sufficient. Second, you will hide the objectionable journalistic form, which your readers will know nothing about until they have gotten so far into your story that they will have to go on. And third, you will be giving the public some *true* matter to leaven the lump of fiction you have written."

"Shall I include my interviews with you?"

"By all means. If you put in the Double Parricide and tell about the wheelbarrow catastrophe, you had better say my sanctum is on the tenth floor!"

"That wheelbarrow story is a little too strong, Vampyre, to mingle with my more modest fiction."

"See there now!" answered Vampyre, "the wheelbarrow story is founded on fact. I actually knew a Hibernian labourer to fall from a scaffolding as high as this window, and to escape with a few bruises. He fell on a wheelbarrow, which was totally wrecked. I am not like you fellows, who weave impossible plots. There is an air of *vraisemblance* about my yarns which you won't find in your hundred and fifty-six pages."

"Did you read any of my manuscript?"

"Ye-es! Oh, certainly!"

"How much? Tell the truth."

"Well, my boy, I read the title, and then turned over until I came to the end of the journal——"

"Which is the end of the book!"

"Exactly. I read the last page, every word. You'll do!" he continued, encouragingly. "I was greatly pleased with the conclusion!"

The more I reflected upon Vampyre's plan the more it pleased me. I could not make matter to stick about in odd places. The story was told, and I feared to mar its fair proportions. In my young days, I remember that great statesmen in legislative halls were sometimes put up to speak "against time." I, imitating their worthy example, have been writing against space.

Oh, injured reader, I have thus led thee along through the foregoing pages, pretending to have an entertaining story to relate, when I was all the time slyly counting the new pages, and rejoicing in the prospect of so much added bulk. No longer will I pursue these devious ways. I am sick of the constructive deceit I have been practicing, the more especially as the end is accomplished which I had in view when I began it. Accept my repentance, gentle reader, and begin the *real* story on the next page, with unruffled composure. Sincerely do I hope that thou wilt enjoy the reading as much as I have enjoyed the writing.

AUTHOR AND PUBLISHER.

CHAPTER VIII.

HERBERT'S JOURNAL.

FIRST IMPRESSIONS.

BATON ROUGE, LOUISIANA, *May* 1, 1836.

I PROMISED my dear Mother that I would keep a journal regularly and systematically; and though I have allowed a week to slip away since I arrived here, it is not too late to begin. I hardly know what to set down for my "first impressions" of Louisiana life and manners; but I want this diary to be as true and faithful a transcript of my real feelings, and as literal a history of my sayings and doings, as I can make it. As it will always be in my power to destroy the record, I need not hesitate about writing with perfect freedom. I may remark one thing at the beginning, which is, that one week's sojourn here has sufficed to make a man of me. I can imagine myself twenty-nine instead of nineteen. As to-morrow will be Sunday, I will have more time and a better opportunity for journalizing, and will therefore postpone the regular beginning of my short story until then.

SUNDAY, *May* 2, 1836.

Just a month ago—that is, on the first of April—I was at work at my desk in the counting-room of Jalap & Julap, wholesale Druggists, of Baltimore. I had had a small fight with Mr. Julap, the junior partner, who pretended to know more about book-keeping than I did, and who consequently undertook to correct some entries I had made. It is worth while to notice here that the quarrel began by Mr. Julap's translation of a French label; or, rather, of a French phrase on an English label. It was on a bottle of English perfumery, and was the well known motto on the English Arms: "*Honi soit qui mal y pense.*" I had remarked that the first word ought to be written "Honni," when Mr. Julap replied that "*honi* was the French for honey, and there was honey in the perfumery, no doubt." I was silly enough to endeavour to set him right, before two or three grinning clerks, and then he fell to abusing me for bad book-keeping, because I had proved him guilty of bad French. He knew about as much of one as of the other, so of course he made an ass of himself. Mr. Jalap was in New York, so he was fuller of authority than usual, and I could not forget that I was always above him at school, though he was six years my senior. The quarrel would have become serious if we had not been interrupted by the entrance of a stranger, and I resumed my work, intending to renew the contest at the earliest opportunity. The new comer announced himself as Mr. Bayard, of Louisiana, and I soon became deeply interested in him and in his discourse. He had that free, off-hand manner for which Western and Southern men are distinguished, and he came from a State that has always figured in my dreams as El Dorado.

"I am looking," said he, after a pause in the conversation, "for a young man who understands book-keeping, and who has some knowledge of drugs and chemicals, to take charge of a store I am about to open in Baton Rouge. Can you, sir, assist me in the search?"

Before Mr. Julap had time to reply I had slid down from my stool, and, approaching the stranger, stammered out, "I will go with you, sir!"

"And who are you?" he asked, half surprised and half amused.

"Herbert Harwood, sir."

"And what does this gentleman say?" glancing at Mr. Julap.

"Oh; he has my consent, sir," replied Julap with a sneer, "and I can safely say that he knows more about drugs and books than he does about French."

"The French will come in good time," said Mr. Bayard, rising and taking his hat, "come to Barnum's Hotel at six this afternoon, youngster, and we will arrange about terms. I like your looks, and foresee that we shall get along famously. Good-bye." He shook hands with me with a kindly smile, nodded to Mr. Julap, and left.

That is about all the story. Of course there was a fuss at home, and of course Mother and the girls cried, and I got a little spoony myself;—but here I am in Baton Rouge, and as happy as a lark.

CARRVILLE, LA., *Sunday, May* 9, 1836.

I am not altogether certain that it is proper, or in accordance with my Presbyterian training, for me to devote Sabbath days to this work of journalizing. Hereafter I will find some other time, for Mother's sake; for I know she would not approve of a work which is neither of mercy nor necessity. But I am just now so full of an adventure which I had to-day that I must write it down to-night. In the first place, we, that is, Mr. Bayard and I,

have moved to the town of Carrville, twenty miles lower down the
river than Baton Rouge, and he intends to open his store here.
Our goods are coming round by sea from Baltimore to New
Orleans, and they will not be at the latter city for two or three
weeks, and in the meantime we have little to do, except fixing
shelves and counters. Mr. Bayard brought me here last Monday,
and left the same day for New Orleans. I expect him back to-
morrow. We came in the steamboat "Firefly," which is the regular packet plying between Baton Rouge and the city. The "Firefly" is owned and commanded by a queer old Frenchman named
Captain Joli. I shall have some funny stories to tell about him,
if we meet often. For example: I was very much hurried on
Monday, and wishing to know exactly how much time I had, I
ran down to the landing early in the morning, and asked Captain
Joli at what hour his boat started? His reply was—

"Ten o'clock, sare, precise! You not here *a quarter before ten*,
you be lef', begar!"

The "Firefly" usually arrived from Baton Rouge a little before
noon, and when there is a shipment of cotton on our landing the
boat remains at Carrville several hours. This was the case the
other day, and Captain Joli, leaving the loading in charge of his
subordinates, spent an hour or so with me. He found me poring
over "La Vie de Washington," and overheard some of my
attempts at French pronunciation, which seemed to disgust him
considerably.

"Pardon, Monsieur Hubbard," said he, "vil you please say
twenty-eight in French?"

"*Vingt-huit.*"

"C'est bon! Now say '*huit*' by himself."

"*Ungweet!*" I answered, honestly striving to imitate him.

"*Mille tonnerres!* I did not tell you to gront like one peeg!
Huit!"

"*Huit!*"

"Ah, that is better. It is ver' strange you not talk good French,
ven you read him so well. Many peoples speak good French here.
S'pose you talk much French every day with Monsieur Carr? I
will give you lesson, too. Dis time, I give you *huit, oui, dixhuit!*
You mus' not say '*wee*,' but *oui*. Do you observe ze difference?"

"Yes, sir. You are very kind, Captain, and I will strive to
profit by your lessons——"

"Ah, you have ze small sword also! Come out in ze yard, and

I shall give you another lesson. Bah! we do not want ze mask. I shall not scratch your face."

"But I may scratch yours, Captain."

"I will take ze risque. Allons!"

I took down the foils, and we walked out into the little enclosure behind the store. There is a large China tree here, and under its shade the gallant Captain gave me my lesson. I have been a pretty good fencer for several years, and was a favourite pupil of our old Baltimore instructor. But he was an Italian, and therefore did not take to sword play as a Frenchman does. Captain Joli put me through the ordinary exercise, correcting slight inaccuracies here and there, and politely complimenting me upon my skill.

"Now, mon ami," quoth the Captain, who began to be fond of me, "regardez! You straddle your long legs too much. Ven I call *fendez-vous!* you stretch about five feet. You must always keep your legs under you, and be ready for retreat. Now strike my breast, *en carte.*"

I gave him the thrust in straight carte. He did not oppose his blade, but simply drew his body back. My foil did not reach him by several inches. He then reversed the proposition, and I avoided his thrust in the same manner. This was a grand attainment. He then put me carefully through the parades of *prime, seconde* and *octave*, and made me expert in the semi-circular parry. We resumed our coats, walked into the store, and while we blew a double cloud of fragrant smoke, the Captain finished his lesson verbally.

"You cannot tell, mon ami, when you may be required to do sword play in earnest."

"Do you mean in a duel, Captain?"

"Yes; all gentlemen have to fight some time."

"I shall never fight a duel, Captain," I answered, positively.

"*Che sarà, sarà!*" responded the Captain, sententiously. I started as he uttered the proverb.

"Where did you learn that, sir?" said I, in astonishment.

"Ah, that is a villanous motto of a villanous race. It means, 'What will be, will be,' and was ze proverb of ze Medicis. I do not know why I repeated it just now."

"It is also the motto of a better race than the Medici," I replied.

"It is blank fatalism!" quoth the Captain, "and it is not true."

"I understand it to mean the same thing as an article of my

creed, sir," I answered, after a pause, " namely : 'God hath, from
all eternity, foreordained whatsoever cometh to pass.'"

"Ver' bad philosophy !" replied Captain Joli. "But to return to
ze sword play. Ze sword has always been ze weapon of a gentleman, and always will be. To be master of it there are only two
or three principles to learn, and ze rest is mere practice. First:
you must look into your adversary's *eyes*, and learn to detect each
change of parade wizout seeing his blade. Second : you must *feel*
his weapon wiz yours, all ze same as if you felt wiz your hand·
Third : you must be content wiz enough defence to deflect his
blade from your body. One inch from your person is just as good
as two yards. If you *know* you are covered, you fight wiz assurance. And if you observe my rules, and practice patiently, you
will become nearly invulnerable."

"Suppose two men meet, Captain, who are equally skilful—if
your theory is true, neither will gain an advantage."

"Ah ! that is not a supposable case. But if it were, one man
would get excited, and poof ! ze other plug him !" The Captain .
reflected a few minutes, and continued, " I have had four experience—ze first time I got a coup in my arm; it hurt like ze diable !"

"And the other times, Captain ?"

"Eh, bien ! I am here !" The Captain rose and took his hat.
"Au revoir, Monsieur ! Ze next time we meet we shall confine our-
selves to *prime* and *seconde*."

When the boat arrived at this place the other day, Mr. Bayard
handed me over to a strange gentleman, who was the only other
passenger for Carrville, saying he would go on to the "City" (as
everybody calls New Orleans), and return in about a week. The
stranger was Mr. Charles Carr. I will try to describé him when I
have more time. As the "Firefly" pushed off from the landing Mr.
Bayard called out, " Good bye, Herbert ; take care of yourself!"
He has always called me by my Christian name (which he pro-
nounces "Hubbard"), and as Carr and I walked up from the river,
he once or twice addressed me as " Mr. Hubbard." I remember
that now, though I did not notice it particularly at the time.
When we reached the hotel, Mr. Carr walked up to the desk in
the bar-room, and entered my name on the register as " Mr. Hubbard, of Baton Rouge." I was so shy and foolish that I did not
correct the mistake, and I am ashamed to add, that I have not
corrected it up to this hour. I have been introduced to fifty people as Mr. Hubbard, and I really feel like crying when I think

how horridly stupid I will look when the truth comes out. Of course, I cannot make everybody understand the case as I understand it. It was awkward to say to the first stranger, "my name is Harwood—not Hubbard;" because it looked as though I thought myself of so much importance; and every time the introductions took place the difficulty increased. I have not even told Carr, who is a first rate fellow, and who would appreciate my peculiar difficulty if I were to tell him just how I feel about the affair. I have concluded to leave the whole matter in the hands of Providence, and don't intend to let it annoy me any longer, if I can help it. Mr. Bayard will be able to work me out of the mess when he comes back.

But all this is not the story I sat down to tell; and I will scratch that down now in as few words as possible, for it is getting late, and I am tired to death and want to go to bed. Well, all last week I was overlooking the men who were fixing up the shelves in the store, directing them as to the width and height, &c., and very lazy work it has been. Every day Charley Carr would ride into town (he lives about two miles off), and spend two or three hours with me, sometimes fencing, sometimes teaching me some new steps in dancing, and sometimes helping me in my French. He fences like some Frenchman I have read about, who could make his sword do everything but talk. I never saw anything like it, and I would give five dollars to see him encounter my old conceited Italian teacher, Mazzi, who used to put on so many airs with us boys, when he twitched our foils out of our hands. Well, well, well! I shall never get to the adventure; I will tell it right straight, without any more circumlocution. Yesterday Carr said:

"Hubbard, will you join a small lot of us fellows in a deer hunt to-morrow?"

"To-morrow will be Sunday," I replied.

"I know that," said Carr, "and as you will not have any men at work here, I thought you could get off on that day."

"But I have no horse," I answered, "and no gun; and besides I don't like——"

"Come, come, sir, you shall have Ret's mare. She is a little skittish, and will be all the better after a good gallop; I don't believe we shall find any deer, though, as the season is so late; but we shall have a pleasant time, and you will see something of the country back of the river. I will send a boy in with the mare early in the morning, and you can stop at our house on your way to the meeting place, and get Herbert's gun and accoutrements. I will have all ready for you."

Who was Ret? and who was Herbert?

As Carr mounted his horse, half an hour later, he turned to me, with a kind smile in his great blue eyes, and said,

"Maybe you don't like to spend Sunday in mere amusement; if your conscience is against the frolic I won't urge you to violate your principles."

"If *you* may do it why should not *I?*"

"Oh, I am a free thinker," he replied, half sadly and half contemptuously.

I was a little provoked as I noticed the shadow of a sneer in his voice and manner, and I, therefore, made no reply. He rode off without further remark, taking it for granted that I intended to go, though I had almost decided that I should not. With my customary tardiness I had allowed him to fall into the mistake, intending to write an excuse and apology this morning when the boy brought the horse.

When I got up this morning I looked out of my window and saw a negro leading a beautiful black mare up and down the street before the door. The mare was curveting and capering about at a great rate, and the man evidently had his hands full. I recognized Carr's servant, Jacobus, who had once or twice brought me messages from his master, and as I watched the gambols of the spirited animal he had in charge, all my good resolutions vanished, giving place to an uncontrollable desire to bestride the magnificent beast. I dressed hastily, and opening the window, called the negro to the sidewalk.

"Have you been here long, Jacobus?"

"Jist come, Mars'r. Jist hitch my hoss yonder, and was gwine to knock at your door, only dis black varmint would not be quiet. Gosh! Mars'r, she'll take you *in a gust* dis day!"

"Did Mr. Carr send any message?" I asked.

"Got um note here, sar," replied Jacobus, pulling his hat off, and taking the missive out of the lining. I believe negroes carry everything in their hats. I descended to the street, and taking the note read as follows:

"DEAR H.—We are to start from Maltby's house, where we are to get breakfast. Jacobus will guide you. Don't ride with spurs—the mare is very excitable to-day.   Yours,   C. C."

I had pulled on a pair of riding boots, with spurs screwed into the heels, and as I could not easily get them out, I mentally promised to keep my heels away from the mare's sides, and mounted. Jacobus noticed the spurs as he held the stirrup, and exclaimed:

"Gosh! Mars'r Hubbard, if you tetch Midnight wid one of dem *squrs* she'll jump clean outen her hide!"

"I can't get the spurs out of my boots, Jake," I replied, "but I will take care she does not feel them."

"Werry well, Mars'r—you best not. You see, sah, Midnight is lady's hoss, and ain't 'quainted wid squrs. Mars'r Herbert rode her once, and jist let his squr tetch her, and she flung him clean over her head. Him not easy flung neither."

"Is Mr. Herbert Mr. Charley's brother?" I asked with some curiosity.

"No, sar," answered Jacobus, "Mars'r Herbert is Miss Ret's brudder."

"And who is Miss Ret, Jake?"

"Him Mars'r Herbert's sister, sar!" replied Jake, innocently, and with the air of a man who was giving valuable information.

We rode on in silence for a mile or more. I was not willing to question the negro too closely concerning family matters, though I was burning with curiosity to know who these new comers on the scene could be. I have seen the elder Mr. Carr once or twice, and am inclined to think that I should admire him very much if I knew him better. He must have resembled his son when he was at his age, though there is a great dissimilarity in their appearance now. Mr. Carr is a grey, grave, old looking man, wonderfully courteous and affable, though seemingly habitually melancholy. I remember that he expressed a great deal of interest in me, when Charley introduced me to him, and that he said something about the beauty of Baltimore, my native city. I suppose he really cared very little about me or my birthplace, and I have credited his apparent interest to his natural politeness. It is a great thing, certainly, to be born a gentleman, and Mr. Carr and I have both had this good fortune.

As Jake and I rode on I noticed the sweet odours of the country much more apparent as we got further from the river. My walks have hitherto been confined to the bank of the majestic stream upon whose broad bosom I have travelled for so many hundreds of miles. Compared with the rivers of my own State, the Mississippi is very dull and uninteresting in appearance. Its waters seem always muddy, and its margins are so low and monotonous. But one cannot see the steamers passing each hour of the day, and hear the *bark* of their high pressure engines all through the night, without getting a large conception of the magnificence of this great highway. About two miles from Carrville our horses stopped to drink in the middle of a sparkling little creek, which seemed more charming to me from its contrast to the yellow river I saw every day, and I promised myself the pleasure of many a walk hereafter to so beautiful a locality. My sable guide informed me that this creek was called "Manahio." This is the name of Mr. Carr's estate, and I presume this little rivulet is the one of which I have heard my friend speak. The name is Indian, and signifies "Bright Water." Carr told me that the streamlet separated his father's lands from another estate, whose name he did not mention, and we have projected a fishing excursion to some of the deep pools of the Manahio, to come off in June or July.

The valley through which the creek flows appeared to me like some dream of fairyland. I have never seen, in my own colder home, anything like the abundant and gorgeous vegetation of these southern forests. As we rode up the hill, rising abruptly from the water, I checked my horse for a moment to admire the scene. I shall not try to describe it—at least, not now. I will only say that I thought of Buckingham's curse—"marriage and a life in the country"—and concluded that the curse might fall upon me, and that it would rest full lightly if I might select this spot for my home and be allowed some small space to seek for my "partner in distress." Just at the ford there are three enormous laurels *(Magnolia Grandiflora)*, their trunks half hidden by the undergrowth, there being no other tall trees in their immediate vicinity. Jacobus had pulled up his horse behind me, and observing my admiration of the scene, he pointed to the magnolias and said—

"Dem is de haunted laurels, sar!"

"Haunted!" I exclaimed.

"'Deed dey is, sar; plenty of people done seen de ghossesses. Mars'r seed 'em one time. Him nebber ride 'long dis road at night!"

"What kind of ghossesses are they, Jake?" I asked.

"Well, sar," answered the African, edging his horse a little

nearer to mine—"it am purty long story, but we got two mile
good yet to git to Mars'r Maltby's—and ef you like to hear
him, I'll try to tell him."

But I am not going to repeat Jake's story to-night—two o'clock,
by Jupiter! I'll go to bed now, and try to finish this interminable
yarn to-morrow. And in order to make the narrative as coherent
as possible, I will begin with the wild legend, which, I am ashamed
to say, makes me feel extremely uncomfortable whenever I think
about it. So I will try to think about home till I fall asleep, and,
maybe, I can dream about Mother.

CHAPTER IX.

THE HAUNTED LAURELS.

MONDAY, *May* 10, 1836.

I FEEL like a stewed witch this evening, and no wonder. All day
I have been harassed by the workmen who are fitting shelves and
drawers in the adjoining room, and who were perpetually wanting
instructions, and Carr has been here, and I have promised to go
with him to Manabio to-morrow night, to return on Wednesday
morning after breakfast. I *must* record yesterday's adventure,
while it is fresh in my mind; and I have provided myself with
two candles, and mean to write while I can keep awake—so here
goes! Jake's story is the first thing in order, and may be entitled
"The Haunted Laurels."

Five years ago Mr. Carr was parish judge, and his neighbour,
Mr. John ———— (the negro called him "Mars'r John" all
through his tale, and I forgot to ask his name), was State's attorney for this parish. At that time there was an unusual degree
of excitement throughout all the eastern parishes of Louisiana,
caused by the persistent efforts of a handful of Abolitionists to
induce slaves to abscond, and it was said, also, to incite an insur-
rection. Very vigorous measures were adopted, some of which
were extra legal, and five or six men were arrested, tried and
hung—most of them under the authority of Judge Lynch. Among
these victims there were two men, father and son, who were arrested under suspicious circumstances, at a plantation in the
neighbourhood. They were strangers, and no white man could be

found, between the date of their arrest and day of their death, who had ever seen them before. I could not get from Jacobus any very coherent account of the trial of these Densons, or of the testimony upon which they were condemned. Letters were found upon their persons, written by a noted Abolitionist who was tried at Baton Rouge the same year, and who is now in the State penitentiary, sentenced to imprisonment for life. This man, Sumner, who was, perhaps, the most guilty, who openly avowed his sentiments in the court room, was the only one who had a regular trial, and the only one that escaped the halter. His offence, however atrocious in intention and tendency, was one exactly provided for in the law of the State, and the penalty was life imprisonment at hard labour. There is little doubt, however, that he would have shared the fate of his accomplices, if he had been tried under Lynch law.

The Densons were chained to one of the three laurels on the bank of the Manahio, near the high road, that they might be visible to all passers by, whose recognition of them might avert an impending doom. Two or three dozen young planters from the neighbourhood, armed to the teeth, kept constant guard over them, and precluded the possibility of escape or rescue. At the trial, held at the same spot, each planter present was a judge and juryman, and the prisoners were allowed to defend themselves. Their defence amounted to little more than a plea of not guilty, and they constantly demanded a regular trial before a constituted court, affirming their ability to prove their innocence, if sufficient time were allowed them. At the end of the week they were both hanged on one of the trees of the haunted group. Before the stern sentence was executed the elder Denson made a special appeal to Judge Carr and the State's attorney, as representatives of the law. He might as well have appealed to a couple of tigers. The legend affirms that Denson then predicted the violent death of these two gentlemen, upon the same spot, within some definite period, and promised that both he and his son would haunt the grove until this dire prophecy was fulfilled.

One morning, within the year, the body of the prosecuting attorney was found at the foot of the gallows tree, dead from a pistol shot in the head. His own pistol was clutched in his hand, and the current belief, at least amongst the superstitious negroes, was that he had shot himself. Jacobus represents this gentleman—"Mars'r John"—as a man of extraordinary courage and prowess. I recollect his exact expression at this part of the story. "Mars'r John," he said, "wor not 'feard of two hundred debbles and ghossesses all at once; and ef he had fair chance in the daylight, he could make ghos' and debble bofe run." All that was known about his death was, that he had left Carrville near midnight for his home. His horse was found in the early morning near his house, and a fragment of his bridle lying near his master's body, which was discovered in the bushes, by tracking the footmarks of the animal back to the haunted laurels. At this portion of the narrative Jacobus was visibly affected, and I fancied that I could detect a strange mixture of grief and horror in his tones. He spoke of the deceased gentleman with evident affection, and I thought he regarded his mysterious death as a kind of swindle on the part of the "ghossesses." He said, for instance: "Mars'r John didn't hab no fair shake wid dem. Dey was 'feard to fight him out in de open road, whar de moon was shinen; so dey tolled him inter dem bushes, and dar dey busted his big heart, and made him kill hisself!" There was something about the weird manner of the negro that made me feel very uncomfortable, in spite of my consciousness that the whole story was susceptible of a matter of fact solution if one could only get at the clue.

So far as Mr. Carr is concerned, the prophecy has as yet found no fulfilment. The narrator did not say much upon this branch of the subject. It seems that he resigned his office shortly after the execution of the Densons. That he has seen something uncanny at the haunted laurels Jake does not doubt, but he asserts most positively that he avoids this road in his journeys to and from town, crossing the stream at another ford, a mile higher up.

He concluded his story just as we reached Mr. Maltby's, begging me to say nothing to "ole Mars'r or Mars'r Charley" about the haunted laurels. "Ef you ebber git chance, sar," he said, as he held the gate open for my entrance into Mr. Maltby's grounds, "and ef you want to know more 'bout dis story, you might ax Miss Ret—kase she jis like her fader, and not 'feard ob de debble hisself!"

A dozen questions rushed to my tongue, but Mr. Maltby's appearance and cordial salutation prevented the utterance of any of them. There! I am heartily glad that I have gotten rid of that horrid legend for the present.

I wonder what Mr. Maltby, and so many of his guests as were

near me, thought of my trencher powers yesterday morning ?
The ride had increased an appetite that was vigorous enough
before, and the coffee was the first Mocha that I had tasted since
I left my dear Mother's table. And to cap the climax, there was
genuine wheat bread in abundance, which is a rarity in this fair
land. Mrs. Maltby said, as we rose from the table, " You have
found the way to Highlands, Mr. Hubbard, and I hope we shall
see you very often hereafter." To which Mr. Maltby added,
" Yes, come out every day that you can get off, Hubbard." These
Louisiana people are very kind and hospitable.

Carr handed me a gun and accoutrements as I remounted Midnight, and renewed his cautions against the use of spurs. I expressed some surprise at the selection of so fiery a beast for a
lady's horse, especially as her trot was none of the smoothest.

" Why, that black rascal has put a curb bit in her mouth," said
Carr; " here, Jake ! take off that bridle and martingale, and put
mine on the mare. She travels better with a snaffle, Hubbard,
and you will find her gait pleasant enough. How came you to
put the curb on the filly, Jake ?"

" Golly ! Mars'r Charley," answered the negro, with a grin,
" how I gwine to know that Mars'r Hubbard kin ride like de
witches ? She done flung Mars'r Herbert todder day !"

" Keep your eye on her, Hubbard," shouted Carr, as the mare
glided ahead; " she is safe enough till she feels the spur."

I have gotten another object to be attained, namely the possession of that mare. I do not know whether money will buy her,
and I am not overburdened with that particular article, if it
would. But I mean to own that mare some of these days ! Her
gait is indescribable. To me, who have been accustomed to trot-
ting horses all my life, it was altogether new. She appeared to
" devour the distance " with a motion so light and easy as scarcely
to move me in the saddle. These Southerners, who consult their
ease on all occasions, think more of a horse trained to " pace "
than of the fatest trotters; and Midnight has been so carefully
instructed that I must consider her matchless. But I am getting
along very slowly with my story.

Mr. Maltby stationed me in a glade of the forest, a mile or so
from his house, directing me to watch for the deer whenever I
heard the cry of the hounds. " You can either dismount," he said
at parting, " and fasten your horse to a swinging branch, or you
can shoot from the saddle if you get a shot. The mare will stand

fire." So saying he plunged into the woods, winding his horn, and followed by all the yelping hounds. The other gentlemen of the party galloped off, to take "stands," as they call these openings in the woods, similar to mine, and in a few minutes I had lost sight and sound of them all. And now I am at the beginning of my adventure, at last. While I sit here in quiet, hearing no sound but the scratching of my pen over the paper, I feel my heart beating more rapidly and my body quivering with excitement as the memories of the few events I have to record come thronging back upon me.

After Mr. Maltby disappeared I fastened the mare to a sapling and started in search of water. I had smoked a heavy cigar after breakfast, and my throat was dry and parched. I soon found a tiny rill issuing from the bushes, and thinking the draught would be cooler and purer if I could find its source, I threw my gun into the hollow of my arm, and pushing aside the undergrowth, I splashed my way through, walking in the bed of the rill. As I advanced, the passage grew more and more difficult, and I should have given up the attempt, but for a lamentable obstinacy of disposition, which always makes me persist more resolutely in an undertaking when obstacles thicken around me. My dear, partial Mother speaks of this trait as "one of my few failings." I went on, therefore, getting my gun entangled in the overhanging vines, getting stung in thorny bushes, and growing more thirsty, and more determined to find the spring, till I had probably got two or three hundred yards from my horse. At last I emerged into an "open" of small circumference, and saw the spring, the water bubbling over a bed of pure white sand, and looking deliciously cool and tempting. I kneeled down, and plunging my face in the water, I took the sweetest drink I ever had in my life. As I raised my head and glanced around I discovered that I was not alone. On the other side of the spring, half hidden by the tree against which he was leaning, sat a man clothed in buckskins. His back was towards me, and I could only see his left arm and leg, and the muzzle of an old looking rifle lying across his thigh. He sat perfectly motionless, as I watched him for some minutes and as he must have heard my approach, I wondered why he did not look round the tree to see who I was. I had half a mind to slip quietly back by the way I had come, and, rising to my feet, with this half-formed purpose, and drawing a step back, I got a partial view of his head, and recognized the straight black hair

4

and copper colored, skin of an Indian. I have so long wished to see a real live Indian in something like his " native state," that curiosity overcame every other feeling and I stepped round the tree and accosted him.

"Good morning," said I, nodding to him as cordially as I could. He raised his head when I spoke and I discovered that he was tolerably drunk. He had a junk bottle in his hand which he held out, offering me a drink.

"Um!" he grunted, " white brudder come to see ole Injin! White brudder welcome! take drink!"

" I have just had a drink," I answered, declining the bottle and pointing to the spring—" it is better than that in your bottle."

" Spring good, whisky better! white brudder want moccasin? Come in wigwam." He rose as he spoke, and thrusting the bottle in the bosom of his hunting shirt, he moved away from the tree, dragging his rifle after him.

" I don't want any moccasins—that is, not to-day; I must go back to the stand now." I began to feel a little uneasy, and to remember a hundred stories I have read and heard about scalps, roasting before a slow fire, and similar nonsense. The grisly rascal was six feet tall, erect and vigorous, and looked as though he could make mince meat of me in a twinkling. Drunk as he was, he walked without staggering. He faced me again and beckoned to me to follow him.

" Nebber mind stand," he said, "no deer to-day. Brudder have some Injin's venison? Injin dry him himself; come!"

" No, I thank you, not this time; good bye!"

" No whisky, no moccasin, no venison!" said he, angrily striking the ground with the butt of his gun—" what for young brudder afeard?"

I began to be angry myself now, as well as scared—angry perhaps because scared. I tried to look as fierce as I wished to feel.

" I am not afraid of anything," I answered; I never drink whisky. If you will bring me a pair of moccasins to town to-morrow I will buy them, and as for the venison—well, I *will* taste your venison. How far off is your wigwam?"

" Here," he replied, once more stalking away from the spring. I followed him to the edge of the opposite thicket until he arrived at the trunk of a tree that had been prostrated by some hurricane, as was evident from the huge mass of roots that stood perpendicularly eight or ten feet above the surface of the ground. A quantity of suckers and vines with long trailing branches and tendrils, sprang from among the upturned roots, and, hanging over the cavity they had once occupied, formed a beautiful bower, which shaded and concealed the rude hut beneath them. The fallen tree had stood on a slight eminence or hillock, and the hollow which its roots had scooped out was still a little higher than the surrounding surface. The hut was formed of long strips of bark, leaning against the base of the tree, and appeared to be watertight; the edges of the bark neatly sewn together and covered in places with pieces of deer hide. I did not enter, but as the Indian pushed aside the rude door I saw two or three pairs of moccasins hanging on pegs, and a bundle of skins lying in a corner. At that instant my attention was attracted by the cry of the hounds, and I was about to hasten back to my stand, when the Indian reappeared, with a piece of smoked deermeat in his hand.

"Nebber mind stand," he said; "dog no find deer, 'spose him find fox!" He listened intently for a moment and added, "him come dis way."

I walked hastily along the trunk of the prostrate tree, until I found a place low enough for me to clamber up, and cocking both barrels of my gun, I looked anxiously for the appearance of the deer or fox, whichever it might prove. The Indian followed me, still dragging his rifle after him. I pointed in the direction of the sounds, for the furious baying of the hounds could now be heard distinctly, and they seemed to be approaching very rapidly.

"Plenty time," said my companion, waving his hand, "fox run dis way, dat way. Dog lose him bimeby. S'pose he climb tree; plenty time."

He propped his gun up against the tree, and, drawing a long knife from his belt, proceeded to cut a strip of venison. Suddenly there was a crash in the bushes beyond the hut, and I saw the body of an animal glancing through them. The Indian dropped the meat, stuck his knife into the tree, caught up his rifle and fired. I heard a fierce growl, another crash, and again saw the beast bounding over a bunch of tangled vines. He was not over twenty yards distant, and I discharged one barrel at him just as he leaped into sight. Another growl, another mighty bound, and there he was before me, and I saw the long, striped body, and thick tail, gliding through the grass, as he approached me. I took good aim, and gave him the contents of the second barrel as the hounds—a dozen of them—came tearing through the bushes.

They were upon him in a moment, and such a babel of growls, barks and howls, I never heard before, and hope never to hear again. I was watching the fight as I reloaded my gun. The Indian was forcing a bullet into the muzzle of his rifle, and I heard him mutter: " Whisky too much! hand shake; no shoot;" when I saw Music, a favorite slut of Carr's, dash at the panther, and retreat on the instant, bleeding and howling dismally. Without a thought, I snatched the Indian's knife from the tree, jumped down and plunged into the melée. I hardly know how it was done, but I pushed in among the dogs, several of them badly torn, and drove the knife into the beast's side up to the hilt. He must have been already nearly dead, as we afterwards found that both of my shots had taken effect—the first in his flank and the other in his shoulder. The thrust finished him, however, and, after a convulsive jerk or two, he rolled over, dead. Just then I heard the clatter of horses' hoofs, and Mr. Maltby and a stranger galloped into the open.

CHAPTER X.

CAPTAIN DELANEY.

THE strange gentleman was a man to be looked at. He seemed to be about thirty-five, though I do not know if this estimate of his age is within ten years of the truth. He had that indescribable *tout ensemble* that belongs to very mature young men. His eyes were black and piercing, his hair black, and his sallow face, closely shaven, showed the black roots of his thick beard, around his chin and over his lip. He was dressed with great nicety, in the everlasting blue cottonade unmentionables, and a brown linen frock coat. His shirt bosom was particularly white and smooth, and one got the idea, from a glance at the man, that he would not rumple or soil it if he wore it a month. He wore a black silk cravat and no collar, a broad brimmed Panama hat and kid gloves. Altogether, he was too nice looking for the woods. As he drew up his horse he looked steadily at me, and I touched my hat. He returned my salutation by removing his own, and bowing gracefully, and I observed that his hair, which was crisp and wavy—I feel inclined to write it "*kinky*"—was arranged with care, parted as if it had been done with a rule and pair of compasses. I thoroughly and excessively disliked him at the first glance.

"Why, what in the world are you doing here, Hubbard?" asked Mr. Maltby, looking with great round eyes at me and the bloody knife in my hand.

"I believe I have been killing a panther, sir," I replied, with as much modesty as I could muster.

"The deuce you have! where is he?" and he threw his long leg over the saddlebow and slid down from his horse. "Here he is, by jingo! shot in two places, and stuck to boot! It was your gun, then, that I heard? and here is a rifle shot, right over his ear. Somebody had a pop at him before you; I heard the rifle, but this only riled him. Was he coming at you? Where did you get that knife? Do you usually carry a toothpick of that size?"

"It is the Indian's knife, sir," said I, answering one question out of the volley.

"What Indian?" said the stranger, speaking for the first time. I looked round to the dead tree, where I had left my hospitable friend, but he was no longer there; I stepped to the hut, pushed the door open and looked in—but my "Injun brudder" had disappeared.

"He is gone," said I, returning from my fruitless search; "he was at my side a minute ago, just as you came. I cannot imagine what has become of him; he was watching me when I stuck the panther; I saw his head over the tree trunk yonder."

"What was he like?" said the stranger abruptly, speaking in a sharp, peremptory tone that was rather offensive. I thought he was not treating me with the consideration due to a man of my age, who had just killed a panther. I was in no hurry to answer, therefore, and putting the caps on my gun, I walked towards Mr. Maltby. I am nearly six feet tall, if I *am* young, and it is not agreeable to be spoken to as if I were a boy. He repeated his question, rather more civilly, and I answered without looking round:

"Like other Indians, I suppose. Mr. Maltby, what am I to do next?"

"Get your horse, and we will call in the standers; no deer to-day, at least not in this drive. I think we had better go home, as the dogs are pretty well used up, anyhow." He mounted his horse, and blowing his horn, the hounds gathered around him, poor Music limping painfully along and whining piteously. "Carr's bitch is badly hurt, I'm afraid; did the beast get her down?"

"No, sir; she darted into the fight and out again like lightning, hurt as you see. It was then that I seized the knife and stabbed the panther." Seeing that he listened with great interest, I went on, telling him the story pretty much as I have recorded it here. When I had finished, he said,

"It was a plucky thing to do, youngster, but I advise you the next time to keep your distance. If that fellow had got a lick at you with his paw you would not have been standing here! The Indian must have been old Misty; he lives hereabouts. Where the dickens has he gone, I wonder? drunk as usual! Well, get your horse and come on; we'll ride slowly, and get the dogs home."

I started through the bushes, but returning to stick the knife back in the tree, I heard Maltby say: "His name is Hubbard—a friend of Carr's—he's genuine wildcat though, ain't he?" I could not hear his companion's reply, but I heard Maltby say: "Lying! no, no! I'll be sworn the boy told the truth." Confound that spruce blackguard! maybe I'll have a chance to pay him off some of these days.

I lost myself, and lost much time in getting back to the mare, and had to betake myself to the rivulet at last, and very nearly retrace my steps. At last I found the stand. The mare was restless, and I had considerable difficulty in mounting, encumbered as I was with the gun. I had fastened her by unbuckling the bridle rein, and rebuckling it round the limb of a sapling. I at last got into the saddle, and was trying to buckle the rein, when she stretched out her neck and twitched the bridle out of my fingers. She was off like a shot—right into the woods!

Under ordinary circumstances I could easily have regained the rein by leaning forward in the saddle, but, as it was, I was kept busy dodging the overhanging branches and managing my heavy gun. Once the muzzle caught in a trailing vine, and as the gun swung round I got a sound knock on the side of my head. I have the mark yet. This accident confused me somewhat, and a few minutes later the catastrophe happened. I had presence of mind enough to shake my feet clear of the stirrups when the mare first bolted, and thereafter I was doing regular riding school practice—holding on with my knees. And while the sparks were still flying from my eyes I saw a tree galloping up to me, and leaning to the right to avoid it, I accidentally touched Midnight with the spur. She swerved suddenly to the left, the tree struck me full in the breast, and that is all I know about it.

CHAPTER XI.

MISTEONO.

WHEN I recovered my senses I found myself alone in that wilderness, and felt as I suppose one feels when recovering from a mighty "drunk." My watch crystal was smashed, and my timekeeper had stopped. I picked up my gun and discharged both barrels, hoping that some of my fellow hunters might hear the report and come to my assistance. But the forest was perfectly quiet, though a moment before my fall I had heard Mr. Maltby's horn and the yelping of the dogs that followed him. The situation was decidedly unpleasant. There I was, as completely lost as though I had dropped down there from the clouds. I reloaded my gun, expecting to be attacked by three or four panthers at once, though Carr has since told me that they are very rare birds in this latitude. I walked about, gradually growing more accustomed to the peculiar position of affairs, and gradually perceiving how serious the accident really was. The most important fact was that I was lost. I could not even identify the tree that had brushed me so nicely from the saddle. I only knew that it was a beech, for I remembered the white spots on the bark. And I counted five or six beeches, all near enough to me, and each looking exactly like all the rest. When I first staggered up I moved about, dizzy and confused, and I don't know how far I had walked from the spot I had occupied between my fall and awakening before I thought of finding my way out of the woods. And then, even if I knew the way, the walk was tolerably long, as I was hurt, and wanted sleep more than anything else. I tried to whistle, but failed; I tried to hum a tune, but broke down with something like a sob. I concluded that the adventure was perhaps a little romantic, but also decidedly disgusting.

At length I sat down at the root of one of the beeches and

endeavoured to collect my energies. I wondered what Miss Ret was like, and what she would think of the loss of her mare; and then I wondered if I should ever see either mare or mistress. I wondered what Carr would think of my manhood. I wondered whether Miss Ret was an old maid of forty or a young damsel of fourteen. She could not be very young, or she could not manage that she-devil of a mare; probably twenty-five. If so, she would think that boys ought not to be trusted with valuable horses. Then I wondered why Carr had not talked to me about her. Was she his cousin or aunt? He called her "Ret," so she could not be his aunt. What did "Ret" stand for? It was very queer if it was her real name. And she had a brother, named Herbert; man enough to own a gun and to ride Midnight. Thank fortune Midnight had thrown *him* before I ever saw her. I wondered what Mother would think if she knew how I was amusing myself at that particular moment. And then I remembered her ideas of the Sabbath, and how I had violated my own convictions when I started on the hunt. And then I vowed, from the very depths of my heart, that I would never misspend the day again. Then I began to wonder whether I should live to see any more bright Sabbaths dawn upon the beautiful earth. I suppose my breast, which is bruised and still sore, hurt me, for I groaned.

"Young chief lose hoss? nebber mind, Injin find him."

I started to my feet, and, turning around, saw my Indian acquaintance standing near me. He was leaning on his gun, and did not look quite so drunk as he was at our last meeting. I noticed the long knife in his belt, so he had been back to his hut since I left it. I did not think about scalps this time, but cordially shook the hand he held out to me. No doubt I looked pale, for I felt very shaky, and when he pulled out the bottle from the breast of his shirt I did not refuse it. I took a mouthful of the whisky, which was horridly nasty, but it seemed to revive me. He nodded when I gave him back the bottle, and put it back in his bosom, and then motioning for me to follow him, he struck off into the woods. He reminded me of a cat creeping along with his noiseless step, and I no longer wondered how he had managed to approach me unheard. Beneath my feet the dry twigs cracked and the dead leaves rustled, while the Indian, a step in advance, moved as silently as a ghost. We skirted a canebrake of some extent, pressed through a dense growth of greenbriar bushes, and at length emerged into the open, a few yards from the Indian's hut. The first sight that gladdened my eyes was Midnight, quietly cropping the grass near the spring. She was secured by a thong, attached to a wild grapevine, which was elastic enough to allow her tolerably wide grazing ground. As she raised her head at our approach I noticed that the vine drew up and kept the thong and bridle clear of her legs. This is, therefore, another lesson in woodcraft that I have learned.

I walked round the tree, and was about to kneel down for a drink at the spring, when Misty handed me a gourd, which he took from a fork in the tree. If any one who may ever happen to see this record, wants to know what nectar tastes like, I advise him or her to get thrown from a horse at about noon on a May day in this latitude (which is about equal to a July day anywhere else), and to lie stunned on the ground for an hour or so, and then to take a mouthful of awful whisky, and stumble through wild vines and thickets for a mile or two, till he or she is just ready to die of fatigue and thirst, and then to get a gourdful (say half a gallon) of pure, cold spring water, and drink it in the shade.

After I had satisfied my thirst, and washed down the scalding taste of the raw whisky, I handed the gourd back to the Indian, who replaced it in the tree, and resumed his position, leaning against the trunk. We took a good look at each other. There was not much trace of intoxication left in his countenance now, and he looked more respectable than at our first interview. His long black hair, which was the only head gear he wore, hung straight down over his face and neck. His little, sharp, black eyes were roving over my person, resting upon my face occasionally, with as friendly an expression as such a countenance could assume. There seemed to be a mixture of perplexity and intelligence in these furtive glances into my eyes, as if he were trying to recall my features to his memory, and were baffled each time. He was grave and dignified, apparently waiting for me to address him.

"Is your name Misty?" I asked. He looked all round the open, then nodding his head, he said,

"Yes. Injin have 'nudder name when he was warrior. Young chief name Hubbard?"

"Why, where did you learn my name, Misty?" I answered with surprise, "and why do you call me young chief?"

"Injin see young brudder kill tiger cat. Young brudder brave, he be warrior bimeby. Injin was chief when he live in the Seminole country. Then he have good name. Misteono was warrior before he drink whisky. Now he drunken Misty."

" Who calls you drunken Misty ?" I asked.

" You hear him. Injin hear him when he hid under the tree yonder. When Cap'n come, Misty hide—no want Cap'n see him."

" Do you mean the man who was with Mr. Maltby ?" I inquired.

" Yes, Cap'n Delaney. Misteono knew him in Everglades—Misty know him here."

" What cause have you to fear him, Misteono ?" said I, giving the Indian his ancient name. A fierce scowl passed over his face as he answered,

"Misteono not feared! time not come yet. See !" he added suddenly, pointing his finger at a snake that appeared for an instant and then wriggled into the bushes ; " Rattlesnake no make noise till he ready to strike."

I unfastened my horse and mounted with considerable agility as I heard the name of the dreaded reptile. They are uncomfortably numerous in this locality, and I have heard enough stories about them from the Carrville people to make me prefer my seat in the saddle to the grassy bank upon which I had been standing. Misteono evidently noticed my trepidation and understood its cause.

" Rattlesnake not get bad for two, tree moons yet," he said, " and he always rattle 'fore he bite."

" How did you catch the horse, Misteono ?" said I, not wishing to pursue the snake subject any further. It is not worth while to deny that I am horridly afraid of all varieties of the serpent tribe ; and I believe that this dread and aversion is the instinctive feeling of all men.

" Him come to the spring to drink. Bimeby he lay down to roll and Misteono catch him before he get up. Know young chief's horse, so take his trail and go back for young chief. How fa' off ? Squaw ride him——" Without waiting for an answer he darted to the bushes just as I heard the faint sound of a horn. I rode in the direction of the sound and soon saw my friend Carr, followed by Jacobus. I shouted as soon as they came into sight, and Carr galloped up to me, exclaiming " Here he is, by Jove !"

There is not much more to tell. It seems that the whole hunting party returned to Mr. Maltby's, and after waiting an hour for my arrival, Carr concluded that I was lost. Learning from Mr. Malt-by that he had left me near the Indian's wigwam he had started with Jacobus to look for me.

"I have been delayed somewhat," he said, "as I came round by Manahio, supposing that you would leave the mare to find the way for you, and I was sure she would go straight home. I was a good deal disappointed, and, indeed, uneasy when I found you had not been there. But when I reached your stand and dis-covered that you had ridden off eastwardly I made up my mind to hunt for you in the wilderness of the Amite."

"I did not have a choice of routes," I answered. "Midnight took matters into her own charge as soon as I mounted and soon unseated me. But tell me, Carr, how shall I reward Misty, who has been a true friend in need."

"Oh, give him a gallon of whisky and he will be grateful while it lasts. What a pity it is that the rascal is such a drunkard! He is one of the best hunters I know. And you ought to see him spiking the fish in the creek by torch-light. You *shall* see him, by Jupiter! We will change our fishing excursion to the pools of the creek to a regular gigging party, and Misty shall be master of ceremonies. What do you say?"

"Agreed," I replied; "but where are you going now?"

"To Manahio, of course," answered Carr, "where you will get some dinner and spend the rest of the day in any way that may suit your fancy."

"Not to-day, Carr, if you please. Let me go home, take a bath and dress my wounds and bruises. I shall be very happy to visit Manahio some other time."

"Well, to-morrow evening then, or"—seeing that I hesitated— "say Tuesday. Give me your gun and ammunition and Jake will go with you as far as the ford. Keep the mare till Tuesday and I will come into town after dinner and ride out with you. Good bye."

I got home safely, took a famous nap after my bath, ate a good supper, and then sat up half the night journalizing. And here have I been doing the same thing to-night, but I'm off to bed.

CHAPTER XII.

The Doctor.

TUESDAY, *May* 11, 1836.

THE postmaster of Carrville, Mr. White, has located his office in a little building adjoining our store. I have allowed him to open a door into the store room, so that I have an oversight of the post-office while I am in our own building. We have a mail twice a week, and I have been sworn in as deputy postmaster, and I find that I shall have all the work to do, which don't amount to a great deal. It takes about fifteen minutes to open and assort the mail, and about as much time to make up the mail that leaves Carrville—so that I have undertaken to do fifty hours work in the year for fifty dollars per annum. In to-day's mail there were two letters for me. One from home; all well and happy except for my absence; the other from Mr. Bayard, who is still in New Orleans. He says there is some reason to fear that the Seagull is lost, with all our goods on board, and asks me for a list of invoices, and a memorandum of the insurance. I have answered both letters, and have placed the insurance policies in the iron safe at the hotel. I find that the total amount of purchases is twelve thousand dollars, and that the insurance is for that amount and ten per centum advance, which is according to custom. So, if the Seagull is lost, Mr. Bayard will make twelve hundred dollars, and the difference of interest between the settlement of the claims upon the underwriters and the maturity of his bills in October next. He concluded his letter in these words: "If the ship is ascertained to be lost, *one of us* will have to go North to collect the insurance and replace the goods." I did not reply to this portion of his letter, because I did not know whether he meant to include me in the "one of us," or whether he referred to a silent partner, to whom I have heard him allude once or twice. It would be too good news if he meant that I might have an opportunity to visit my dear home so soon.

There are two gentlemen in this place of whom I have been intending to say something ever since I began this diary, and I may as well take the present opportunity to put down my impressions concerning them. Of course, I know very little about them, but they have both been very friendly in their intercourse with me, and

I like them particularly. The first is Mr. Robert White, our post-master. He is a quiet, gentlemanly fellow, about thirty years old; rather good looking and moderately lazy, or, perhaps, I ought to say, indolent. I met him on the night of my arrival, and was pleased with him from the first. Carr tells me that he owns no plantation in this neighbourhood, though his wife has one some-where in what they call the "Téche Country." I suppose this means the lands lying on or near the Bayou Téche. He lives in a pretty little house on the outskirts of Carrville, and I spent a pleasant hour there one afternoon last week. I called him lazy just now, but when I remember the beautiful garden around his house, which he has adorned with his own hands, and which he is all the time improving, I am forced to recall the slander. Still he seems to be lazy about everything else. He won't do anything about the post-office that he can escape. When he proposed to open the door of communication between the office and our store room, he said:

"I don't intend to work much among the mails. I did not ask for the appointment; and I should like you to undertake the prin-cipal part of the duties at whatever price you think reasonable. You can do all the mail work in an hour each week. The revenue it yields me is very trifling, but it will be advantageous to you to have it located near your store. What do you think would com-pensate you?"

"Fifty dollars per annum," I answered.

"Agreed!" said Mr. White, and that was the bargain.

The thing that made the strongest impression upon me the other evening when I called at his house, was the profound affection he and his wife entertain for each other. There was no violent de-monstration, but it was constantly apparent. The mere inflexions of their voices, as they called each other's names—"Robert" or "Mary," attracted my attention all the time. I do not believe that I can describe them, or even express what I think about them, but I only know that I have never seen a man and his wife so cordially devoted to each other as Mr. and Mrs. White seem to be. They have no children. I shall probably have more to say about them hereafter. Perhaps the best indication I can offer of the impression their unity of sentiment made upon me, is the fact that I never think of them separately.

The other gentleman is Doctor Markham, the only physician in this neighbourhood. And now that I have written his name, I am at a loss to begin a description of him. He is probably a year or two younger than Mr. White, and is undoubtedly a right down good fellow. His office is opposite the store and I see him frequently during the day, sometimes mounting his horse to start out on his round of visits, and looking as if he had not fully made up his mind whether to start or not, or which foot he would put into the stirrup. Sometimes, when he comes home, his horse stops at his door and he sits awhile in the saddle, as if debating in his own mind whether or not he had better dismount, or call his little nigger "Sam" to help him down. He is the slowest man I ever met, and yet he is a man of excellent sense and sound judgment. His practice is large, and probably would be profitable, if he were not too lazy to attend to collections. This morning, as he was riding away, he called out to me across the street:

"Hubbard! I wish those drugs of yours would come, I am almost out of calomel!"

"I can get some for you, doctor," I answered.

"Where? How?"

"From Baton Rouge. I can send by Captain Joli, and have it here in a day or two."

"So you can!" he exclaimed, after meditating a few minutes. "I wish you would send for half a pound." And then he paused again, and added, "Hey! No! Say a quarter of a pound. Maybe it is not good!" Another pause, and then—"No, you had better get a pound! When yours comes I can use this for external applications. Get up!" And away he went.

He came back about noon. I have had toothache for a day or two, and to-day it was dreadful. So when the doctor returned, I walked over to his office and followed him into it. He shook hands with me and handed me a chair with great politeness. Then he took off his hat and coat, and bawled out for "Sam." When the young African appeared, the doctor told him to "get some water in the other room." The boy moved with great activity to obey his commands, and presently I heard the doctor splashing in the water in the next room. He came to the door in a short time, rubbing his face with a towel, and wiping his hands as though he never intended to consider them dry. At last he looked at me attentively and said:

"What ails you, Hubbard? Your face is a yard long!"

"I've got the toothache, doctor."

"Hey! Where is it?"

"In my mouth, sir," I replied with a sickly attempt at a smile. "The deuce it is !"

He pulled open a little drawer and took out two or three horrid looking implements. The pain suddenly subsided, and I began to think what an ass I was to come over there at all. But I was ashamed to back out now, so I allowed him to examine my grinders.

"Does it ache much ?" asked the doctor, after he had found the ailing tooth, and poked about it in a very unpleasant manner.

"No, sir; it don't ache at all now." He laughed, and I plucked up courage to ask: "Do you think it ought to come out, doctor ?"

"Yes; it will probably ache until you get rid of it; but if you don't want it out, I'll put some kreosote in the cavity; maybe it will get easier."

"Will it hurt me much to draw it ?"

"Yes; it will hurt like blazes," he replied, with charming candor. "The gum is inflamed and sore; but it will soon be over, and I think you will survive the operation." And here he laughed again.

"Work your fiendish will upon me !" I exclaimed, in a rage. He put his arm around my head, and passed a lancet around the gum. Then he seized the tooth in the forceps, the heavens and the earth came together with a crash, and the doctor stood over me, flourishing the extracted molar in triumph above my head. Slow as he is about most things, he was fast enough this time.

"There !" he said, kindly, "you bore that like a stoic. I expected you to howl a little. It hurt, didn't it ? Here ! take a sip of brandy. I don't often recommend brandy, either. Will you have another tooth drawn ?"

"No, I thank you, doctor. I am sorry to deny you the gratification, too; but the next time I submit to such an operation it will be after I have endured the pain three hundred and sixty-five days."

"It won't be a wisdom tooth, then," quoth the doctor. "Here, I'll lend you a book;" and he took a volume from a shelf. "It is old Burton's Anatomy."

"I am much obliged to you, doctor," I answered, "but I have the book, and have already read it through."

"The deuce you have ! Burton's Anatomy of Melancholy ! read it through ! What d'ye mean ? Have you laid it aside as a work accomplished ?"

"No, indeed; I read a little every time I get a chance. One does not *finish* Burton with one reading."

"How old are you?" said the doctor.

"Not quite twenty-one;" replied I. And then I thought it was a small business to pretend to be older than I was, so I added: "the truth is, doctor, I am not quite twenty. I am about nineteen and a half."

"Well, you will be older in a few, years, if you live; besides, there is not much difference between nineteen and twenty-one. A man don't have any sense until he is thirty-five or forty, anyhow."

"I did not think you were so old, doctor," I rejoined with a bow.

"Who? I? Oh, I don't profess to be very wise; and there are exceptions to all general rules. Are you going? Well, I'll call over to-night and have a talk with you."

"I am going to Mr. Carr's to-night, but any other time——"

"Why, so am I! I have to see that boy again to-day. Well, then, I'll meet you there, if I am not able to ride out with you. Good bye!"

I have written all this about Doctor Markham, because he can thus describe himself better than I can describe him. Mr. White says his patients are all very much attached to him, and that he could "take his choice" among the young ladies of the neighbourhood, if he were inclined to marry. When I know him better I intend to find out why it is that he keeps single; but I hear Carr's voice, and now I must get ready for our ride. I suppose I shall have to wear a black coat, hot as it is. We won't have the doctor's company, as I saw him ride off an hour ago.

CHAPTER XIII

RET.

WEDNESDAY, *May* 12, 1836.

I FEEL so bewildered, and (I don't know why) also so dispirited to-night, that I am half-inclined to put my diary away again and go to bed. There is some unfathomable mystery enveloping me, and the matters I have to record are so strange to my mind that I kept awake all last night, thinking and wondering. I believe I have made up my mind to consult Mr. White, and to be guided by his advice. He is a good man, and I can trust him with the whole story. Since I came in from Manahio, this morning, I have had very little to do, and I have spent the day in thinking over the events of last night. The workmen have gone at last—the store being finished; and I have been alone here all day, as Mr. White went to Baton Rouge early this morning. I cannot go to sleep, if I go to bed, so I will write until I feel drowsy, anyhow.

After Carr and I crossed the creek yesterday afternoon we turned into a broad carriage road, which followed the course of the stream for more than a mile. We arrived at the grounds around the house, which is not far from the Manahio, at sunset. Like all residences in this State, the house is surrounded with a broad veranda, and for eight or nine months in the year the spacious "galleries," as they term them, are the living rooms of the family. As we rode up the gravelled road, approaching the house, I saw several persons on this open porch, and my heart beat with mingled curiosity and bashfulness as I perceived that a young lady was one of the party. She was dressed—pshaw! what do I know about her dress! I only noticed that it was black, and looked blacker in contrast with her fair neck and arms. I suppose I ought to call these "alabaster." She has brown hair, brown eyes, generally sad looking, though sometimes bright and sparkling. I don't know whether she is handsome or not. Probably she is, or would be, if she did not dress in black. She is eighteen. I heard Mr. Carr say that she was two years older than her brother, and he told me that he was sixteen. But I am anticipating.

Jacobus took our horses, and as we ascended the steps Mr. Carr came forward to meet us. He shook hands with me, inquired if I felt any ill effects from my late accident, and then presented me to the young lady, who stood near him.

"Mr. Hubbard, my dear; Miss HARWOOD, sir!" I bowed and stammered something, as the lady returned my salutation, and Mr. Carr, who had me by the arm, led me to a youth seated in an arm chair, and finished the ceremony, and nearly finished *me*, by adding: "Mr. HERBERT HARWOOD, sir! The boy had his right arm in a sling, and he put out his left hand to me, saying: "Midnight gave me a tumble, too, Mr. Hubbard. Please excuse my left hand!" He is a bright looking fellow, and decidedly good looking, too. I don't know what I should have said or done in my confusion, if Dr. Markham had not come up, and shaking my hand, inquired: "How is the toothache now, Burton?"

What under the shining sun does it mean? My name is not a very common name, and here I find a boy bearing it, while I have lost it. There certainly *must* be some wonderful mystery about the business. How has it chanced that I have never heard the name of this brother and sister before? I remember, when the negro told me the story of the haunted laurels, he spoke of their dead father constantly as "Mars'r John." While I lay awake last night, thinking confusedly of that ghost story and of these young children and their sorrows, of the melancholy expression of the girl's face, and the horrid burden she constantly bears, in the knowledge of her father's death, perhaps by his own hand; and then her brother's name, Herbert—a name given to me in memory of my father's uncle, and so uncommon that I have never known a single individual who bore it—while I thought of all these matters, I vow that I almost fancied the room was haunted. I was foolish enough, at last, to get out of bed, dress myself, excepting my boots, and sit at the window, smoking cigars, and listening to the murmur of the Manahio, which I could hear distinctly in the stillness of the night. But I am not telling my story very coherently.

At the tea table I sat next to Miss Ret, which is the universal name of Miss Harwood, and had some slight opportunity to look at her and converse with her. She looks actually beautiful when she smiles, which she does very rarely, however. Doctor Markham asked her brother if he felt disposed to ride Midnight again, and if "he would like to have his other shoulder put into place?"

"I am ready to take another ride whenever Ret will lend me her mare," replied Herbert; "but I am not the only one she has thrown;" and here he glanced slyly at me.

"I was not exactly *thrown*," replied I, "the mare brushed me off by running on the wrong side of the tree. Besides, *I* had no bridle. You must be tolerably courageous, Miss Harwood, to undertake the management of Midnight."

"Oh, she never misbehaves with me," she rejoined, with a smile; "perhaps she is like most of her sex, restive under masculine restraint."

"I am always uneasy, however, Miss Henrietta," said Mr. Carr, "when you mount that animal, and I have nearly concluded to forbid your use of her for a year or so. She will, perhaps, be more discreet when she is more matured."

"Now, father," said Charley, "you must not lay an embargo on Ret's rides. Herbert was thrown because he would spur Midnight, and Mr. Hubbard—by Jove! *he* had spurs on Sunday, too! I had forgotten all about them! Look at him; he is actually blushing; make a clean breast of it, my friend! She threw you because you spurred her. Hey?"

"No! Yes! that is——" and everybody, Miss Ret included, began to laugh. I told the story of the accident as soon as they got quiet enough to listen, but I am perfectly satisfied that they all blame the spur. Anyhow, they laughed again when I had finished. It is just possible that the accidental touch of my "armed heel" hastened matters somewhat.

"How old is your mare, Miss Harwood?" I asked.

"Four years on the first of July next," she replied. I was about to say something concerning her accuracy in dates, when I observed the smile fade away from her face, which became deadly pale. I thought everybody looked rather grave, and wondered what impropriety there could be in the question and answer. There was a few minutes' silence after her reply, which seemed to be embarrassing, and it was at last broken by the young lady herself remarking that both her brother and I had met with our disasters on the Sabbath.

"Do you really believe, Ret," said Charley Carr, "that the day had anything to do with the occurrences? Because Midnight must then be more religiously inclined than any of us. Besides, you are in some sort responsible yourself, as the mare is your property."

"You know very well, Charley," retorted Ret, "that the animal was used on both occasions without my knowledge or consent, and you also know that I should have objected, if my opinion or will had been consulted." This was said with a quiet dignity, and she looked beautiful once more, though she did *not* smile.

"I am obliged to confess," said I, interrupting Carr's rejoinder—"that my first thought, when I recovered from the effects of the fall, was, that I deserved my fate for violating the Sabbath. Moreover, my firmest resolution at the same time was to avoid all similar abuses of the day hereafter." They were all looking at me when I said this, Miss Ret very kindly, Mr. Carr very curiously, and Charley and the doctor very incredulously. I went on bravely: "I am not particularly pious, and I know I do a great many worse things ; but my Mother would be deeply pained if she knew how I had spent that day."

"That's right, Burton," said the doctor, patting me on the back, "and I'll knock anybody down that says you are wrong."

"The resolution was a good one at least," observed Miss Harwood, "whether the motive was proper or not. I mean," she added apologetically, as we rose from the table, "I mean that you might have had even a *better* motive than love for your Mother." Once more she looked superbly lovely.

"Perhaps I have, or *may* have," replied I, in a low tone. She heard me, but nobody else did. She is a wonderful woman, considering her age! My answer was somewhat equivocal, and her look showed that she so regarded it. We were all seated on the gallery a few minutes later, where we found a Mr. Gowrie, an old Scottish gentleman living at Carrville, who had just arrived. The discussion was resumed by the doctor, who observed that all days were necessarily alike to him, inasmuch as people " got sick on Sunday, and had to be visited and prescribed for." I waited for somebody else to answer him until Carr asked : " What have you to say to that, Hubbard ?"

"I don't know why you appeal to me," I replied, "but it is only necessary to say that good people hold that works of necessity and mercy are allowable on the Sabbath. The doctor's vocation includes both classes."

" My idea," quoth the doctor, "is, that men should cultivate a thankful, and, if you please, a devout frame of mind all the time. I don't believe in any religion that one puts on only one day in seven."

" That is to say, the Sabbath is the product of mere human superstition," I replied, " or, at least, that actions which are wrong on Sunday are equally wrong on any other day."

" Exactly," said Charley Carr. There was a short pause. Miss Harwood looked inquiringly at me, as if she expected me to say more. She sat just opposite one of the windows, and the light from the room shone on her face. I could not resist the look. I was foolish enough to fancy that it said, " Answer him," in a tone that was at once imperious and gentle. Mr. Carr appeared restless, and tired of the conversation. Master Herbert was whistling softly; nevertheless, I ventured one more shot.

"You seem so well satisfied with your conclusion, Carr, that it is almost a pity to disturb your serenity, but I will just say another word: if we are creatures at all, we owe allegiance to the Creator, and He has expressly commanded a special observance of one day of the week. He has forbidden certain things on the Sabbath which He enjoins upon us during the week."

"That is verra weel put, young gentleman," observed Mr. Gowrie, "but it does not contain all the argument." We were all slightly startled by this remark. Mr. Gowrie had walked out from the village, and declined the invitation to supper when Mr. Carr found him on the gallery, saying he had already supped. He had been listening very quietly to the conversation, and this was his first remark. There was something pugnacious in the tone, which awakened the doctor's pugnacity in turn.

"I should like to hear an argument, Mr. Gowrie," said he, "if there is one."

"It is no' easy to state it in full, but the septenary division of time seems to be written upon the nature of humanity. It is found among heathen tribes, who never heard of either Jewish or Christian Sabbath."

"But that proves nothing about the establishment of a special day for religious observance. Does it, Burton?"

"I beg to refer you to Mr. Gowrie. My side of the debate is in his hands now, and I am well content to leave it there."

"D'ye happen to know," said the Scot, "why the Sabbath came to be observed at first?"

There was a slight pause, and then a sweet voice answered, "For in six days the Lord made heaven and earth, the sea and all that in them is, and rested the seventh day; wherefore, the Lord blessed the Sabbath day and hallowed it."

"Preceesely. The young leddy has given the best possible answer. If you believe the words she has quoted have authority, I suppose there need be nae mair argumentation."

"I have an objection to put in just there," said Charley Carr. "The day, you observe, is not the day referred to in Miss Harwood's quotation."

"And I have another slight objection," quoth the doctor. "I happen to be a geologist, and, therefore, I can never believe that this earth was made in six days."

The Scot settled himself in his chair, took a pinch of snuff, cleared his throat, and answered:

"I'll just tak' one objection at a time, and begin with yours, doctor. Geology is a fine science, and I cherish a great respect for it, but it is no' quite so auld as revelation. Then, its professors dinna agree verra weel amang themselves. I know of a dispute, in which a few millions of years are involved, between twa of your maist famous professors in Scotland."

"But they agree in rejecting the six days story, anyhow."

"Ay, ay," answered Mr. Gowrie, "they agree in many points; but I am no' certain about the sax days mysel', and, in fact, I dinna care a bawbee whether it was sax days or sax million ages. D'ye happen to have a copy of the Scriptures at hand, Miss Harwood?"

Miss Harwood rose, stepped through the window into the room, and reappeared in a moment with a Bible in her hand, which she offered to Mr. Gowrie.

"If I may be so bauld," he said, "I'll trouble you to read the passages I want; my eyes are no sae young as they were forty years ago."

"With pleasure, sir," replied she. "I can see perfectly by this light."

"Weel," began the theologue, dogmatically, "there were twa things which God gave to man in Eden that he brought out wi' him. He left somewhat in a hurry and brought very little else. The first was the marriage relation, the second was the Sabbath."

"That is a striking remark," said Dr. Markham, "and I am pleased to admit it; but the six days——"

"Bide a wee, we'll hae the sax days soon enough. Please to read a varse or twa of the second chapter of Genesis, Miss Ret." She read three verses, and Mr. Gowrie stopped her. "There is the whole story *ab initio*. I tak' it for granted that you young gentlemen will admit that these varses contain the whole original account of the institution of the Sabbath."

"Yes," answered Charley and the doctor in a breath.

"Weel," said Mr. Gowrie, very slowly and composedly, "there is na word aboot the sax days there."

Miss Harwood read the verses again. There was a pause. Everybody appeared reluctant to "tackle" the Scotsman. He looked very grisly, as he sat there in the dim light, audibly chuckling.

"I cannot see the force of the omission, Mr. Gowrie," said Miss Ret, at last. "Will you please explain?"

"Certainly, so far as I can. I think the Sabbath was hallowed because God *rested*, not because He *worked*. He could have made the world in sax minutes, if He pleased, or He may have wrought through countless ages. It maks no differ in either case, as it is the Rest we celebrate on the Sabbath."

"Mr. Gowrie," said the doctor, elaborately, "I am sure you err in calling the day 'the Sabbath.' It is probably owing to the misfortune of your Presbyterian education. The day observed by Christians (except Seventh-day Baptists), whatever their mode of observance, is in no sense of the word 'the Sabbath,' which is a peculiarly Jewish institution, and belongs to the seventh day of the week alone. If you observe the seventh day you observe the Sabbath; if the first day, be as rigid as you please, it is 'Sunday,' or 'the Lord's day,' if you like, but not 'the Sabbath.' You might as well call Easter 'the Passover.'"

Here was another pause. At first I thought Mr. Gowrie was floored, but happened again to hear his truculent chuckle. I looked intently at him, saw his eyes twinkle, and waited for his answer.

"I dinna ken whether you'll hae the patience to hear the answer ——"

"You can't get off so easily, Mr. Gowrie," said Charley, delightedly; "we'll listen to you all night, if necessary."

"Less time will do, Maister Charley, and I am the mair willing to answer the doctor, because I answer yon objection of yours at the same time. Will the young leddy please read a varse or twa from the fourth of Hebrews?"

"What verse, sir?"

"Aweel, begin wi' the fourth varse."

And Miss Harwood read:

"For He spoke in a certain place of the seventh day on this wise—'And God did rest the seventh day from all His works.'"

"That is to say," said Mr. Gowrie, expounding, "He so spoke in the second chapter of Genesis, which Miss Ret has already quoted. Now, in the 5th chapter of Deuteronomy and at the fifteenth varse, Moses says the Lord commanded this observance because He had brought the tribes out of Egypt. There was always before the mind of the Jew the Rest of the land of Canaan, after his toilsome wanderings throughout the forty years, and the constantly recurring Sabbath was, to the Jew, an earnest, and pledge, and type of that Rest. But in the eighth varse of this fourth of Hebrews the writer says Joshua did not obtain the true Rest, because

God *afterwards* spoke of *another* day. Nothing could be more clear and explicit than this statement. Now, doctor," and he produced a little volume from his pocket, "I'll just trouble *you* to read the next varse—the ninth."

"The doctor took the book, and stepped to the window. "Why, it is Greek!" he exclaimed.

"Preceesely," answered the Scot composedly, "and a verra fine tongue it is."

"I am rather rusty in Greek, Mr. Gowrie," said Markham, "but I'll try. The ninth verse, fourth chapter—here it is! Um, um!"

"Ye need na' read the Greek, doctor, please translate into English."

"Well," said the doctor, "it reads somehow thus: 'There remains therefore a rest and a Sabbath-keeping to the people of God.'"

"And the next varse," said Mr. Gowrie, "gives the reason. It is because Christ also has ceased from His work, and entered into His rest," to wit, on "the first day of the week, when He arose from the dead, preceesely as God ceased and rested on the last day of the week." He rose as he spoke, and with great dignity continued, "it is easy to preach from so clear a text as this. If the Jew had a Sabbath, sanctified by the completion of God's great work of creation, surely the Christian has a Sabbath, sanctified by the completion of God's great work of redemption. And I'll just add, doctor," and he turned suddenly upon the medico, "if you will take the trouble to look at the twelfth chapter of the Acts, at the fourth varse, ye'll just find that the writer there calls the Passover Easter. Your illustration was unfortunate. Gude night, Miss Ret, I am verra much obliged to you for listening so patiently. Gude night, gentlemen." And chuckling at a great rate, he went crunching on the gravel towards the gate. In a moment he was hidden by the trees, but we heard him once or twice chuckling in high glee.

We all laughed. The discomfited appearance of the doctor was very funny, but did not seem to disturb him at all. He sat there where the Scot left him, meditating. At length he sighed softly.

"I tell you what it is, Burton," he said, "any man who tackles a Scotch Presbyterian on Theology had better keep out of reach of the fool-killer. I thought I had him down, but I hadn't!"

"Some of Mr. Gowrie's positions are new to me," I answered, "but his whole argument was tolerably strong."

"Mr. Gowrie is one of the most remarkable men I have ever met," observed Judge Carr; "he is very thoroughly educated, and has more than once given me from memory long 'quottations,' as he calls them, from classical authors, that were perfectly accurate. He is also very fond of lighter literature, a very severe critic of modern poetry, especially that of Moore and Byron, but with sound judgment and rare taste. He is an excellent business man, exact and scrupulous in all his dealings, seeming to take delight in the dryest details of commercial affairs. Once or twice I have, for mere amusement, engaged him in controversy upon theological subjects, and I must say that he has always forced me to believe that his points were well taken, and, in fact, impregnable. He has a sly way of yielding points which appear to be vital, and then coming down suddenly, and with tremendous force, in an unexpected quarter. His curious dismissal of the 'Sax days' appears to illustrate this peculiar habit."

"What do *you* think of Mr. Gowrie's positions, Mr. Hubbard?" said Miss Harwood.

"It seems to me," replied I, "that his statements were all perfectly logical. A quaint remark of his just occurs to me. I was speaking to him this morning about an infidel book that has recently appeared, entitled 'The Free Thinker,' and his comment was 'ay, ay, I hae perused yon book. The maist remarkable thing I found in it was the title. The author, instead of being 'free,' is in bondage to the maist extraordinary ignorance, and there is no sign in his book of any 'thinking' of any sort." I turned to Charley and added, "You may as well abandon your flimsy theories, *mon ami*, and rely upon the immutable facts of an existent Deity, and *therefore* a Divine Revelation."

"You are taking for granted every thing that you ought to prove," said Carr; "the existence of a Deity, the fact of a Divine Revelation, and——"

"Oh! Charley! Charley!" Miss Ret is certainly in love with my friend, I think, and she is as evidently disgusted with what he calls his 'free thinking.' I don't believe, however, that he is settled in his infidel opinions, but rather suppose he talked for the sake of argument. I'll have it out with him hereafter."

His father interposed at this point:

"We have been waiting for this opportunity, Mr. Hubbard, to hear from you an account of your adventures last Sunday," he said. "Charley tells me that you did not give him more than the outlines of your story, so if you please we will postpone polemics, and listen with great pleasure to your account of the panther hunt."

"If *you* please, father," said Charley, "I would like to ask Hubbard one question before we change the subject. Why did you go on this unhallowed expedition last Sunday? I presume the views you have just expressed are not altogether new to you?"

"I hardly know why I did not decline your invitation when it was given. I recollect that I offered some objection and I think you did not give me time to refuse. However, I *had* determined to send you a note of apology by Jake, but——"

"But what?" said Miss Harwood.

"But my good resolutions vanished before the desire to bestride your mare as soon as I saw her. After I once mounted, I confess I did not think much of the day until Midnight and I parted company."

"There!" said Charley, triumphantly, "I said it was all your fault, Ret, or your mare's fault, which is the same thing. *She* is a dumb brute and not responsible."

"I want to hear about the panther now," replied Miss Harwood. Her brother ceased whistling, and drew his chair up. I had a very attentive audience. They all listened with a flattering silence while I narrated the panther story. I tried to say little about the actual encounter, which was no great shakes after all. The brute must have had some forty buckshot in his body before I gave him the *coup de grace*. When I finished the recital Carr observed that my account did not exactly agree with Mr. Maltby's. "He said that you rushed in and knifed the brute while he was still fighting the dogs."

"I believe I did," I answered; "it was all over in a minute. I saw Music dash at the panther and get an ugly scratch, and you know she is a pet of yours and mine. I suppose I was induced to take an active part in the dispute on her account."

"Mr. Maltby says he would not have stood in your shoes for the best plantation in the State. The panther was more dangerous because wounded, and poor Music can testify that he was not quite so nearly dead as you suppose."

"Please tell me, Mr. Hubbard," said Herbert earnestly, "what you thought when you *went in*."

"I don't remember," replied I, laughing at his earnestness. "I had not much time to think. I saw the dogs flying about, and when I first got a good view of the panther he was on his back, fighting with all four of his feet. As I ran up a dog passed me and darted at his throat, and in the struggle that followed he turned over on his side. I think I put my foot on his fore leg and thrust the knife into his body, just behind the shoulder."

"That was just it," said Charley Carr. "Maltby thinks it was the pluckiest thing he ever saw or heard of. It is curious, by-the bye, what became of the beast. Maltby went with one of his boys in the afternoon to skin him, but could not find hide or hair. Old Misty could not be found either, nor has he been seen since Sunday."

"There was a person with Mr. Maltby on Sunday," said I, "called Captain Delaney, I think——"

"Delaney!" said Miss Harwood, with a start.

"Yes; at least the Indian told me that was his name. I mentioned his because I wished to know if any of you could tell me anything about him."

"Captain Delaney lives in New Orleans," said Mr. Carr. "He comes to this parish occasionally. When he is in this neighbourhood he stays at Mr. Maltby's. I think he is related to Mrs. Maltby."

"Is he in the army, sir?" I inquired.

"No—that is, he *was* a captain of volunteers in the Florida war, and he still retains the title. At present he is a——"

"A sportsman," said Charley, when his father paused, as if he were hunting for a word to describe the sleek gentleman's occupation. "Sportsman" in this latitude means simply a gambler.

"I was going to say a gentleman of leisure," continued Mr. Carr. "He seems to have plenty of money always. Charles calls him a 'sportsman,' I suppose, because he plays for money, but I think he has never been suspected of unfairness. Most of the gentlemen in this vicinity have played with him, and though he generally wins, his good fortune is attributed to his superior luck, or skill, or both together."

Here the doctor started up, saying he must "be off." Jake brought his horse to the step, and after he had deliberated some five minutes, he finally made up his mind to put his left foot in the stirrup. He mounted while he was making his farewell speech.

"Do you keep yourself quiet for a day or two longer and you shall have your fiddle again. You had better get Burton here to give you some lessons. He plays like the witches! Good evening. Never mind the gate, Jake. Mr. Hubbard will open it for me. Come, Burton, walk down to the gate; I want to speak to you."

As soon as we got out of earshot of the occupants of the porch, the doctor, who is very thoughtful and considerate, began:

"I only wanted to say to you, Hubbard, that you must not allow yourself to admire Miss Ret too much. She is mortgaged to our friend Charley, I suspect."

"Much obliged for the warning, doctor," replied I, laughing, although I felt rather provoked, "but there is not the slightest danger in my case."

"I don't know about that, Burton. She is the finest girl in this State, or in any other, that I know of."

"No doubt. Nevertheless I am safe enough.

"The devil you are! D'ye mean that your young affections are already placed?"

"Yes—upon myself. I am not young enough to fall in love with the first pretty girl I see. Besides, Miss Ret is not so remarkably beautiful. Oh, please tell me what there was about my question that was *mal apropos.* I mean, when I inquired how old Midnight was."

"Nothing amiss on your part. The mare was foaled on the night that Mr. Harwood—— died. I'll tell you about it to-morrow. Here's the gate. I advise you to go back by that walk to the left. I hate to be crunching over gravel when I can get on the soft grass. Good night."

I turned off the carriage road as the doctor advised and presently came to a beautiful little bower, covering a rustic seat. I sat down here and puffed at my cigar, thinking over all the matters I have been scrawling down here. It is probable that the time slipped away faster than I imagined while I was indulging in my "maiden meditations, fancy free." At last I threw away the stump of my cigar and was about to resume my walk when I heard footsteps on the carriage road, which was near the path, and as they drew nearer I heard Miss Harwood's voice. She has a remarkably sweet voice, and I paused to listen.

"The doctor calls him Burton," she said.

"That's not his name, though," said Charley Carr. "Stop, I have a note from him in my pocket now. I can read it by moonlight." He fumbled in his pocket and I heard the rustling of the paper. "It is signed 'H. H.,'" said Carr, in a tone of vexation.

" ' H.' does not stand for ' Burton,' " said Miss Ret.

" It must be ' Henry,' " observed Carr.

" Maybe it's ' Herbert,' " said my namesake, and then the young rascal began to hum—

> "Old Mother Hubbard,
> She lived in a cupboard."

" Hush !" said his sister, " he might hear you and perhaps he would not like it. I think he must be a namesake of mine, brother ; your name is not very common."

" I shall call myself ' Henry' hereafter, anyhow," said I, advancing ; " Miss Harwood has not left me a choice."

They all laughed, though I thought the young lady was somewhat embarrassed, as she observed,

" We did not know you were so near."

" The doctor recommended the walk to me, and I was tempted by the beauty of this arbour to rest while I finished my cigar. I have overheard very little of your conversation. Dr. Markham calls me ' Burton' sometimes, because we both admire an author of that name."

" I can very easily find out Hubbard's Christian name," said Charley, " as some of the Carrville people will know it."

" Very well," replied I ; " in the meantime I am to remain Henry Hubbard, at your service."

" Your initials are the same as mine, Mr. Hubbard," said Herbert, " and Ret's too. Isn't that funny ?"

" Yes. But I know something still more unaccountable ; and that is, that I am acquainted with a Baltimorean whose name is precisely identical with yours."

" Herbert Harwood !" exclaimed all three.

I watched them to see what effect the announcement would produce. Carr and Herbert expressed nothing but surprise, while Miss Harwood appeared to be discomposed. Maybe this was only my fancy. But she said immediately—" we are keeping Mr. Hubbard standing all this time. Let us go back to the house." Charley and her brother walked on ahead, and I had the honour of walking by Miss Ret's side. I think she lagged a little behind purposely, to say to me, " At another time I will be much obliged to you for a fuller account of—— your Baltimore acquaintance. It is possible that Herbert and I may have relations there of whom we know nothing, or very little." ·

I made no reply to this. I thought once or twice of bolting out the secret of my identity with these possible " relations," but there was some inflexion in her voice, or something in her manner, that kept me silent. It's of no use for me to try to say what it was. I don't know. But I *will* know, if it pleases heaven!

Ten o'clock came pretty soon. Charley escorted me to my sleeping apartment, in which everything was nice and comfortable, and left me, wishing me "pleasant dreams!" I hunted for the dreams till midnight, and then got up and dressed. My room opened on the second story of the verandah, and I spent most of the night sitting at the window and on the door-sill, smoking, wondering, dreaming perhaps, but not sleeping. I left this morning before anybody was up except Jake, who got my horse for me.

CHAPTER XIV.

HERBERT.

THURSDAY, *May* 13, 1836.

I HAVE been thinking a great deal about Miss Harwood to-day, and trying to recall all that I have ever heard about my father's family. I think there must be some relationship between this young lady and myself, as I cannot otherwise account for the interest I take in her and all belonging to her. It would be quite absurd to suppose that the short time I spent in her society was long enough to create any special—I was going to say—regard, independently of an instinctive recognition of *kinship*, if there is such a word. It may, and probably will turn out that I am her forty-seventh cousin—that is always supposing my—friendly feeling to be the result of a blood relationship, recognized by me through some mysterious faculty of the mind. In that case, however, the—liking, if I may so call it—ought to be mutual, and I am bound to confess that I cannot remember that she gave any evidence that way; though I think I remember all her looks and words. I have not much to record as the events of to-day. If Mr. White had returned I should have had some talk with him about the matter. I don't know now whether I had better tell him about my change of name or not. I wrote a letter to Mother about it to-day and tore it up afterwards. I don't know what to think about an engagement between her and Charley Carr. While she appears to be devotedly attached to him, I could not see any tokens of very flaming love on his part. It would be truly horrible for such a girl as she is to marry a man who did not half love her! But what business is it of mine? I'll quit writing on the subject.

I have been in the post-office all day. There are not many applicants for letters here, except on the day after the mail arrives, so I have been uninterrupted most of the day. At dinner at the hotel I noticed a stranger on the opposite side of the table, and intended to look at the register to ascertain who he was and where he was from. He is a slight, pale young man, a little bald, wears near-sighted spectacles, and looks as if he had burned any quantity of midnight oil. I forgot about the register when I came out, and was seated behind the counter in the post-office smoking my after-dinner cigar, when the stranger entered the office.

"Is there a letter for 'Hamilton?'" he asked.

"Yes sir!" replied I, going to the letter box and selecting it. It was addressed to "the Rev. Philip Hamilton, Carrville, La."

"You have a good memory, sir," he observed politely. He opened the letter, read it rapidly and then put it in his pocket.

"I remembered your letter, sir," said I, when he had got through with it, "because it had the Baltimore post mark." He was turning away as I spoke, but came back immediately.

"Ah!" he said, with considerable interest. "Are you from that city?"

"Yes sir, it is my birth-place."

"The hotel keeper told me you were Mr. Hubbard;" here he bowed. "I asked your name, because I fancied that I saw in your face a resemblance to—— some one I have met in Baltimore;—perhaps a relation of yours?"

"I have a Mother and two sisters there, sir, and no other kindred that I know."

"Ah! then I must have fancied a likeness. Good afternoon, sir."

"Won't you walk in and take a smoke with me?" said I. "I can't invite you into the post-office; but if you will step into the street and come in at the door at the right, we can fumigate the whole of the adjoining house."

"Thank you, you are very kind." So he came in. I gave him one of my regalias, and we were soon puffing away in the empty store room.

I found my new acquaintance very entertaining. He is very fond of a joke, and cracks a good many himself. Most of the preachers that I have known have been so grave and solemn that I have always fought shy of their society. Mr. Hamilton asked me some questions about Baltimore; said he had been there within a month, though he knew very little about the people. He preached twice in one of the churches there, Doctor Nevius', I believe, and had become a little acquainted with some of the members of that congregation. He is going to preach in the Presbyterian Church, in Carrville, on the next Sabbath, and I intend to go hear him. He knows everything, and I hope we shall be good friends.

This evening, after tea, I went into the playing room at the hotel, and saw Mr. Maltby and Mr. Carr playing a game called euchre, with Captain Delaney and an ugly fellow that I have seen in town two or three times. I have heard that he is an overseer on some plantation in the neighbourhood. His name is Beckett. I spoke to Maltby and Mr. Carr, but did not notice the others. They seemed to be playing a pretty high game; that is, Mr. Carr and Delaney were betting ten dollars a game. I only staid a short time. The game is somewhat like whist; the best cards, however, are the knaves of trumps, and of the other suit of the same colour. I did not like to see old Mr. Carr gambling, though almost everybody out here does it. They did not keep the play up very late, as I saw Mr. Carr, Maltby and Beckett, riding out of town an hour or two ago. This was the first sight of Delaney that I have had since last Sunday. I heard him say that he was going to New Orleans to-morrow. I hope he will stay there.

FRIDAY, *May* 14, 1836.

Ah, me! Let me recount things in order. First, the mail last night brought a letter for " Judge Carr." It was postmarked New York, and had come " by express mail, postage seventy-five cents, prepaid." Next, Charley came in this morning, and went on to New Orleans in a transient steamboat. By-the-bye, Delaney went in the same boat. I showed the letter to Charley, who requested me to send it out to Manahio, if opportunity offered, or if none presented, and, if " I would be so kind," to ride his horse out, with the letter, in the afternoon. We both concluded that the letter was important, as it had come out of the ordinary course. Third: Mr. White returned last night, and took possession of the Reverend Mr. Hamilton, moving him, bag and baggage, from the hotel to his pretty cottage. After dinner they both came in, and when I told Mr. White about the letter, he said he would remain in the office with Mr. Hamilton, and if I would like the ride, I had better act upon Charley's suggestion. So I found myself, early in the afternoon, on the banks of the creek and near the haunted laurels.

This was the first time, since I heard the legend, that I had the chance to take a near look at this locality, so I turned off from the road, and pushing through the undergrowth, I reached the trunks of the big trees. They stand near the bank of the creek, in a triangle, the sides of which are probably eight or ten yards long. My first thought, after I had fastened the horse to a swinging branch and dismounted, was, that the little area would be a splendid place for a quiet duel. The ground is level and smooth, and the bushes, which were thick enough outside of the trees' shadow, would conceal the combatants effectually. I looked in vain for some traces of the tragedy which had been enacted on this spot; but it is probable that time has effaced such dismal memorials, if they were visible five years ago. It was here, too, that John Harwood died his mysterious death, and I felt the old melancholy feeling coming over me, which took possession of me, and kept me awake the other night. I don't know why I should not be affected by the sad countenance of his orphan daughter, and I am not ashamed to own that I *am* affected, whenever I think of her (which is pretty nearly all the time). The thing that plagues me most is the conviction that Charley don't appreciate her, and, therefore, will never be able to comfort her—bah! what a dreadful ninny I must be!

The day was hot, and I took off my coat and vest, half disposed to take a bath in the creek. While I was thinking about it I heard a horse neigh, and presently I heard the tramp of his hoofs. My horse neighed in reply, and in a minute or two a Spanish pony poked his way through the bushes, bringing on his back no less a personage than Master Herbert Harwood.

"Hello! Mr. Hubbard! Why, what the dickens are you doing here?"

"That's just what I was going to ask *you*," replied I, shaking his hand. He slipped down from the saddle, and throwing the stirrups over the cantle, he let the pony go, saying: "Here's some elegant grass, Dick, and you may eat your belly full. I never hitch Dick; he always stays where I leave him. I have to turn the stirrups over, though, for once he tried to get *on himself;* at least, I found him with his hind foot in the stirrup. I am going to bathe in here, please; so are you, ain't you? That's jolly! I've got two towels." By the time he had got thus far, he had wriggled himself out of his coat, and was fumbling at his collar-button with his left hand. I perceived that his right arm was not of much use to him, though he had gotten rid of the sling.

"Let me help you," said I, unfastening his button.

"Thank 'ee! My arm hurts me a little, and the doctor says I must not use it much, yet awhile. Now, sir; please pull my shirt right over my head! Thank 'ee! I can manage the rest. Boots and trousers come off together, you see! Why don't you undress?"

He slipped off his drawers and stockings, and waded out into the stream, and was pretty soon up to his neck. He did not attempt to swim, but wading back towards the bank, he crawled up on a log, one end of which was resting on the shore. It gradually sank with his weight, until only his head was visible above the water. I was getting out of my boots when he recommenced his harangue.

"I say, Mr. Hubbard! You know Jake went in after Midnight the other morning? I mean the day after you were out at Manahio?"

"Yes."

"Well, he found she was hard to lead, so he got on her back, and she gave him an awful hyste!"

"Was he hurt?" I asked. He made no reply, but I heard him splashing in the water. I had my back towards him, and was tugging at my last stocking, when it suddenly occurred to me that he had slipped off the log. I ran down to the edge of the creek, saw the log bobbing up and down, but the boy had disappeared! I was stripped, with the exception of my drawers, and without a moment's hesitation I plunged into the stream. As soon as I got into the current I allowed my body to float with it, diving whenever the water was too deep for me to see the bottom. The laurels stood in a little cove, and there is a strong eddy just along the bank; I suppose that is the reason the creek is deeper there than at the ford. It is probable that Herbert was carried back, up the stream, by this return current, as I found, after I had floated and swam twenty or thirty yards from the log, that the creek was too shoal for his body to get lower down. Accordingly I put forth all my vigour, swimming along the bank, until

at last I saw his arm, and then his white body above the surface
for an instant, near the spot where I at first entered the water.
In another minute his arm was around my neck, nearly choking
me, and I was half swimming and half crawling towards the bank.
I scrambled up somehow, and laid him down on the grass. He
was not entirely insensible, though he still clutched me round the
neck, and I had some trouble to get rid of his convulsive grasp.
Altogether, I was pretty well used up. However, I began to rub
him vigorously with a towel, trying to remember what was the
proper treatment for half drowned people. He muttered something about " hurting his arm," and I propped him up in a sitting
posture, handling him as tenderly as I could. Gradually a little
colour came into his cheeks and light into his eyes. He had not
been three minutes in the water.

" I say!" he began, after looking all round—" at sun and stream
and plain"—as if he were trying to decide where he was—" I say,
why didn't you come when I called you ?"

" You must have called me while you were under the water, old
fellow. How came you to get under ? I saw you wading just
before you disappeared."

" I slipped off the log yonder, and it struck me on my lame
arm, and then I kept falling down, down, till the current caught
me. But I thought I called you to help me."

" I thought you were astride of the log until I looked for you,
and when I found you were not, I jumped in, and have been as
far as the ripple and back again. I found you at last close by the
bank."

" Well, then," said Herbert, " I've been drownded!"

" Not quite," replied I, laughing, " but you were not very far
from it. Can't you swim ?"

" Yes, a little, but my arm hurt me so ! I say !" he continued,
his lips quivering and the tears springing to his eyes—" I say,
you have saved my life !"

" Maybe so, but never mind that. How do you feel now ?"

" Oh, I'm all right now, only a little weak. Would you mind
helping me dress ? Thank'ee! But I'll dip myself in the water
first. I've gone and muddied my legs !"

While he was performing his ablutions I took off my drawers,
and wringing them out, hung them on a bush in the sun. They
were nearly dry by the time I had got him dressed. His tongue
seemed to be the only member that had not lost its usual vigour,
as he talked incessantly.

"Look here, Mr. Hubbard! honour bright! didn't you hear me sing anything while I was in the water?"

"Not a note."

"Not 'Old Mother'"—he paused.

"'Old Mother Hubbard, she lived in a cupboard?'" replied I. "I heard you sing that the other night."

"Did you mind it? Ret gave me fits about it."

"Of course I didn't," I replied, "you may sing it to me as often as you like."

"That's a jolly good fellow!" and here he insisted upon shaking my hand while I was trying to get his shirt over his head. "Well, I thought I sung that while I was in the creek. It's a *dog on* ugly name though, ain't it?"

"Yes, but I have another name and——"

"May I call you Harry?" he shouted, "oh, that's prime! but you are such a big fellow that it don't seem polite. S'pose I call you cousin Harry?"

"That's the very thing," answered I, poking his arm into his shirt sleeve, "and I'll call you Cousin Herbert."

"Will you? Oh, ain't that jolly?" and he pulled his arm out to shake hands again. "Well, I call Charley Carr 'Cousin Charley,' and he's not my cousin, you know."

"No, I don't know; I thought Mr. Carr was your uncle."

"No, he ain't; no relation at all. He is guardian for me and Ret. We've always called him uncle, but he ain't."

"Well, now, do you hold still till I get you dressed, and we can talk as we ride. I am going to Manahio with you."

"Just shake hands once more, Cousin Harry. Thank 'ee! now I'll be still as a mouse." He kept his word, and we were soon dressed. As we rode along the beautiful shady road, which I believe I've mentioned before, my new cousin did an immense amount of talking, and I learned from him many things that I have been wanting to know. I avoided asking him about his family, because I intended to get the information I wanted on that point from his sister, if I ever had an opportunity. This opportunity arrived sooner than I expected or hoped. When we reached Mr. Carr's house I saw Midnight in Jake's custody, with a side saddle on her sleek back.

Mr. Carr came out on the gallery, welcomed me very politely, and expressed his acknowledgments for "my kindness" in bringing the letter. After he had read it, I proposed taking his reply.

back with me, as I could send it to New Orleans by this evening's boat and it could go by express mail immediately, from the city. His answer to this offer was, "that the letter could only be answered in person, and it was doubtful whether the matter was of sufficient importance to warrant a journey to New York." Herbert had vanished into the house, and now reappeared with his beautiful sister, who was dressed in a riding habit. She walked straight up to me, as if she were about to knock me down, and holding out her little white hand, which I took clumsily enough, she said—

"Oh, Uncle! Herbert would have been drowned if Mr. Hubbard had not saved him!" There were tears in her eyes and her voice.

"How! what! when?" exclaimed Mr. Carr, with astonishment.

"I was taking a swim, sir," said Master Herbert, "and I slipped off a log, and hurt my arm, and then I suppose I fainted; anyhow, cousin Harry had to swim ever so far before he found me."

"Your cousin Harry!" said Mr. Carr, "what cousin Harry?"

"I believe that is to be my title, henceforth, sir," said I. "Since I had the good fortune to pull Herbert out of the Manahio, he has been looking out for a name for me, and I am very well satisfied with the one he has chosen." All this time I was holding Miss Ret's hand, like a booby. I suppose I looked at her with a very warm, *cousinly* glance, and perhaps I squeezed her little hand. I daresay; I was mad enough to do anything, for she was looking at me with her big brown eyes, in which the tear-drops still glittered —anyhow, she drew her hand away, and I think she blushed—a little.

"You have not yet told me how all this happened," said Mr. Carr, looking alternately at me and Herbert; "how did it chance that Mr. Hubbard found your bathing place?"

"I was already there, sir," I answered.

"Where?"

"At the Haunted Laurels."

"The Laurels!" said Mr. Carr, staggering back as if he had been shot. Miss Harwood ran to him, as he sank into a chair, and I kept on talking, hoping they would all think that I had not noticed his extraordinary agitation.

"Herbert would have been in no danger, sir, if he had not hurt his arm. I think you had better prohibit similar excursions until he gets over his escapade with Midnight. By-the-bye, Miss Harwood, you are going to ride her this afternoon ?"

"Yes, sir, I was going to Harwood with a message from uncle. But it will answer as well to-morrow; won't it, uncle ?"

"Yes, yes, replied her guardian—"put the mare away, Jake, and Mr. Charles's horse, also—Mr. Hubbard will stay with us this evening."

"Don't postpone your ride on my account," said I, rising, "but rather allow me to ride with you—that is, if you are going towards town. I have to be there this evening to attend to mail business, otherwise I should be too happy to remain."

"Are you well enough for me to leave you, brother ?"

"Oh, I'm all right," answered he, swaggering about the gallery, " only I want the sling again."

" Well, then, we will go, if you are ready, sir," to me. " Jake, bring the horses." And a few minutes later we were pacing down the drive, Jake following at a respectful distance. He was gorgeously attired, and had a livery band around his hat, and seemed proud of the honor of attending upon his future young mistress. We passed out of the gate and I waited for her to say something that would lead to the questions I wanted to ask her. As we came in sight of the creek I inquired about the depth of the water.

"The stream is fordable in many places," she replied ; " there are some deep places which they call 'pools,' but I think they are two or three miles lower down, near the mouth of the stream."

"It is deep at the—the place where your brother was bathing."

" You mean at the Laurels ; yes, I have heard that it was deeper there. How did it happen that you were there to-day ?"

" I was on my way to Manahio, with a letter for Mr. Carr, and turned off to look at the trees. I was resting under their shade when your brother came."

"Herbert says you risked your life to save his! Oh, Mr. Hubbard, I have not much left to live for, and if my brother had died there to-day, I think I should have died too !"

" I don't deny that I was instrumental in saving his life, but I ran no risk. I can swim across the Mississippi. You need not look so gratefully at me. The gratitude is due elsewhere. If I had not been drawn to the spot, by what seemed only idle curiosity, but which both you and I know was direct and special Provi-

dence—Herbert would have been drowned." She covered her
face with her hands and we rode on in silence. After a time I
said : "You implied, the other night, that you would tell me
something about the Baltimore Harwoods, or rather that you would
ask me some questions about them."

"Oh yes. Do you know them well ? How many are there of
them ?"

"I know them very intimately. There are four persons only in
the family—Mrs. Harwood, Miss Alice, Miss Grace and Mr. Herbert. I know they have no relations—at least not on this side of
the ocean."

"Alice ! Herbert !" she exclaimed, "and the family of English origin ?"

"Yes, their immediate ancestors were English."

"Do they resemble us ? I mean me or my brother ?"

"I cannot say that they do. And yet, when you smile, you *do*
look like dear Grace."

"'*Dear* Grace !' Oh, indeed ! Mr. Hubbard ! I perceive now
why you were so eager to talk about your Baltimore friends. Like
me, is she ? I take that for a compliment, anyhow. She must be
particularly lovely in your eyes !"

"You are entirely mistaken," I stammered.

"Come, sir !" she said, still laughing merrily, "Do you mean
to say that you are not in love ?"

"I am afraid I am," I answered, and I believe I groaned.

"Well, don't distress yourself, I won't pursue the subject, Mr.
Hubbard."

"I wish you would not call me Mr. Hubbard !" I exclaimed pet-
ulantly.

"I think I might follow Herbert's example, and call you Cousin
Harry, if you like that better. I am beginning to believe that
your friends are truly cousins of mine, and I would only be anticipating a little if I gave you that relationship." All this was said
in a gay tone, very different from her usual manner. The ride
must have put her in good spirits.

"If you *will* honour me so much, Miss Harwood, I will be extremely grateful." She looked surprised, and I continued, "You
don't know how I hate to be called Hubbard, but I will tell you
the next time I see you—that is—I *think* I will. And now, if you
will explain to me the possible relationship between you and—my
friends in Baltimore, you will confer a great favour upon me. I

have powerful reasons—I might say I have a *right* to know all you can tell me."

We had by this time arrived at a fork in the carriage road, one branch of which is the direct road to Carrville, the other leading across the Manahio, by a ford more than a mile above the Laurels. She turned her horse into this road, remarking that "I could get to town that way." I followed her across the creek, wondering what she was thinking about the matter, and what she was going to say about my request for the history of the Harwoods. She was evidently thinking upon the subject, and arriving at some conclusion.

"I believe I understand you," she said at length. "You shall have all the information I can give you. You *have* a right to ask on two accounts. You have saved my brother's life, and there is no one living that can be affected by the history I can furnish you, unless it should happen that the Baltimore family—but they are *your* friends—" She considered a moment, and then added: "Promise me that no member of *that* family shall know what you learn from the papers I give you."

"I cannot. It would not be possible for me to keep such a promise."

"Well, promise me that you will reveal what you learn from them to no one except your *wife.*"

"I may safely promise that; I shall never have a wife."

"There is something very strange about this matter," said Ret, with an air of great perplexity. "I suppose it is not proper for me to ask what it is?"

"I can tell you this much," I replied desperately: "I think I love a lady, or that I *would* love her if I dared. But I have reason to think—or know—that she loves my friend. I have been told that there is even an engagement."

"I was going to ask you if your friend loved her, but if there is an engagement between them——"

"I don't know. If I *knew* that he loved her as she ought to be loved, I think I could endure it." She listened with great interest, and I was encouraged to go on. "At times I doubt whether she has the kind and degree of affection for him that a wife ought to have. My ideas on the subject are peculiar, and perhaps romantic. If I should ever marry, I should require my wife to love God supremely—and then to give *me* every other thought and feeling of her heart, and, in requital, I would love her as no man ever loved before, or ever will again."

"And you doubt whether these feelings are mutually entertained by Miss Harwood and your friend?"

"I do."

"If your suspicions are well founded," she said, speaking slowly and deliberately, "they ought never to marry. And if you could be certain that your feelings have not warped your good judgment, you would be justified in using any lawful means to avert the doom that awaits them. Your friendship for one and your love for the other, equally demand your interference to break an engagement which, if fulfilled, will entail a life of misery upon both."

She said this with great earnestness. We had entered a beautiful avenue, and were approaching a house far superior in appearance to any of the residences I had seen in the State. It is built in the style of English cottages, with pointed gables, and looks like pictures I have somewhere seen, probably in some book of architectural designs. A broad verandah extends along the wide front, and the windows opening upon it descend to the floor, having inside shutters, which fold back against the frames. Jacobus took our horses, and we stood on the floor of the verandah, looking at the beautiful prospect before us.

"This is Harwood, sir," said Ret, "and I bid you welcome to my father's house."

She rang the bell, and the door was opened by a little coal black African, who showed a mouth full of ivory as soon as he saw us. I heard him bawling out from the back of the house, after we had passed into a drawing room on the right of the hall, "Oh, mammy, mammy! Here Miss Ret done come, wid a nudder gemp'lum! Uncle 'Cobus, too!"

"It is a wonder that 'Uncle 'Cobus' was not the first to be announced," said Ret, laughing; "here comes Aunt Chloe."

A fat, middle aged negress came waddling into the room, dropping me a curtsey, and a "Sarvant, Mars'r!" as she passed me. She waddled over to Ret, and, shaking her hand, said, "La! Miss Ret, I'se right down glad to see you! But dis room ain't bin dusted to-day. Ef I'd knowd you was gwine to come, I'd hab it all fix up!"

"Never mind, Aunty," said Ret, "I am only going to stay a little while. Send Phany for Mr. Beckett."

"De oberseer done gone to town, Missee," replied Chloe.

"Well, then, I'll ride over again to-morrow. Tell him I'll be here at four o'clock; and, Aunty, please to bring me the black key box. It is on the table in my room." While Aunt Chloe was absent, Ret said, "Since my father's death we have lived altogether at Mr. Carr's. There is no one about the house excepting Chloe and her son, Phany."

"Phany?" said I; "that is a queer name."

"His name is Aristophanes. The negroes like big names for their children, and father always gratified them by getting the longest names he could think of. Thank you, Aunty." She unlocked the box with a key that was attached to her watch chain, and taking a bunch of keys from the box she opened an iron door in the jamb of the fireplace. She took a package from this recess, and, relocking the door, replaced the keys in the ebony box, which she gave back to Chloe, instructing her to return it to her chamber.

"These letters," she said, giving me the package, "are arranged according to their dates. You will, perhaps, have to read them all if you desire to know the full history of the Harwoods. Some of them are old, and the ink has faded, but they are all legible. I have read them several times. *You* will understand, when you read them, why I wished to impose the restrictions——"

"I wish you could trust me," I said, earnestly, "and let me judge how much of the story I may reveal, and how much of it I should consider private and confidential."

"Well," she said, after a pause, "read the letters, and if you think afterwards that you should be freed from your promise, I'll—consider it."

I assisted her to mount Midnight, and when we passed out of the avenue into the road, she observed that there were two ways by which I could reach Carrville; "The most direct route is a succession of blind paths, and you might easily get astray in the woods. If you have the time to spare, you had better ride round by the Laurels—I am going home that way."

"I have the day before me," I answered; "my mail duties do not begin till late in the night. I would go back to Manahio with you if it were not for this package. I am dying to get at it."

"What have you heard about the Haunted Laurels?" she asked, as we rode along. "Do not hesitate to tell me, I know the common legend, and should like to correct any wrong impressions you may have."

I told the story as I heard it from Jacobus, only saying that Mr. Harwood had been found there dead, from a pistol shot.

"It is partly true and partly false," she remarked, when I had finished. The Densons were almost undoubtedly guilty; but my father rather tried to deliver them from the doom they suffered. They did not threaten Mr. Carr or my father with any unusual calamity; but one of them, the elder, said just before he died: 'We will haunt these Laurels for five years to come, and cheat those cursed Harwoods, yet.' Sometimes I think my father attached some particular meaning to the threat, but he never said so." I expected her to say something about her father's death; but she did not, and I did not dare to ask her then. When we reached the Laurels, she said she wanted to see the scene of Herbert's accident, so we rode through the bushes, which I endeavoured to separate for her passage. I pointed out the places where he had disappeared; where I sought for him; where I found him; and where we landed. We went back to the road, and I held out my hand at parting.

"I have said nothing to you, sir," she said, her dear eyes once more overflowing, "about my gratitude. I hope you know that I can never forget what we owe you."

"Pray, Miss Harwood, say no more about it. I have great cause of gratitude to God, who allowed me to be instrumental in saving your brother, since you——" I was going to say she might think kindly of me for Herbert's sake; but I stopped. She seemed to understand me, however, but she said nothing; and so we parted.

Since I came home I have concluded not to read the letters. It would be dishonourable. She does not know who I am, and she would not have given them to me if she had known my name. I opened the package and looked at the address and signature of the first letter. It is dated "H. M. S. Orpheus, off Malta, December 1, 1800;" and was signed "Herbert Harwood." I therefore know that the letter was written by my grand uncle, and although I was burning with curiosity, I resealed the package, which I shall take back to her to-morrow, if I live. She said she would be at Harwood at four o'clock. So will I. What will come of that interview only Heaven knows. I am resolved to — be guided by circumstances.

CHAPTER XV.

KINDRED.

SATURDAY, *May* 15, 1836.

WHEN I sat down last night and opened the package of letters, I was in a state of excitement which I can neither understand nor describe. The tones of my dear cousin's voice—for she
is my cousin, I know—and the light of her eyes, were still with me;
and I felt my heart—nay, I feel it at this moment—thumping my ribs,
as though it wanted to get out and go after her. I suppose there is
something about her forlorn condition as an orphan that excites my
sympathy. All the intense curiosity I felt to dive after the mystery that was hidden in the letters, did not keep me from spending
a solid hour in recalling all her looks and words. Alas! I can
find nothing in them that indicates any interest in me. She regards me, no doubt, as a poor devil of a clerk, who has come to
this far off country to make money, and who has been fortunate
enough to get some slight claim upon her, by pulling her brother
out of the water. This is the exact state of the case, and I were
a double distilled goose to suppose anything else.

The letters were all open, one laid upon another, and I looked
only at the date and signature to the top letter. I endeavoured
not to see the address; but I think I *did* see "My dear John." I
immediately replaced the wrappers, and adding a new one, I got
sealing wax and secured the package, which I addressed to "Miss
Henrietta Harwood, Manahio."

After dinner Mr. White was here, and I asked him if he would
be postmaster while I "took a ride." He consented, and I was
astride of Charley's horse, and cantering out of town pretty early
in the afternoon; of course I was an hour or two too early. When
I crossed the creek I looked at my watch, and found it was only
two o'clock. Half an hour would take me to Harwood, or to Manahio, either, so I had an hour and a half too much time. I rode on
slowly, keeping the main road, and thinking of yesterday's ride, and
trying to invent some pretext to take me to Manahio, so that I might
accompany Ret in her ride to Harwood; but I was too stupid to
concoct an excuse that would satisfy me. I would adhere to my
original plan, which was to be at the latter place at about four
o'clock. Presently I heard the hoof strokes of a horse behind me;

but I did not look back until he was near enough for me to hear the rider say—

"Charley Carr's horse! Hello! Hubbard!"

It was Mr. Maltby.

"How d' ye do?" he said. "You are going to Highlands to dine with me? That's first rate."

"I have dined, thank you," replied I; "but I will ride a little way with you. Are you from town?"

"No, I have been down the creek, trying to survey a little. My land joins Judge Carr's and Harwood, at a point near the creek, and none of us have any fences up. I want to cut some timber, and *don't* want to cut any of my neighbour's in mistake."

"Do the lands of the Harwood estate lie on this side of the creek?" I inquired.

"Yes, a portion of them. Harwood is an original section, and the survey of that estate is perfect. The line crosses the creek at the ford, and I think it just takes in the big laurels."

"Isn't it a fine estate, Mr. Maltby?"

"Oh, yes; poor John spent much money in improvements, and was considerably involved when he died. It won't make much difference to the children, however, as Judge Carr holds the mortgage."

"How much is the mortgage, and what is the value of the estate?"

"Harwood is worth one hundred thousand dollars. Carr's mortgage is for fifty thousand. He advanced money to John, and I think he also holds bills of sale, giving him the ownership of the niggers, or of part of them. There was some arrangement made, by which one half of the estate should go to Herbert, uninvolved, and Ret won't want any estate, you know, as she is going to marry Charley."

"But suppose she does not, what estate has she then?"

"Just none at all, I reckon. But the match has been settled long ago, and it will be first rate on both sides. Ret is a splendid girl, and you know what Charley is."

"Yes." I tried to keep up an appearance of indifference, but I was on fire. "When does the wedding come off?" I coughed, to hide the trembling of my voice, as I asked the question.

"Pretty soon, I reckon. Maybe Charley has gone to the city to get his toggery now?" here he looked at me inquiringly.

"I don't know. He did not tell me."

" I think I'll persuade Carr to settle that mortgage on Charley; for if the Judge bets as high all the time as he did t'other night he'll be flat broke before he dies."

"I noticed that he was betting pretty high," I said; " ten dollars a game, wasn't it ?"

"Ten dollars a game, and twenty-five on the rub," replied Mr. Maltby, "and he did not win any rubs that night. He must have lost a thousand at least."

" He must have a strong back to stand many such losses," I observed.

" Well, I shouldn't wonder if he was short of funds now. He has been going it tolerably strong with Delaney single-handed, and I must say that Delaney has the devil's own luck!" He hesitated, and then added, "look here, youngster, all this is confidential, mind you! D'ye remember last Sunday, when Delaney and I found you after you killed the panther? Well—he had been playing euchre all the morning with Carr, and must have won like thunder!"

I looked at my watch and found it was three o'clock, so bidding Mr. Maltby good-bye, I rode back to the creek, and thinking I might overtake or be overtaken by Midnight and her mistress, I pushed on at a good pace. But I reached the long avenue without seeing any traces of her, and concluding that I would go on boldly and wait for her, I fastened my horse near the house. I rang the bell and Aristophanes showed his black visage in a few minutes.

" Well, Phany, has Miss Ret come yet ?"

" No Mars'r—walk in, sar !" and he ushered me into the drawing room. I sat down in the arm chair where she sat yesterday, and tried to resolve to do right. Maltby had made me happy and most miserable. She was poor! Heaven be thanked! But she was soon to be rich by a marriage, which I felt ought not to be solemnized. What should I do ? What is my DUTY ? I covered my face with my hands, and made a baby of myself.

"Lor' bless us! Is you sick, young mars'r ?" It was Chloe.

"No, Aunty!" said I, starting up and wiping my eyes, "not very. I have had a dreadful pain just here in my side; it is better now. Don't tell any one that you saw me crying over such a little affair;" and I slipped a dollar into her hand. "How soon do you expect Miss Harwood ?"

" She not gwine to come to-day, sar," she replied. " 'Cobus bin here for oberseer to go over dar. Missee Ret sick !"

"Sick! Good Heavens! How sick?"

"Only headache," 'Cobus says. "S'pose you ride over, sar?"

"If I could do any good—pshaw! what a fool I am! here, Aunt Chloe, is a package which Miss Ret gave me yesterday. Where shall I put it? It is important, and I want to put it in a safe place."

She pulled open a drawer in a secretaire in the room, and I placed the letters in it, closed and locked it, and put the key in my pocket.

"I will give the key to Miss Ret, Aunty," I said, as I came away; "did Jacobus go to town after doctor Markham?"

"Lor' no! Mars'r—Miss Ret don't want doctor for headache! yah, yah, yah! S'pose I git you somethin' for pain in your side, Mars'r—am got some first rate yarb tea!"

"Never mind, Aunty, I am pretty well now. Good-bye." I got my horse, and gave Phany a quarter as he stood grinning at the gate, and—here I am back again. I am learning a hard lesson— I am learning to *wait*. Oh for patience, and wisdom, and strength, and manhood!

SABBATH, *May* 16, 1836.

One week ago I was in the green woods at this hour, careless and indifferent about everything except present enjoyment. I was looking forward with a pleasant curiosity to the time when I should know who Ret was and what she was like. What changes one short week has wrought! I am a different man to-day. I am ten years older. I used to have a theory upon which I reposed with great complacency. It was this: no contingency can occur in which I need be doubtful as to my course, so long as my reason will show me what is honourable and right. And now I am perplexed with doubts. I decide finally upon a course, and give my resolve to the winds an hour later. I find myself saying to myself—"Let us wait for the emergency, and then it will be time enough to decide." But I hear the church bell.

CHAPTER XVI.

A Parting.

MONDAY, *May* 17, 1836.

WHEN I went to the church yesterday I arrived in time to
assist Miss Harwood to alight from Judge Carr's carriage.
Herbert followed, greeting me warmly, and then Mr. Carr. The
latter invited me to sit in his pew. Mr. Hamilton was already in
the pulpit. His manner and the tones of his voice attracted me,
from the utterance of his first short prayer. His text was "Deny
thyself," and I have certainly never heard such a discourse as he
delivered. My attention was riveted. I heard every syllable of
the sermon, which was spoken, not read, and I could now write
down in order the divisions of the discourse, and the arguments
and appeals occurring under each head. I believe a profound and
salutary impression was made upon my mind, for I no longer feel
doubtful or desponding, though I am far from happy. I can wait
for the emergency, and think I shall do right when the emergency comes. After the sermon Mr. Hamilton announced that
there would be service in the afternoon at "Harwood Chapel,"
and, as we came out of the church, Mr. Carr suggested that I
should ride out with them, and if I felt disposed, "I could attend
the service at the chapel." Herbert seconded the invitation on
the instant. I did not accept immediately, waiting for some indication of Miss Harwood's wishes. I did not get it. She looked at
me inquiringly, and I accepted, saying I would get Charley's
horse and overtake them. I rode beside the carriage, talking and
listening. Ret was quiet, answering when spoken to, but volunteering no conversation. When dinner was over she disappeared,
and Herbert and I walked about the grounds, he chattering and
I smoking. I had observed at dinner that I would go to the
chapel if "any of them" were going, and Ret replied that she
would go on Midnight. I was impatient for the hour to arrive. It
came at last, and we started, she and I—no groom, for Sunday is
the negro's holiday. If I dared to make such a choice, I could
wish that my life ended when that ride was over. I was weak
enough to be happy while it lasted.

"Where is Harwood chapel?" I inquired, as we entered the
avenue leading to Harwood.

"It is on an edge of the plantation, beyond the house. We go very nearly by the same road as that we passed over the other day. The chapel was built by my father, for the accommodation of the blacks belonging to the three plantations, Manahio, Highlands and Harwood."

"Then this afternoon's service is for their benefit?"

"Yes, but there is always a good attendance of whites, and they are always particularly welcome."

"I hope you have entirely recovered from your indisposition of yesterday?" She looked surprised. "Chloe told me you were sick."

"Where did you see Chloe?"

"At Harwood. I was there yesterday, hoping to meet you. I took back the letters. The package is in the right hand drawer of the secretaire in the drawing room. Here is the key."

"Have you read all these letters?"

"I have read none of them. I opened the package and saw that one of the letters was written by Captain Sir Herbert Harwood, of the British navy, and I know that he was the grand uncle of Herbert Harwood, of Baltimore."

"I have suspected as much," she replied, taking the key; "but I cannot understand why the knowledge of this relationship decided you to return the letters unread."

"Because you were not willing that your relations should know anything or *everything* that may be revealed in those letters. I could not read them, if I regarded my own honour, because one at least of that family would know all that I could learn from them."

"I thought I made an exception of that *one* member," she said, smiling. "I think if you had read the letters you would have justified my course. However, we will talk about it hereafter. There is the chapel."

Half a dozen well dressed negroes surrounded us as we rode up in front of the building, taking possession of the horses, and overwhelming us with polite attentions. Mr. and Mrs. White, Mr. and Mrs. Maltby and Mr. Hamilton were standing apart, in the shade of the trees. We joined them and entered the chapel together. It is a plain building, weather-boarded on the outside and white-washed. The "white folks" occupied the front seats, and the house was soon filled with a well behaved and attentive audience. The singing was positively wonderful, though somewhat marred by the necessity to "line out" the hymns, after the Methodist fashion. The overseer, Beckett, whom I saw playing cards in town the other night, was there, and I caught him eyeing me curiously once or twice. Mr. Hamilton preached a plain, simple and beautiful Gospel sermon, which was understood by the most untutored of his listeners. It was near sunset when we started on our homeward journey, and we rode slowly, enjoying the calm beauty of the early summer. I talked about the discourse of the morning, and expressed my admiration of the minister in very warm terms.

"I have enjoyed to-day's sermons very much," she said, "but I did not suppose that a discourse on self-denial would have been considered so appropriate by you."

"Ah, you don't know how much I have been strengthened in my better purposes by Mr. Hamilton's teachings this morning. Neither do you know how much I need all the support I can obtain, to keep me in the course of honour and duty."

"I do not know, of course, what particular temptations you may be called upon to overcome, and if I did, I am not qualified to counsel you."

"Pardon me, Miss Harwood, but you alone can give me the counsel I need. Don't look at me with such an astonished expression, or I shall never find courage to go on. I am reluctant to say what is upon my mind anyhow, because the kindness with which you have listened to me hitherto is due to the slight service I was able to render your brother. Don't interrupt me, please! I mean to say that you would never have allowed the present terms of intimacy to exist between us if it had not been for that fortunate accident."

"There are no accidents," she replied.

"I am rejoiced to believe it, and I regard your brother's peril, from which I was permitted to rescue him, as the interposition of a kind Providence in *my* behalf. Otherwise I might never have known you as well as I know you now."

"I understand you," she said, gently, "and although you speak slightingly of your instrumentality in saving Herbert, I know from your own description, as well as from his, that you exposed your own life to danger. If another had been there, instead of you, my brother would probably have died. You have spoken very much in riddles about the matter that interests you. May I ask you one or two questions?"

"A thousand."

"Less than that will do," answered she, laughing. "Suppose you knew that the father of Grace Harwood had been guilty of an act of peculiar infamy, to which he was instigated, and in the performance of which he had been aided by her mother——"

"If there is a living man who will dare to say so," I replied, while I struggled fiercely to keep down the raging tempest her words had raised in my bosom, "I will slay him like a dog."

"There is no living man that I know of to encounter your sinful anger. The testimony to this sad story comes from the grave."

By this time I was perfectly calm. I had reflected, even while she was speaking, and had decided that some strange mystery was to be cleared up. That such a foul charge could be true of the noble gentleman I dimly remembered, or of his widow, my angelic Mother, was simply *impossible.*

"I was excited by your cruel words, doubly cruel coming from you, to speak intemperately. Pray, forgive me. I am perfectly cool now."

"I do not blame you," answered Ret; "your anger was natural, considering the relations you sustain to that unhappy family. I think I shall burn that package of letters——"

"I charge you not to do so," said I, "interrupting her. "Miss Harwood, do you believe that I am an honest man and a gentleman ?"

"Undoubtedly I do," she replied, astonished at my vehemence.

"Then I implore you to intrust me with those letters once more, and without any restrictions. Nay, let me have them, with the full certainty that every line shall be read by Herbert Harwood, the son of the man whose memory they blacken."

"You don't know what you ask. You require me to send unutterable misery into the midst of a family of innocent children. If I had destroyed those papers before I saw you, none of this could have happened."

"It is you who are in error," I answered; "*you* don't know how fatal the mistake would have been if you had destroyed this record. I am young, but I have a man's heart and a man's arm. I will right this dead man's memory and clear the stain upon this living woman's name. I devote myself to this work, body and soul. Oh, if you had known that loyal gentleman! Oh, if you knew that spotless lady! You would then know, as I know, that no infamy could ever attach to their names. It is you, *you* who shall admit it! I swear it to you before heaven!"

"I cannot withstan you," she answered, as we entered the grounds at Manahio, "you shall have the letters, and do with them as your honour and conscience shall dictate. You said just now that I was interested in you on Herbert's account. I am much more interested in you on your own. Oh, I am *so* sorry—" and I saw the tears in her eyes by the fading light, as I assisted her from the saddle, "I am *so* sorry that I should have been instrumental in making you unhappy."

"If I ever know happiness again, in this life, it will be you who shall confer it upon me. When may I have the letters?"

"To-morrow—no, on Tuesday. Mr. and Mrs. Maltby will be here all day to-morrow, and I cannot be absent. Can you wait till Tuesday?"

"Yes, yes. I will come for them on Tuesday afternoon, shall I?" and so it was settled. We went into the house. I staid to tea and then rode home in the night.

TUESDAY, *May* 18th, 1836.

I don't know how much time I shall have to write, but while I am waiting for the steamboat, I may as well get as much as I can recorded. Last night there was a mail from New Orleans, and in it a letter from Mr. Bayard for me. He says the loss of the Sea Gull is confirmed, and he wants me to join him on board the "Queen of the West," which he expected to arrive at Carrville some time to-night. She is bound for Wheeling or Pittsburg, and I am to go on to Baltimore and New York to collect the insurance and replace the goods. I went over to Mr. White's this morning, and announced my intention to leave Carrville to-night, and begged him to take charge of the Post-office to-day, and let me off. He growled a good deal at the prospect of making up and assorting mails for two months, but set me free soon after breakfast. By ten o'clock I was at Manahio. I found Judge Carr in his library among a huge pile of papers, and accounted for my appearance by saying that I was going to New York, and came to offer my services if I could transact any business for him there. "You said, sir," I observed, "that the letter I brought you the other day could only be answered in person, and I thought I might be able to represent you, if you would like to entrust me with the business." He was evidently pleased with the attention, and expressed himself in polite terms, as under great obligations to me. Selecting the letter from the mass of papers before him, he requested me to read it. It is as follows:

" NEW YORK, *May* 1, 1836.

" DEAR SIR :—I have at last got entire control of the mine, and, according to agreement, I offer you one-fourth interest. The total cost, with expenses, is about two thousand dollars; your proportion being, of course, one-fourth of that sum. I am sure the profit will be good, and it may be enormous. If you accept, let me hear from you (with remittance) on or before 30th June. I shall not be able to keep the stock beyond that date.

" Very respectfully yours,

" GEORGE CALLAHAN."

" Now, Mr. Hubbard, it is not a long story. Mr. Callahan is a stock broker in Wall street. About a year ago I was in New York, and he and two other gentlemen were negotiating for this mine. From his representations I was induced to promise to take a fourth part of it if it should prove as good as they predicted. If I could go there I would be governed by circumstances. If I was not satisfied that the investment was a good one I should not hesitate to decline it; and I would not be misled by the visionary schemes of speculators. Will you, can you spare the time necessary to look thoroughly into the affair ? If so, take the letter and act for me according to your judgment."

" I will attend to this business with great pleasure, sir," I answered, " and if the money must be paid I shall have control of a sufficient sum from the insurances I am to collect, and you can either settle with me when I return or remit it to New York."

" I thank you very much, sir," he replied, rising as I was about to leave him. " I suppose I need not ask you to dine with me, as you say you must hasten back. Good-bye, sir; I hope you will have a pleasant trip, and that we shall soon have you back again."

As I rode away I saw Master Herbert with a fishing rod strolling down the drive. I had not asked for his sister, because I intended to go straight to Harwood and wait for her, as I knew she would go there for the letters. I called out to the boy as I approached him—" Hello, cousin Herbert, don't get drowned again to-day; I shall not be able to pull you out. Farewell! I am going North to-night."

" When are you coming back ?"

" In about two months. Is your sister home ?"

" No. She went to Harwood half an hour ago."

"Well, I must be off. Tell Charley good-bye for me."

I reckon Charley's horse thought some bad words as he flew along the road to Harwood. I threw the bridle to Jake, who was fastening Midnight to the rack, and walked up on to the verandah, and through the French window into the drawing room. Ret was seated at the secretaire fitting the key to the lock when I entered. She started, and uttered some exclamation when she saw me.

"I hope you will pardon me, Miss Harwood, for coming so abruptly, but I am much hurried. I am going away to-night."

"Going away!" She pushed the chair back, and looked at me earnestly.

"Yes; I start for Baltimore to-night—on business. I shall be away two months, perhaps longer; I hope you will not forget me."

"I shall not forget you," she answered, very quietly.

"You will give me the letters?" She opened the drawer and handed me the package. "Thank you. If I never come back I will destroy them. If I do come back I will return them to you."

"I understood you to say that you would be back this summer," she said, in the same quiet tone. "Why do you now say you may not return?"

"Because I will not look upon your face again if I fail to unravel the dark mystery that is hidden in this packet."

"There is nothing in the letters that can possibly affect you," said Ret; "if you fail to disprove the things that trouble you, there are many compensations, even in this life, for all its disappointments."

"There is more than life involved in these fatal letters. I would rather die a thousand deaths than believe what you say they reveal. But I shall not fail! Farewell! and may you be as happy as I wish you to be. If I am not permitted to see you again, you may perhaps be happier in the reflection that one miserable man is less miserable because he can remember you and your kindness."

"Must you go?" she said hurriedly, as I moved away.

"Yes, better that I should! Words are trying to break from me that should not be spoken! Will you forgive the presumption if I ask you one question, personal to you alone?" She did not answer, but looked steadily at me. "Well, I will not ask it. I prefer leaving you with a kind expression on your face. Do you wish me to succeed in my effort to make you think as I think of your kindred in Baltimore?"

" I will pray for your success every day while you are gone—and also that you may have grace to endure that which you cannot avert or change."

She paused—then said suddenly—" What did you wish to ask me ?"

" I heard that you would be married very soon, is it true ?"

She became pale as a lily—then blushed very red. I thought she *pouted*.

" I do not expect to be married very soon."

" Not this summer ?"

" Not this summer."

" Thank God !" and I rushed out of the house. I wonder if she thinks I am a lunatic.

There is the steamboat bell !

A BUNDLE OF LETTERS.

LETTER I.

H. M. S. ORPHEUS, }
OFF MALTA, *December* 1, 1800. }

To JOHN HARWOOD, Esqr., London.

My dear John:—I hear bad news of you, my boy. You and Barnard have been quarrelling again! What shall I say to you, you young lubber ! If I could only get at you with a rope's end I should die happy. I know you will have excuses enough, but there can be no satisfactory excuse. How is it that Allen, who has always been a good lad, can avoid these quarrels, while you, you fiery young puppy, are always getting into them ? When I was at your age I never had any fights except with my brothers. If I had lived in the same house with *cousins* I think I should have lived at peace the year round. Your father and Allen's father used to combine forces to thrash me, but they never did it, my boy ! I suppose it is all right and natural for brothers to fight a little, but it is heinous for cousins to squabble. Now, just for the sake of argument, let us suppose a case. Suppose it were true that Barnard was always in the wrong, and that you were always in the right ? Even then you might consider your aunt's peace of mind, and endure a little for her sake. But I won't scold any more.

There is some prospect of relief from this cruising ground for the old Orpheus. I am told that my ship will be ordered home soon, and it is hinted that I shall have sailing orders in another direction. It will be very pleasant to be among you young scamps, even for a few months, and if I have no more ill accounts in the meantime, there will be a grand distribution of guineas at Harwood House when I come! I don't expect this hint to have any salutary effect upon you, however, but just let Barnard know what is in prospect, and perhaps he will behave better. I expect *you* to keep straight from love to your old uncle. If you are still bent upon your American explorations, I shall not oppose you, though it *is* a wild goose chase. But youngsters won't learn in any other school than the school of experience.

There is a regular Levanter blowing to-day, and the ship is rolling tremendously, so that writing is no easy task. If the wind holds, and I get my orders, I can slip through the straits in a jiffy!   Your affectionate uncle,

HERBERT HARWOOD.

LETTER II.

H. M. S. ORPHEUS,
 OFF MALTA, *December* 1, 1800 }

To LADY ANNE HARWOOD, London.

Dearest Anne :—I enclose two letters to the boys, which you will please seal and deliver to them, after possessing yourself of the contents. From your account, I feel sure that Barnard is altogether to blame, and Allen's letter, which I also enclose, strengthens this impression. You will see from my letter to John, that I have hopes of seeing you in a few months, and if the necessary repairs are put upon the ship, I shall perhaps be with you the greater part of next year. I need not tell you, dear wife, that the prospect is very cheering to an old sea dog, who has been knocking and being knocked about the world for two long years, in which time he has been far from home and kindred. The changes in the Government, to which you refer, cannot affect me very materially. If we are going to have a peaceful time, and I am no more to hear the roar of the Orpheus's broadsides, I shall hang up my sword in the library at Harwood

House, and retire upon half pay. To tell you the truth, I am concerned about those young whelps at home. John is so violent and impulsive that I am continually expecting to hear of some mad exploit of his that may embitter his whole future life. I know that all his instincts are generous and noble, and if he is properly managed and controlled, he will add honour to the old name. I understand your hint about promotion, &c. Women are always ambitious! But I am entirely indifferent about such vain gewgaws. It is enough to belong to the race from which I sprang, and I really believe I accepted the little title I received with the peaceful stroke of His Majesty's sword only to please you. Sir Herbert Harwood, knight, is no greater personage in my opinion than plain Captain Harwood was; and, as for money, we have more than enough for all probable contingencies. You know my income has nearly doubled since I received my inheritance, and I have been able to lay aside £5,000 for each of the boys and Alice, without impairing my estate one bit. I want this to go to Allen, as good as it was when I received it, and, maybe, far better. Allen does not know anything about my will; of course, you will not tell him. There will be another mail bag in a week or so, by the Chester, and I will write again.

Your devoted husband,

HERBERT HARWOOD.

LETTER III.

LONDON, *October* 9, 1800.

To CAPTAIN SIR HERBERT HARWOOD, H. M. S. Orpheus, Mediterranean Squadron.

My dear Uncle:—Aunt Anne does not know that I am writing to you, and I thought you could tell her yourself, if you wish her to know what I write about. I have been here about two weeks; all the rest are at Harwood House, and I shall be able to get back in a few days. Dear Uncle, I am sorry to say that Barnard and John don't get along together at all, and I wish now that you had carried out your plan, and sent them to different schools. I don't care which one goes with me, but I hope you won't send us all three together. Barnard has got Aunt Anne's permission to go down to Scotland to shoot. He was invited by the young Laird I wrote you about last month, Macailan, of Linmuir. You know his place is somewhere near Glasgow. Uncle, he is another bad fellow, and a great deal worse because he has plenty of pocket money. He and Barnard are very intimate, and I think Alice likes this Scotchman very much. I don't believe Aunt Anne will tell you about the last quarrel between John and Barnard. It was all on account of Macailan, who came in to dinner one day quite drunk! He is only seventeen or eighteen, though he is a big fellow. Aunt Anne had Lord and Lady Morton to dinner that day, and John tried to persuade the other boys to stay in their rooms, as they were not fit to be seen in respectable society. He offered to stay with them, and so did I. Macailan swore at us dreadfully, and said he meant to " walk down with Leddy Morton, who was na fit to be married to sic an auld pike as my Lord." Barnard encouraged him, and told John he was a low fellow, and not a proper person to associate with gentlemen. I managed to get John away that time, but after dinner he and Barnard had it out. Macailan behaved so improperly at the table, that Aunt Anne had to reprove him, and at last told Barnard " to take Mr. Macailan out with him, as he was evidently not well." We were all four out in the park in the evening, and before we came in John had thrashed both of them. The Scotchman could not use his fists at all, but Barnard fought pretty well. John is such a tiger when he is in a rage that all the school boys are afraid of him ; but he is not a bit quarrelsome, and only had four fights last half. I had more than that myself.

I don't think Aunt Anne will allow Barnard to invite his friend to Harwood House any more. It surprises me that Alice should see anything to admire in him; but she accompanies him and Barnard on all sorts of expeditions, whenever Aunt Anne will allow her to go. I wish you would not send me any more cheques, dear Uncle, until I ask you for them. I have more money now than I know what to do with. If you had not forbidden it, I should like to divide my surplus cash between John and Barnard; but Alice is my banker, and she has ever so many guineas of mine now stowed away for hard times.

Your affectionate nephew,

ALLEN HARWOOD.

LONDON, *November* 1, 1800.

To Master BARNARD HARWOOD, Linmuir, near Glasgow, Scotland.

Sir :—I see no impropriety in answering the questions you put in your letter of 15th ultimo. There is no need to mark communications of this sort "private and confidential," inasmuch as all letters addressed to lawyers upon private business are so regarded. There is no entail. Sir Herbert has full control of his property. If, however, he should die without a will, the estate, or that portion of it which your uncle received by inheritance, would descend, first, to your cousin Allen, next to your cousin John, and lastly to yourself. You young gentlemen occupy precisely the same position with regard to the estate as that occupied by your respective fathers. Lady Harwood's annuity would probably absorb about one-half of the revenues. In regard to Miss Alice More, there has never been any formal and legal adoption, and I presume Sir Herbert's will would make provision for her. She is the daughter of a brother officer of Captain Harwood's, who was killed in battle, when both he and Captain Harwood were lieutenants. She has no inheritance whatever, that I know of. If Sir Herbert had made a will, and the instrument was in my charge, you are aware that I could not with propriety reveal to any one any of its provisions.

I am, sir, very respectfully, your obedient servant,

TITUS PARCHMENT,
Solicitor, &c.

H. M. S. ORPHEUS, }
OFF MALTA, *December* 10, 1800. }

To LADY ANNE HARWOOD, London.

My dear Anne :—I have only time to write a line by the Chester, and that is to announce that the Orpheus follows in her wake. I received my orders to-day, and shall set sail for old England to-morrow. The Chester will beat us a week or more. I shall go direct to London, and thence to Harwood House. If these plaguey orders had only come a month sooner, I might have eaten Christmas dinner with you.

Your devoted husband,

HERBERT HARWOOD.

LETTER VI.

LONDON, *December* 20, 1800.

To BARNARD HARWOOD, Esq., Linmuir, near Glasgow, Scotland.

Sir :—I am not in possession of any information in regard to a settlement of £5,000 upon you or upon Miss More. If Sir Herbert has made, or intends to make any such settlement, he has kept the matter entirely to himself. I would respectfully suggest, if you deem it advisable and proper to institute an investigation on this subject, that you direct your inquiries to your uncle himself. While your motives may be perfectly justifiable, you at least lay yourself liable to unfavourable impressions, produced upon the minds of your friends, by your continued attempts to obtain the information you want, outside of your own family.

I am, sir, very respectfully, your obedient servant,

TITUS PARCHMENT,
Solicitor, &c.

LETTER VII.

LONDON, *December* 20, 1800.

To BARNARD HARWOOD, Esq., Linmuir, near Glasgow, Scotland.

Sir :—We never reveal the condition of any of our accounts to second parties. Should Sir Herbert Harwood desire to know the balance in our hands, he must, under our invariable rules, apply to us directly, or through his known solicitor, Titus Parchment, Esq.

We are, sir, very respectfully, yours,

CARY, BULLION & CO.,
Bankers.

LETTER VIII.

HARWOOD HOUSE, *December* 21, 1800.

To BARNARD HARWOOD, Esq., Linmuir, near Glasgow, Scotland.

Dear Barnard :—We are all surprised, and some of us grieved, that you should decide to be absent at Christmas. Mother thinks it possible that father may be home, as we know that his ship has been ordered to Portsmouth. Lord Morton says he may be here any day now. I burnt your letter to me, as you requested. Are

you sure that you know your own heart on that subject？ I am
too old for you, Barnard; five years older than you are, and you
are only fifteen. If it were possible to get your uncle's consent to
such a marriage, you would have to wait at least six years, and
then I would be twenty-six. I do love you very dearly, certainly,
but I have never thought of you as a possible husband. Do you
know that I shall have positively no fortune at all？ My poor father
had nothing but his pay, and all that I have had since his death
I have received from my second father, Sir Herbert. It is possible that he would give me a portion, if I married with his consent,
but I am sure he would think your proposal to engage yourself to
me nothing else than insanity. I am not mistaken about the
£5,000 laid aside for you and your cousins. I saw one of father's
letters, in which he said he had put this sum away for each of you.
You will have to return to us before long, as your uncle will certainly be home within a month. We will talk further about your
absurd proposals. when you come.

Affectionately yours,

ALICE MORE.

LETTER IX.

LONDON, *June* 1, 1801.

To SIR HERBERT HARWOOD, Bart., Harwood House, Essex.

Dear Sir Herbert :—I am very happy to address you under your
new title, which, I see by the papers, has at last been conferred
upon you. You will allow an old friend to say that he is disappointed. I expected you to change your knighthood for something
better than a baronetcy. However, it may be only a stepping
stone. I have obeyed your instructions, and have taken a thous-
and shares of Wheal Pentland in the name of your nephew, Mr.
Allen Harwood. Your cheque for £5,000 exactly pays for the
stock. I hope his trip to Cornwall has not damaged his intellect.
Though as you require me to keep the secret of this investment,
perhaps he don't know how rich he is to be. I have filed the certificate with your other papers in my possession. Will you allow
me to say (in confidence) that your nephew, Barnard, will be all
the better for your presence in England, if you will keep him out
of bad company？

Faithfully your friend and servant,

TITUS PARCHMENT.

LETTER X.

NEW ORLEANS, LOUISIANA, *May* 1, 1803.

To LADY ANNE HARWOOD, Harwood House, Essex.

My dear Anne:—We are back in this Frenchified city, after a
regular cruise up the muddy river on which it stands. John is so
infatuated that he declares his desire to remain here all his life. I
have been with him I don't know how far up the river, and have
bought him a lot of land back in the country. It is pretty much
wilderness now, and I must admit that it is very beautiful. He
has called it "Harwood." It has cost a good lot of money, though
the property dealers here say it was a great bargain. I have consented to let him remain here, as he is so eager to begin to work
his "plantation." By-the-bye, John is an American citizen by
birth, you know. I wonder if that will account for his preference
for this half-civilized country! My poor brother, who was sent to
Canada on some public business, contracted the disease of which
he died in that cold latitude, and his wife died in the States when
John was born. John has resumed his law studies, and will remain in this city most of his time, until he passes his examination.
He expects to be "admitted" in two years. There are not so
many formalities to get through with, and I suppose the examination is not so rigid here as at home. The birth of my son and
heir has not affected the prospects of any of the boys, except
Allen, who has a small fortune already, though he does not know
it. Do you remember that he came from Cornwall two years ago,
with flaming accounts of some copper mines? I invested his
£5,000 in mining stock, and it has more than doubled in value
already. I intend to keep this secret till all of them are of age.
I suppose I shall have to give up my project of getting Barnard
into the Navy, as he seems to have no bias in that direction.
But as he has become so steady and well behaved he shall choose
his own profession. If the predictions of the knowing ones of
New Orleans may be relied upon, John's fortune is also made, as
the prospective value of his estate up the river is enormous.

I am happy to hear such good accounts of my youngster, the
future Sir Charles. Since I have acquired a title to transmit, I
may as well give it to the embryo baronet in advance. I hope
he will value it as lightly as his father does.

Your devoted husband,

HERBERT HARWOOD.

L E T T E R   X I.

LONDON, *July* 10, 1804.

To SIR HERBERT HARWOOD, Bart., Harwood House, Essex.

My dear Sir Herbert:—With this I send by special messenger the lead-covered box containing the ancient coins and jewelry; the box has probably never been opened since it was bequeathed to Mr. Allen's mother until to-day, when I took an inventory of its contents. Some of the diamonds must be of great value, and the coins are also very rare and would fetch double their weight in guineas any day. You will remember that the box was sent to me from the executors of Lady Denham, for transmission to Mrs. Lacy Harwood, who died before the packet was sent. Since that sad event I have had charge of it, keeping it by your directions as guardian, until Mr. Allen should attain his majority. The only other property belonging to the estate of Lacy Harwood, Esq., or rather to his son and heir, Mr. Allen, is the certificate of 1,000 shares of Wheal Pentland. I have enclosed this certificate in the box also, with the inventory of jewels and coins. The key is fastened to one of the handles, and the box has been sewed up in a strong linen case by Mrs. Parchment under my supervision. I have also inclosed it in thick outside wrappings, corded it and sealed it. If you receive it with the seals intact, you can rely upon the safety of the contents.

Very sincerely, your friend and obed't serv't,

TITUS PARCHMENT.

(The following was written in Sir Herbert's hand at the bottom of this letter :)

I have not opened the box. It is on the hypothenuse just nine feet from its juncture with the base.

HERBERT HARWOOD.

April 30, 1808.

L E T T E R   X I I.

NEW ORLEANS, *May* 10, 1808.

To LADY ANNE HARWOOD, Harwood House, Essex, England.

My dearest Anne:—Allen and I will return to England by the next packet. John is fairly settled on his plantation, living in a comfortable log house, which he affirms to be superior in accommodation to all the buildings in this city. He is practising law, and is very popular with his neighbours. I have not bought a plantation for Allen, as I cannot discover that he has the slightest desire to possess one. He has enjoyed himself as much as possible, with John and his friends, hunting wild beasts in the country back of "Harwood," and narrowly escaping with his life in two separate encounters, one with a bear, the other with an Indian. The latter adventure however happened on the west bank of the big river. He shall tell you and Alice the story himself. I have kept the secret of his little fortune from him, and everybody else excepting you and Parchment. I wished him to come to some decision about his future before I put him in possession. I think this is the last trip I shall take in this direction. I was compelled by circumstances to put Allen's lead-covered box in a place of security, and have made a memorandum on Parchment's letter, which I will explain to you when I get home.

If you should be correct in your suspicion that Macailan wishes to marry Alice, I shall be glad to give my consent. The lad has become quite steady, and with a good wife like Alice (who is too old for him, though), he will become settled. I take it for granted that Barnard has given up his boyish notion. The birth of my two boys has made some change necessary in my intentions, but I still propose to give Barnard a good start in life. He is quite old enough now to make up his mind.

Your devoted husband,
HERBERT HARWOOD.

LETTER XIII.

LINMUIR, *August* 1, 1808.

To LADY ANNE HARWOOD, Harwood House, Essex.

My Lady :—Can you spare dear Alice for a few weeks ? I have set my heart upon having her with me while the young gentlemen are here. Macailan expects Mr. Barnard about the middle of the month. If he comes, and you can oblige me so much, he can escort Miss More. I would offer my son's services, as he is now in London, but suppose you would prefer the other arrangement. I will promise to allow her to return at whatever time your ladyship may appoint.

I am your ladyship's servant,
HESTER MACAILAN.

LETTER XIV.

LONDON, *August* 3, 1808.

To BARNARD HARWOOD, Esq., Harwood House, Essex.

Mon Cher :—My mother is going to invite Miss Alice to Linmuir, and as I am so disreputable a scamp she will arrange for you to attend her to Glasgow. You are to go down on the 15th. I have not been able to learn anything from the old wretch of a lawyer. Denham was with me when I called on him. He was speering about some lead-covered box which was left by will to your dear Uncle. Lacy's widow by his stepmother. Denham is such a close fellow that I could not pump much out of him, but I think he claims some jewels, which he affirms were in the box, and which he says were "family jewels," and not in her power to bequeath. The lawyer gave us no satisfaction; he did not even admit the receipt of the box, and referred Denham to his mother's executors. From the few hints he dropped, I conclude that Denham was about as fond of his stepmother as the devil is of holy water, or as you are of your cousin John. Sir Herbert and your nice cousin Allen will be here in a week, and old Parchment politely invited me to reserve my inquiries till they arrived!

I am off to Linmuir to-morrow.

Yours,   MACAILAN.

———

LETTER XV.

LONDON, *August* 4, 1808.

To LADY ANNE HARWOOD, Harwood House, Essex.

My dear Lady Anne :—Although Sir Herbert will be here in a few days, I think it advisable to notify you that I have been applied to by the son of Sir Mark Denham, who claims some property (personal) which was bequeathed to Mrs. Lacy Harwood by Lady Denham, the stepmother of this young man. It is possible that he may apply to you in Sir Herbert's absence, and I only wish to say that the claim is entirely ridiculous. It is well known that Sir Mark Denham married his second wife solely for money, and it is also well known that every pound of her property was settled upon her. I drew the marriage settlement myself. There has never been any controversy about her real estate, which went

8

to her heir-at-law, or about her money, stocks, etc., which were distributed according to the provisions of her will. Nobody knew anything about the contents of this particular box until I opened it at Sir Herbert's request, about four years ago. It is as clearly Allen's property as his coat is. If this young Denham should apply to you, I would respectfully advise that you give him no information whatever. I can imagine no possible way by which he could learn that the box contained any articles of value except through Sir Herbert or some member of his household. Should Sir Herbert go to Harwood House before I see him, please show him this letter

With great respect, your ladyship's obedient servant,

TITUS PARCHMENT,

Solicitor, etc.

LETTER XVI.

LONDON, 10*th August*, 1808.

To SIR HERBERT HARWOOD, Bart., Harwood House, Essex.

*Sir :—*In reply to your inquiry, left at our banking house last night, we have to inform you that the exact balance standing at your credit is £11,080 18*s.* 4*d.*

Very respectfully yours,

CARY, BULLION & CO.,

Bankers.

LETTER XVII.

LONDON, 28*th September*, 1808.

To SIR HERBERT HARWOOD, Bart., Harwood House, Essex.

*Sir :—*Your cheque for £1,000 to order of Mr. Allen Harwood was presented by that gentleman yesterday and paid. According to our invariable rule, we hereby notify you that your account is overdrawn to the amount of £224 6*s.* 8*d.* The dividends that will be paid in on 1st proximo will, however, place your account largely in credit.

Very respectfully yours,

CARY, BULLION & CO.,

Bankers.

LETTER XVIII.

LONDON, *September* 28, 1808.

To SIR HERBERT HARWOOD, Bart., Harwood House, Essex.

My dear Uncle:—The ship will sail this forenoon, and I write this on board. I have drawn the money for the cheque, and have it now buckled around my waist. As soon as we get fairly out at sea I shall place it in my trunk, as the weight of the belt makes it a very undesirable part of my dress. My dear, kind uncle, I may not live to see you again, and I would not willingly die without saying how deeply I feel all your kindness to me. I know from Aunt Anne that you intended me to be your successor in the possession of Harwood House and of most of the fortune you have added to your original inheritance. I know you will believe me when I say that I rejoice with all my heart that those plans of yours were disarranged by the birth of my dear little cousins, Charles and Allen. And now I am going to communicate an old secret to you. You know that I accumulated a considerable quantity of guineas in the hands of my trusty banker, Alice; well, after I came from Cornwall, seven years ago, I took this money and invested it all in Wheal Pentland. I sold out yesterday, and there is another thousand pounds in my belt, besides your munificent gift. So you see, dear uncle, that I am rich. I tell you the secret now because I know you will be better satisfied to allow your estate to go to the boys unincumbered with any unnecessary legacies. Barnard told me you had laid aside a sum for each of us, but as I am already provided for so amply, you can mark me off. You cannot obliterate the lessons I have learned from your example, uncle, nor can you take back the education you have given me.

What do you think of my having a young lady confided to my care, all the way to Calcutta? She is the orphan daughter of a dissenting minister, who died here six or eight months ago. She has an uncle in India, who has invited her to his home, and her friends here are now in the cabin with her. They introduced me a little while ago. She is very pretty and interesting, and I mean to fall in love with her during the voyage. Her name is Miss Devere.

I am just informed that the steamboat is about to leave the ship. Good-bye, my dear uncle.

Your attached nephew,

ALLEN HARWOOD.

LETTER XIX.

LONDON, *October* 3, 1808.

To LADY ANNE HARWOOD, Harwood House, Essex.

My dear Anne:—I have only time to write a line. It is a forgery of one cheque for £10,000. I start for Scotland by the coach in five minutes.   Your devoted husband,

HERBERT HARWOOD.

——

LETTER XX.

GLASGOW, *October* 10, 1808.

To LADY ANNE HARWOOD, Harwood House, Essex.

My dear Wife:—The news I have to communicate to you will plunge you into affliction. I cannot doubt any longer that Barnard and Alice have conspired to perpetrate a most infamous crime. When I reached London last week I went directly to the bank, and demanded a sight of the cheques I had drawn since they furnished me with their last statement. All were right excepting one for £10,000. This cheque was a remarkably correct imitation of my hand, and I should not think of doubting the signature if I did not know that I had never drawn such a cheque. It is payable to Barnard Harwood's order, and endorsed by him. I asked no questions at the bank, but went directly to Parchment and stated the case. He recommended me to start at once for Glasgow, and recover the money from my nephew, without making any stir. It would kill me if the boy's villany should be generally known. I met Mr. Macailan at the coach office in this town, and he informed me that Barnard and Alice were married before they arrived at Linmuir together;—that they had gone to London after spending a few days with them, and had taken passage for Leghorn. He knew nothing about Barnard's supply of money, except that he declined a loan which the Scotchman says he offered him. Barnard told him that he could not live without Alice, and that I had violently opposed their union, so they were forced to abscond.

How much of this account is true I cannot determine. I know that part of it is false. Lord Morton has been here just a week, and he saw Barnard and talked with him since his arrival at Glasgow. He informs me that Barnard and Alice were staying at the same inn with him. I have been there and found his portfolio, containing a number of letters. I suppose he left it in the hurry of his departure. I shall remain a few days, and if I discover no satisfactory traces of them I intend to return to London and get Parchment to put one of his bloodhounds on the scent—only to discover the whereabouts of the unhappy pair, however. I shall acknowledge the cheque. They have only stolen that which I have long intended to give them; but their heartless disregard of you and me, and of the name they bear, cuts me to the quick.

Your devoted husband,

HERBERT HARWOOD.

LETTER XXI.

LONDON, *December* 2, 1808.

To SIR HERBERT HARWOOD, Bart., Harwood House, Essex.

My dear Sir Herbert:—My clerk, Mr. Blinker, has just returned from Scotland, and I hasten to lay before you the result of his investigations, promising that you may rely upon the accuracy of his statements, and the soundness of his deductions. My instructions to him, which have been faithfully observed, precluded the possibility of exciting any suspicions upon the minds of the parties with whom he came in contact; and now that the facts are elicited, there is no reason to suppose that any one will ever hear of the transactions, excepting those immediately concerned. I have instructed Mr. Blinker to furnish me with a written statement of his proceedings, and I now enclose that statement. You have only to account for your nephew's marriage and absence from England, and I presume you have already decided to allow the simple truth on this point to go to the world, namely: that your nephew, having married contrary to your express wishes, has gone abroad with his bride, having *received* the portions you had laid aside for both himself and your adopted daughter.

I am, my dear Sir Herbert, very faithfully your friend and servant,

TITUS PARCHMENT.

P. S.—I beg you to observe that I have taken my son, Alfred Parchment, into partnership, as indicated in the annexed circular. In any emergency, during my absence from London, you may safely intrust to him any business that would be confided to his father.

LETTER XXII.

To Titus Parchment, Esq., Solicitor, &c., London.

Honoured Sir :—In re, Sir H. H. and others. Acting under your instructions (verbal), I have obtained all the information you required concerning the payment of a cheque for £10,000 drawn by the aforesaid Sir H. H. to the order of, and endorsed by Mr. B. H., and also concerning the subsequent movements of the said B. H and others.

My brother, Silas Blinker, is a clerk in the banking house of C. B. & Co., and as it was necessary that I should obtain the facts without asking questions to excite suspicions, I was compelled to spend two consecutive evenings at my brother's house, and allow him to reveal voluntarily all that I now proceed to communicate. I was also obliged to lay three separate wagers (in a friendly way), and to lose all three, involving an outlay of eighteen shillings. This amount and other small amounts you will find in the enclosed schedule of expenses.

On the fifteenth day of August, of the present year, Sir H. H.'s coach stopped at the banking house before mentioned, at 11.10 A. M. Five shillings were expended in the wager relating to the accuracy of this date. Mr. B. H. descended from the coach, leaving Miss A. M. inside, and entering the front office, presented the cheque, remarking that he was in haste, as he wished to catch the Oxford mail, which started precisely at noon. The cheque was paid as soon as he had written his name across the back. The other thirteen shillings were expended in two wagers, one as to the identity of Miss A. M., and the other as to the fact that there was no Oxford mail that left the city at noon. There was a mail to Uxbridge, which started from the Red Ox Inn at that hour. I went on the third day direct to Glasgow, according to your directions, stopping only once, at Dumfries, where I saw the marriage of B. H. and A. M. duly registered, according to the Scotch law, under date of August 19th, 1808. I put up at the Thistle Inn, in Glasgow, at which place Mr. and Mrs. B. H. had spent ten days, . namely: from the 25th of September to the 5th of October. They had been to the wild country called "the Highlands" for nearly a month previously, and had spent three days at Linmuir, before they came to the Thistle. They went from Glasgow to Liverpool, and took passage and sailed in the ship Tempest, for Baltimore, in the United States of North America. The ship sailed on the 11th of October.

The most of this information I obtained from the agent of a Scotch gentleman, who lives near Glasgow, and although I asked no questions whatever, *he* asked a great number of me, and the evidence in the case I was obliged to gather from the inquiries he propounded. As I was careful to corroborate everything by additional testimony, you may rely upon the facts stated.

This 2d day of December, 1808.

Very respectfully your humble servant,

SAMUEL BLINKER.

LETTER XXIII.

LONDON, March 26, 1810.

To SIR HERBERT HARWOOD, Bart., Harwood House, Essex.

My dear Friend :—It is my painful duty to communicate to you intelligence of the most sorrowful character. Your noble nephew, Allen, is no more. The account of the circumstances attending his death I have obtained from the master of the ill-fated ship in which he sailed for Calcutta. I know that you have long been ill at ease, as no news of this vessel has reached England since she was spoken off the Cape, more than a year ago. She was attacked in March of last year by a French privateer, and escaped capture after an obstinate fight of several hours' duration. She carried four guns, and the men fought with a valour becoming British seamen. One of the masts of the privateer was at last carried away by a fortunate shot, and the Indiaman escaped in the darkness of the night. But poor Allen had been very severely and probably fatally wounded early in the action, and when the storm arose in the night, he was lying helpless in the cabin, apparently near his end. The ship had been much damaged by the Frenchman's shot, and was altogether unseaworthy, when the master and crew decided to abandon her in the boats, as she was evidently sinking. A young lady passenger, a Miss Devere, refused to leave the wreck unless Allen was also taken, and from the shipmaster's account, the two boats, all they had that could live in that sea, were already overladen. He also refused to forsake the ship, and the crew, probably mutinous, had pushed off and left the three to their fate. Later in the night, when the storm had somewhat abated, he was able, with the young lady's assistance, to lower the small boat, into which he managed, with great difficulty, to get some water and provisions. He says he was in the boat stowing the kegs, when a sea struck her, and parted the line by which the boat was fastened to the ship. By the time he had got out his oars he had lost the ship in the darkness. The brave fellow endeavoured to keep near the vessel until daylight, when he could find no vestige of the Hesperus in sight. He admits that he might have drifted to a considerable distance from the wreck in the night, but says positively that she must have gone down within a few hours after he left her side. He was picked up three days afterwards by the same privateer, and was compelled to do an ordinary seaman's duty on board, until a few months ago, when the privateer was captured by a British man-of-war. He came to London from Portsmouth only yesterday, and was brought to me by Lord Morton this morning.

There are two facts connected with this melancholy story that afford some slight gleam of comfort. As soon as the character of the privateer was ascertained, Allen was the first to propose a determined resistance; and volunteering to assume any post that the master deemed him competent to fill, he was given command of one of the guns, and fought with the bravery of a lion, until he was carried senseless into the cabin. He fell, my dear friend, as you would have him fall, fighting the enemies of his country. The other fact is, that the intercourse of five or six months had produced a profound mutual attachment between Allen and Miss Devere. This young lady must have been a very superior woman, well worthy of the devotion of such a man as Allen. Consider, my friend, that while *we* have been so sadly bereaved, *they* went through the dark valley together.

With great sympathy your friend,

TITUS PARCHMENT.

LETTER XXIV.

LONDON, *April* 1, 1810.

To JOHN HARWOOD, Esq., Baton Rouge, Louisiana, U. S. America.

Dear Sir:—I am requested by Sir Herbert Harwood to write to you in his name, to inform you of the sudden death of your aunt,

Lady Harwood, and also of the loss of the ship Hesperus on her voyage to India, with all her passengers and crew, excepting the master of the vessel. Your cousin, Allen Harwood, was passenger in this ship. Lady Harwood's health has been failing for some time past, and the intelligence of Allen's death probably hastened her demise. Under this double affliction Sir Herbert is nearly inconsolable. He has just been offered the command of a ship, and I have no doubt he will accept the position. There is no probability that the war will terminate for years to come, and Sir Herbert will find in the active duties of his old profession the most agreeable deliverance from the scenes of his recent sorrows. He desires me to convey to you the assurance of his affection. If he accepts his appointment, he proposes to leave his little boys under the joint guardianship of Mr. Titus Parchment and

Your obedient servant,
MORTON.

LETTER XXV.

LONDON, November 14, 1810.

To JOHN HARWOOD, Esq., Baton Rouge, Louisiana, U. S. America.

My dear Sir:—Captain Sir Herbert Harwood died on 30th ultimo, of wounds received in a naval engagement, off Cape de la Hogue. By his will I am instructed to send you his writing desk and contents, which will go by the packet that sails from Liverpool to New Orleans on 20th instant. I am inclined to think that Sir Herbert had a presentiment of his approaching death, from the papers I find since I have entered upon my duties as executor. The present baronet, Sir Charles, and his brother, are with Lady Morton in Devonshire. Please acknowledge the receipt of the writing desk. If you happen to know the address of your cousin Barnard, who has never been heard from since his marriage and departure for Leghorn, will you please inform him of the death of your lamented uncle? I have sealed up the desk, and know nothing of its contents.

Very sincerely your obedient servant,
MORTON.

LETTER XXVI.

LINMUIR, NEAR GLASGOW, *February* 6, 1811.

To JOHN HARWOOD, Esq., Baton Rouge, Louisiana, U. S. A.

Sir :—I received your communication dated December 26, 1810, and have at last concluded to notice it. I am, however, at a loss to conceive by what right you have addressed me on this subject, or any other. I know nothing whatever of the movements of Mr. Barnard Harwood. He told me, the last time I saw him, that he was going to Leghorn. He may have gone there, or to the States, or to the devil, which is about the same thing, in my opinion. As you appear to have adopted that contemptible country, you will probably not agree with me.

Yours,   HECTOR MACAILAN,
of Linmuir.

LETTER XXVII.

LONDON, 14*th May*, 1811.

To JOHN HARWOOD, Esq., Baton Rouge, Louisiana, U. S. A.

Dear Sir :—In looking carefully over the memoranda left by my father, who was very methodical and precise, I can find nothing about the box you mention, excepting the following entries in his " estate book." I give you the entries entire:

" June 8th, 1785. Received of William Lipscomb and Thomas Dale, executors of Lady Denham, widow of Sir Mark Denham, Kt., one box, covered with sheet lead, contents unknown, for transfer to Mrs. Lacy Harwood, widow, to whom said box was bequeathed by said Lady Denham."

" June 10th, 1785. Mrs. Lacy Harwood died at Harwood House on 8th instant. I am directed by Sir Herbert Harwood, Kt., and Captain R. N., to retain the box in my possession, it being now the property of Allen Harwood, infant son of Mrs. Lacy Harwood, deceased."

" July 10th, 1804. Sent the above mentioned box to Sir Herbert Harwood, Bart., by the hands of Samuel Blinker, having taken inventory of contents by Sir Herbert's directions. Inventory enclosed in the box with other papers belonging to Allen Harwood, Esq."

These are all the memoranda on the subject. In regard to any claim that may be set up by Mr. Mark Denham, I happen to know that all the property, real and personal, of Lady Denham, was entirely at her own disposal, and could not have been inherited by her stepson, even if there had been no will.

I am, sir, very respectfully yours,

ALFRED PARCHMENT,
Solicitor, etc.

___

LETTER XXVIII.

BALTIMORE, *May* 11, 1811.

To JOHN HARWOOD, Esq., Baton Rouge, La.

Dear Sir :—There is no such person as Barnard Harwood residing in this city, nor has there been for the past ten years, unless he moved in the humblest circles. I have examined the marine lists for the year 1808, and no ship of the name you mention entered our port in that year. Please remit me twenty dollars, which will cover all the expenses of the search.

Very respectfully, yours, etc.,

THOMAS R. SMITH,
Attorney-at-Law.

___

LETTER XXIX.

NEW ORLEANS, La., *May* 3, 1812.

ｒ HARWOOD, Esq., Baton Rouge, La.

·ar Harwood :—We are as certain to have war, within a
ths, as that we live. There is no remedy. I am making
all my preparations to move to Manahio, and shall be able to get a weekly mail, at least, to the village, Carrville. Let us decide to go quietly to work on our plantations and wait for this storm to pass. I have a young son, who made his appearance a few weeks ago. I wanted to give him your name, but my wife is obstinate, and insists that he shall bear his father's. There will be no law business, either here or at Baton Rouge, that will be of sufficient importance to us to keep us away from home. Don't think of the folly of building your house this year, and don't delay

your marriage on account of the small dimensions of your present domicile at Harwood. Your house is better than nine-tenths of the country houses in this State.

Yours, very truly,

CHARLES CARR.

P. S.—Maltby has just been in and informed me of your intention to take the above advice *before you get it.* He says you will be married this month, and that you intend to go direct to Harwood. Accept my congratulations, which are about as much in advance as my good counsel will be in arrears.

LETTER XXX.

NEW ORLEANS, *October 17th*, 1831.

To JOHN HARWOOD, Esq., Carrville, La.

My dear Harwood:—Allow me to introduce to your acquaintance the bearer of this letter, Mr. Edward Delaney, late of Pensacola, Florida. He has some business to transact in your neighbourhood, and I shall gratefully acknowledge any attentions you may be able to show him. He is a distant relation of my wife's family, or at least she supposes he is, as she is related to the Delaneys, some of whom reside in the Flowery State. I think Mr. Delaney wishes to gain some information from you relative to the two abolitionists who were hanged near Carrville last summer.

Very truly yours,

FRANK MALTBY.

LETTER XXXI.

PENSACOLA, Fla., *January* 10, 1832.

To JOHN HARWOOD, Esq., State's Attorney, etc., Carrville, La.

My dear Friend:—There is a Scotchman, named Gowrie, who has some sort of a mercantile establishment in Carrville, who can tell you more about Mr. Delaney than I can. He lived here eight or ten years, and I am comparatively a newcomer. I have heard, however, that he is a widower and appears to be rich. He plays

high, and wins, generally. There is some rumour about his having committed acts of great cruelty among the Indians in the
Everglades, where he had an indigo plantation, probably five or
six years ago. He sold out there, I am told, because an Indian
chief had a fierce quarrel with him and his life was in danger.
Those Seminoles are becoming very troublesome. Don't get into
any quarrel with Delaney. He is a bad fellow when crossed, and
very prompt with his pistol. He shot the Indian I mentioned
above, upon small provocation, and wounded him very severely,
thus exciting the enmity of a whole tribe, and making the neighbourhood too hot for himself and very uncomfortable to the other
planters. He is here very rarely now-a-days, and seems to come
merely for the purpose of visiting his wife's grave. He has no
children. Yours sincerely,

RICHARD TALBOT.

LETTER XXXII.

NEW ORLEANS, *April 3d,* 1832.

To JOHN HARWOOD, Esq., State's Attorney, etc., Carrville, La.

Dear Sir :—I have found the three bales of cotton that were
missing. They were in the warehouse of Messrs. Campbell & Co.,
the marks and numbers almost obliterated. I was able to identify them by my mem. of shipment. The person you speak of was
living in Pensacola when I first arrived there. He had a house
in the town, and lived alone. His wife had been dead several
years. This is all that I feel at liberty to communicate by letter,
but may be able to answer any proper questions when I return to
Carrville, next week.

Very respectfully, your obedient servant,

ANDREW GOWRIE.

The following letters were enclosed in a separate wrapper,
which bore this endorsement: "Since the death of the two Densons I found the enclosed papers in a negro cabin on my plantation. I endeavoured to save the lives of these miserable men at
the Lynch trial, but I stood alone. These new papers only serve
to make their guilt more apparent, though I still regret that I
was not able to obtain for them the regular legal trial they
demanded.

June 20, 1832. JOHN HARWOOD."

LETTER XXXIII.

NEW ORLEANS, 1*st May*, 1830.

To MATTHEW DENSON, Baton Rouge, La.

Friend and Brother :—The good cause is progressing. I leave this city to-morrow, and will join you at the place you have selected for your field of labour early in next week. Lose no opportunity that may offer for informing our brethren in bondage of the remedy for the evils they suffer. All that is now needed is concert of action. The remedy we propose is desperate, but the disease is worse.

Your fellow worker,

C. SUMNER.

LETTER XXXIV.

NEW ORLEANS, *July* 8, 1830.

To MATTHEW DENSON, Baton Rouge, La.

Dear D. :—You are running a great and unnecessary risk. Let the niggers take their chances until the other matter is settled. I own that I should not go into mourning if you could persuade them to kill all the planters in that particular neighbourhood. If we could manage them afterwards, they could, perhaps, aid us in our search. Don't write to me under *any* name. If you can find the *thing* we will divide fairly, but *I* know that this part of the world will be very unhealthy afterwards. With an old friend I may venture to dispense with the formality of a

SIGNATURE.

LETTER XXXV.

NEW ORLEANS, *July* 18, 1831.

To MATTHEW DENSON, Baton Rouge, La.

Dear D. :—Your messenger reached here in safety, and if he were wise he would not return. He, however, avows his determination to share your fate. I tell you again, you are incurring a *terrible* risk. If you suppose that you can escape, through any legal quibble, dismiss that delusion from your mind instanter. You can never obtain a regular trial, but will be strung up to the nearest tree if you are caught. That madman, Sumner, is already in jail—fortunately for him—and all the rest of his gang are known and will be caught. Burn this up. I am not a coward, yet I am shaking now with apprehension. If you do not *instantly* give up *all* the schemes for the present, and work your way into another State, through the woods—or any way off the public roads—we shall meet no more on this side of Tophet! Yet you are such a headstrong devil, that I *know* you will not profit by my advice. I swear to you that I will hunt for the valuables when this fanatical scheme and the schemers are both disposed of and forgotten, and I will divide fairly with you, as agreed. I swear it to you, by the name I bear, or ought to bear. I can tell you nothing about the trees. I only know that there are some in the neighbourhood, as you will find to your cost, when you are dangling from one of them. I will repeat to M. the exact conversation that was overheard, and you can draw your own conclusions. Once more, I charge you—fly!

NEMO.

LETTER XXXVI.

NEW ORLEANS, *August* 1, 1831.

To MATTHEW DENSON, Carrville, La.

You are lost, both of you! It is possible that this may reach you in time, and only possible. Sumner—the damned fool—had a list of names and "fields of labour," and these are found. You and your son are therein located in Carrville. If it chances that you are still free when you get this—look not behind you!

NEMO.

LETTER XXXVII, AND LAST.

June 20, 1832.

To HENRIETTA HARWOOD, Harwood.

My Darling Child:—I have selected the letters in this packet, and arranged them in order, addressing them to you. Most of the day has been given to this occupation, and the task is now finished. When you receive this, which will not be until your father has exchanged this world for a better one, I wish you to keep the letters together, and to read them when you will, and to dispose of them thereafter as your excellent judgment and your enlightened conscience shall dictate. And while I wish *you* to know all of the story therein unfolded, I do not desire my dear boy to know any part of it. Since your mother's death you have been my most constant companion, and my most intimate friend, and I feel that this intercourse will grow closer and more intimate as your mind expands—if it should please God to spare me. But if it is otherwise ordered, my daughter, let it comfort you to know that your whole life has been one unchanging comfort to me; and also, that I confide your brother to you, with a strong and abiding conviction that you are fully equal to the responsibility of the charge. Darling Ret, your father thanks God for the gift of his precious daughter every hour of his life.

You will know from Judge Carr, to whose legal guardianship I have confided my children, what I have thought would be best for you, in regard to your settlement in life. Need I say, dear child, that this is only an expression of my opinion, and by no means intended to bind you, should you make a different choice. Only one word of counsel, darling, do I leave with you on this subject. Never marry until you are *sure* that your husband is the "foremost man" of all your world. Do not be misled by outward attractions of any sort. You come of a high race, and should never mate except with a gentleman of rare honour. But I can freely trust you in this also.

Besides you and Herbert, I have no living kindred in America—that is, I do not know that I have. If I have, they are not such as you will wish to know or acknowledge. I have two young cousins in England—or had twenty years ago—as you will understand from the letters. Farewell, my daughter!

Your loving father,

JOHN HARWOOD.

P. S.—There is a man called Delaney, whom you have seen once or twice—I find myself instinctively recoiling from him. Trust my instinct, Ret, and avoid him.

HERBERT'S JOURNAL,

RESUMED.

CHAPTER XVII.

Mr. Denham.

BALTIMORE, MONDAY, *June* 14, 1836.

I HAVE been home nearly a week, and have enjoyed myself as much as was possible, under all the circumstances. Most of the time has been spent in Insurance offices and in the stores. I have almost finished my Baltimore work, and expect to start for New York to-morrow. It is possible that I may be detained there 30 or 60 days, as the underwriters there may insist upon the time mentioned in their policies. Mr. Bayard has gone to St. Louis, and will remain there the rest of this year. He has given me *carte blanche*, and I am to employ any assistants I may want when the goods reach Carrville.

Mother and the girls know most of my Louisiana history—it is barely possible that I mentioned Miss Harwood as little and as slightly as I could. I cannot endure that even my Mother should know all that I might reveal. I have not spoken of the letters at all. Grace got me into a corner yesterday, and asked me some extremely embarrassing questions. I was rascal enough to pretend that I was in love with Maltby's little girl! and I praised her to the skies. She is a little slip of a girl, about fourteen—a mere child! Grace asked me the colour of her eyes and hair. I hope I told the truth, but am not certain. At last she asked me " what sort of a *bonnet she wore !*" I did *not* swear, but the exclamation I uttered got me off without cross-examination. Mother gave me a lecture—I don't know how long—about my change of name, as if I could help it! I have prevailed on her to promise, however, that she will write to Mr. Henry Hubbard when I go back, and I have promised to resume my name "as soon as possible." Dear Mother is kind to me, and yielded at last, against her judgment. Alice don't want to hear much, except when I happen to speak of Mr. Hamilton. She is such an old blue stocking that she listened with great attention while I repreached the two sermons I heard. She heard him all the time when he was in Baltimore, and was introduced to him at somebody's house, where he happened to call. If she had known he was going to Louisiana she would have sent some message to me! That would have been a nice business! I daresay he saw some family likeness, when he said I reminded him of some one he had met here. Dear me! I said nothing about his self-denial sermon fitting me so exactly. I spoke of Miss Harwood as the promised wife of Charley Carr all the time. Oh! how earnestly do I long to believe that I lied every time I did it! Mother asked for my journal once or twice. I told her the last time that there was only about one week's record in it, and that I could give her a verbal history in less time than it would take to read the record. Oh, Ret! my whole life is compressed into that short week!

TUESDAY, *June* 15, 1836.

My trunk and I arrived at the steamboat wharf just five minutes after the boat started. So I left my baggage at the office and walked back to my Mother's house, carrying my little portfolio containing my letters and this journal, and some *other* letters. I have made it a rule to keep this always under my own eye since I left Carrville. On board the "Queen of the West" I left it in my trunk, but carried it in my hands from Wheeling to Baltimore.

I let myself in with my latch-key, and, walking softly, intending to pounce upon Mother and the girls suddenly, I slipped into a little closet adjoining the drawing-room. I had been there but a few minutes when the door bell rang. As I could get out of the closet into the hall if the visitor entered the drawing-room, I seated myself and waited patiently for the "call" to be over. When the servant opened the door I heard a man's voice, saying:

"Does Mrs. Harwood reside here?"

"Yes, sir, walk in."

"Give her this card, and say I will be obliged if she will favour me with a few minutes' conversation," and he walked into the parlour.

I soon heard my Mother's silks rustling, as she passed the closet door, and when she got into the parlour, I thought I would slip out and go back for the girls. Before I got out of earshot, I heard the visitor say:

"Mrs. Harwood?"

"Yes, sir! Mr. Denham, I believe?"

I resumed my seat.

"Yes, madam, I am Mr. Denham. I have called to see if I could find a relation of the late Sir Herbert Harwood, of Harwood House, Essex."

"My husband was the nephew of Sir Herbert Harwood, sir," replied my Mother.

"I suppose so, madam, from information I received."

"Resume your seat, sir," said my Mother, and they sat down. The idea of going away flashed across my mind, as I did not like being an eavesdropper; but I was rooted to the spot by the next words.

"I am not at liberty to say all I know, madam," resumed the visitor, "but it will perhaps be sufficient to say that your son— you have a son I think?"

"Yes, sir; Herbert!"

"Precisely, madam. Mr. Herbert Harwood is particularly interested in the matter. For the present, however, I am obliged to act very circumspectly; and I may add that your son especially should know nothing of what I may say to you." There was a pause.

"Proceed, sir," said my Mother, at length.

"Pardon me, madam. Do I understand you to agree that what I reveal is to be considered confidential?"

"My son has just left the city, sir. He may not return for several weeks. You will have to allow me to decide when I have heard what you say you have to reveal." There was another pause.

"I see you distrust me, madam, and I will frankly state the case to you. I am a lawyer, and my personal interest in this business depends entirely upon the success of my effort to place your son in possession of a large sum of money. Now, if he should hear too soon of this good fortune, and deem it advisable to make any personal effort to secure it, he would almost certainly derange my plans, and probably lose the fortune altogether."

"My son is a man, sir; and a gentleman by birth and education. You may safely rely upon his honour."

"Undoubtedly, madam!" replied her interlocutor. "You shall judge for yourself whether or not to include him in our confidence——"

"I do not comprehend what you mean by our confidence, sir." My Mother is a regular queen when she chooses to put on her majesty. I could hardly refrain from peeping into the room to see how Mr. Denham took that shot.

"I perceive that there is no confidence on *your* side at least, madam," said he; "and I fear the whole business will fall through for want of it. It is absolutely necessary that I should see all papers that your husband may have left. I do not object to the presence of your son or yourself while I make the investigation. Nay, I only ask that you, or either of you, should read the papers in my hearing. If I am to proceed in the case thereafter, I must insist upon full liberty to act without the interference of any one."

"My husband left no papers relating to his connection with the family of Sir Herbert, excepting those written by himself——"

"Those are precisely the papers I want, madam," said Mr. Denham eagerly.

"The only papers in my possession, sir, are contained in a packet addressed to my son."

"No doubt, madam; they are all important in this matter."

"Well sir, I can do nothing without consulting my son. If you desire it I will write to him by the next mail. I can have an answer in about a week."

"I must content myself with your decision," said he, rising. My Mother rang the bell, and he passed into the hall. As the servant opened the door I peeped into the passage, and saw his crisp, black hair, the nicely fitting kid glove, and the glossy silk hat he was adjusting on his wicked skull.

It was Captain Delaney.

As my Mother walked up the hall I emerged from the closet and met her.

"Herbert! my son! what has happened?"

"Nothing, Mother. The boat left me, and I must postpone my journey until to-morrow. Please come into the drawing room again."

"You are ill, Herbert? your face is pale, and——"

"I am quite well, dear Mother. You had a visitor just now?"

"Yes—a Mr —— Denham," she said, glancing at the card in her hand—"the most intensely disagreeable man I ever met!"

"What makes you say so, Mother?"

"His *tout ensemble;* the glance of his sharp, black eye; the tone of his voice; the motion of his gloved hand; his seeming determination to accomplish his purposes—*coute qui coute.*" Oh, excellent Mother!

"I have heard all your conversation, Mother. Please forgive me. I was in the closet all the time he was here. Don't scold me, please, but listen. I know this man. I have seen him in Louisiana, and have heard more than I have seen. He is now working out some devilish plot affecting me, or—— John Harwood's children. Oh, Mother! help me to circumvent him."

"Why are you so excited, Herbert? where are you going?" I went into the closet and got my portfolio; I laid it in her lap, and then putting my arms round her neck I hid my face in her loving bosom.

"I have not dealt candidly with you, Mother. Read all of my journal, and all the letters, and you will then be able to counsel me. I am ashamed of myself, Mother; I should have told you everything. Where are the girls?"

"They are both out—will not be home until evening. Suppose you go after them; they are at Mrs. Leland's. Go, my son, and I will read while you are all away. Mrs. Leland will be very glad to have you. Come home early." So I went.

When we got home Mother was in her own room. It was about ten o'clock, and the girls soon retired. I took my candle and came here into my chamber. My Father's portrait is hanging over there by the window, and I was standing before it, looking into his eyes and trying to remember how he looked when I last saw him, when Mother came into the room. She laid my portfolio down on the table and held out her arms to me. She held me in her embrace a moment, and then we sat down.

"My poor boy!" she said at last, "does your Father's picture say anything to you?"

"Yes, Mother. It tells me that I am the son of a noble gentleman and of a matchless lady! I don't need any other lesson."

"I have read your journal, Herbert, and all those letters. You have acted well, my son, and I am proud of you."

"I think you may trust me, Mother. And now I want my Father's letter—may I have it?"

"It is here, in your portfolio. It was to be given you when you were of age. I think that time has come, dear, hasn't it?"

"Yes, ma'am."

"Do you want to read it to-night, Herbert?" she said, as she kissed me at parting.

"Yes, Mother. We will talk about it to-morrow. Let me light you. Good night!"

CHAPTER XVIII.

ALLEN HARWOOD'S LETTER.

BALTIMORE, *May 1st*, 1826.

My Beloved Son :—It is proper that you should know some part of the history of your family, and while you are now too young to understand the story, the time will probably arrive when it will be full of interest. I am admonished by many unmistakable tokens that my career is nearly ended. Yours will be only begun, my son, when you read these lines. May it be as happy as your Father's has been, and far more useful.

My grandfather was the second son of John Lacy Harwood, Baron Morton of Lavington, Devonshire. The Harwoods are a very old family, and have always piqued themselves upon their ancient name. From the wars of the Roses down to the accession of the House of Hanover, it has always happened that the branch of the family from which you spring has espoused the cause which modern historians have pronounced to be right. There have been many vicissitudes in their history, but through them all the Harwoods of Essex and Devonshire have ever maintained their reputation as valiant soldiers, wise statesmen and spotless gentlemen. Therefore, the cumulative power of the example of these worthies has been felt through succeeding generations; and all the members of the family that I have known, with one exception, have acknowledged and been governed by this influence. In this democratic land there is a growing disposition to ignore and despise all the claims of lineage and blood; but I charge you, my son, to live and die worthily, to let the controlling emotions of your moral nature, the words of your lips, and the acts of your life, all accord with the record of the race from which you have descended.

The lordship of Morton, with the Devonshire estates, the principal of which is Lavington, were all conferred upon my father's grandfather, John Lacy Harwood. My grandfather was a younger son of the first Baron Morton of Lavington. He died in 1760, leaving four sons, namely: Herbert, Lacy, John and Barnard. My earliest recollections go back to about 1790, when my uncle Herbert was the only survivor of these four gentlemen. My father, Lacy Harwood, died soon after my birth; my uncles, John and Barnard, died before 1790—leaving, each of them, a son, whose sole inheritance was his father's name. My uncle Herbert was an officer in the Royal Navy, and died about fifteen years ago, after winning a victory that cost him his life. You bear the name of this noble gentleman, my son, and I trust you to transmit it to your children without stain or blemish.

My grandfather's estate, according to English law, descended to his eldest son, and the portions of both of my cousins were very small. We were all three brought up in our uncle's house, and I should have inherited his fortune if he had died without issue; but he left two sons, who were born to him, after we three had arrived at manhood. My cousin John had an estate somewhere in Louisiana, bought for him by our uncle, who had been created a baronet by George III, and whose estate had reached a value nearly double the amount of his inheritance. He was munificent in his gifts to his nephews, and intended to purchase a similar estate for me after the birth of his heir. But I had long desired to win a fortune for myself in India, and my kind uncle yielded to my wishes.

Before I proceed with my own story, I have a few words to say about my cousin Barnard, and about his wife, Miss Alice More, who was Sir Herbert's adopted daughter. What I say to you on this subject I wish you alone to know. So far as I am aware, your Mother and I are the only living repositories of these secrets, and I communicate them to you, hoping you will be warned by an evil example, as you will be stimulated to good by that of your grand uncle. The history of his life is a part of the history of his country, and in all her glorious annals I could find no name to bestow upon you that was more worthy than his.

From his early youth Barnard was fierce, wilful, imperious, exacting and revengeful. This much I know. I am obliged to *think* he was also covetous and even dishonest. He was the one bad product of a goodly tree. At school, and at home during the holidays, he was a perpetual thorn in the sides of John and your father. I avoided quarrels with him by avoiding his society, but he and John spent their early lives in one long battle, with occasional hollow truces. About the time I attained my majority, uncle returned after a long absence from England, and placed Barnard at a different school, and shortly afterwards John was finally settled in Louisiana. Just about the time of my departure for India, Barnard and Alice were privately married in Scotland, and sailed for Leghorn, it was said, immediately. I do not know what to say of Alice. I loved her very dearly, and I am now disposed to believe that she was misled and overruled by Barnard, whose one redeeming trait was his profound affection for her. Their marriage was opposed by Sir Herbert on account of the disparity in their ages, Alice being five or six years older than her husband. Neither of them had any fortune, as we were all alike dependent upon Sir Herbert's kindness, and it was because I was not willing to take any part of his inheritance from his natural heirs that I determined to seek my own fortune in the East. I try to think of you, Herbert, as a matured man, while I write this, and to believe that you will appreciate the sacredness of the secret I am about to tell you. I am afraid that Barnard obtained whatever money he had by a direct robbery. This was enough of degradation, it would seem; but to crown the act with peculiar infamy, he chose for his victim the kind, unsuspecting uncle, in whose house he had lived from his infancy! I do not *know* this, but there is not the shadow of a doubt upon my mind concerning the sad story. I have told it to you, trying to distinguish between facts and suspicions, because it is possible that you may some day encounter your unworthy relative. He is able to deceive you or any one, but with this knowledge of his character you need not be deceived, if you should ever chance to meet.

I come now to my own history, and have little more to say. Your mother will communicate all you may desire to learn. I first saw her on the voyage to Calcutta, and learned to appreciate her value before we had been many days at sea. Like me, she was an orphan, and poor. She was going, a passenger in the same ship, to India, at the invitation of her uncle, who was in moderately prosperous circumstances. On the voyage the ship was attacked by a French privateer, and although not captured, was so badly damaged that she was abandoned by her crew in the midst of a storm. I had been severely wounded and was supposed to be dying, and the crew refused to transfer my almost lifeless body to the overladen boat. Alice, *my* Alice, your noble Mother, refused to leave her affianced husband while the vital spark still lingered, and the master of the Hesperus also resolved to share our fate. The crew left us, and were no doubt drowned an hour afterwards. The master was swept away in a small boat, which he was supplying with provisions for our escape, and was afterwards picked up and saved. We were rescued, Alice and I, from the sinking vessel by an American merchantman, and your Mother saw the wreck sink before we had reached the deck of the Chesapeake. We saved, that is *she* saved my baggage and her own, and our joint fortunes amounted to a little more than ten thousand dollars. Before we reached this city, to which the Chesapeake was bound, we had spoken two British cruisers, and I had sent letters to my uncle, informing him of my safety, by both of them. I afterwards learned that he had died before either of these letters reached England, if they ever did.

The day of our arrival in Baltimore was the happiest day of my life. Your mother and I were married at the office of the British Consul, and the certificate she now has bears his signature and official seal. I commenced the business from which I am now re- tiring with the capital I had saved from the wreck of the Hes- perus, and the blessing of Providence has so far attended me that I am able to leave my family in the possession of a modest com- petence. You will have to make your own way in the world, my son; if you desire riches you must earn them. In this land, strict attention to a vocation and economy in expenditure will rarely fail of obtaining enough for any reasonable wants. I wrote to my cousin, John Harwood, addressing him in New Orleans, and in- formed him of my marriage and my happiness. I received in reply a letter from a Mr. Denham, an English gentleman, who stated that poor John had died just as the last war between England and this country began. He had contracted a disease—some malig- nant fever, and died on the eve of his own marriage.

Next to my uncle, whose kindness and affection followed me through my whole life, and to whom I am indebted for all that I have, John Harwood occupies the highest place in my memory. Though he was ever rash, impulsive and passionate, he was also ever brave, generous and true. I loved him very dearly, and if he had lived, it would have been my pleasant duty to bid you honour him, as you can now only honour his memory. I visited him with Sir Herbert at his home in Louisiana, just twenty-three years ago, and we three gentlemen explored a portion of the western bank of the great river, hunting during the day and sleeping in the open woods at night. It was then a wilderness, and there were occa- sionally parties of unfriendly Indians, from the farther West, who roved in small bands almost within reach of the settlements on the banks of the Mississippi. I was once attacked by a scout of one of these wild tribes, and should probably have been slain in the encounter but for the courage and address of my cousin John. The savage had surprised me, and mastered my rifle, and we were struggling on the ground, my strength gradually yielding under the pressure of the iron muscles of the Indian, when John suddenly arrived and rescued me. I shall never forget how he dashed upon the truculent savage, tore him from my relaxing grasp, and wresting the knife from his hand killed him with his own weapon. Mr. Denham's letter informed me that he was engaged to settle his estate, by the guardian of Sir Charles Harwood. I presume the title to the property had remained in Sir Herbert Harwood, though I know that it was my uncle's intention to convey it to John. If Mr. Denham's letter had not so explicitly stated the contrary, I should have gone South to look after this property, for my children's sake; but this gentleman could have had no conceivable motive to deceive me, and I am forced to conclude that my uncle had retained the title deeds.

My story is ended. It is not probable that you will ever see any of the members of the family whose history I have just recounted to you. I have few memorials to leave you. The most valuable is my watch and seal, bearing the Harwood arms. The watch is even now somewhat antiquated, and when you are old enough to wear it it will no doubt be out of fashion; but, if it has no other value, the inscription on the case—"From Sir Herbert Harwood, Baronet, to his dear nephew and heir-at-law, Allen Harwood, London, 1801"—is a rich legacy, because it reminds me of my loving uncle, and will serve to remind you, my dear son, of both him and

Your loving father,

ALLEN HARWOOD.

CHAPTER XIX.

WHEAL PENTLAND.

WEDNESDAY, *June* 16, 1836.

MY Mother and I have spent most of this morning in mutual explanations, and we have enlightened each other amazingly. She began, after reading my Father's letter, to unravel the Denham mystery. The rascal Denham, or Delaney, has been prowling about the neighbourhood of Harwood, to find and carry off the box of jewelry which he supposes to be hidden there. It is *my* box, so he is trying to steal from me. His object in getting my Father's papers is evidently to eke out the imperfect information he already has, and which he probably obtained from Barnard Harwood. We have concluded to meet him as follows: I shall write to my Mother, as soon as I reach New York, declining to treat with Mr. Denham without some more definite statement, and inviting him to correspond with me upon the subject through my Mother. I want a letter from him, because I think he is the writer of those letters to the Densons, and, if so, I can prove it by comparing them. I don't know what will be the next step, but I am going to keep the secret of my interest in the matter from Captain Delaney by keeping my Hubbard name awhile longer. If I escape meeting him here, I shall have the advantage when we meet again in Louisiana, as I will know *his* secret but he will not know mine. I shall try to be in time for the steamboat this evening.

NEW YORK, SATURDAY, *June* 19, 1836.

After prowling about this big city all day I feel rather tired. There will be some delay about collecting the insurance money, and I don't know how long I shall be detained. I wrote the letter to Mother as soon as I arrived here, and expect to have a reply some day in next week—probably about Wednesday. The largest amount of our New York Insurance is in the New York and Baltimore Consolidated office, and I spent about three hours there to-day. When I got access to the secretary I found him poring over some huge account books, and apparently very much perplexed. He soon disposed of my business by appointing to-morrow for the investigation of my claim; and remarking that he was very much annoyed by the state of his accounts, I offered my assistance. He has to make a semi-annual report on the 1st of July, and there is a large error in his balance sheet which he has not been able to find. I told him that I was an accountant of considerable experience, and that I would look for the mistake while he examined my insurance claim. He agreed at once, and I went to work. It is only necessary to say that I have thus far discovered nothing, except that the mistake *must* be in one of three or four large accounts. Mr. Hardy, the secretary, is not much of an accountant, and he has been wasting valuable time and labour in looking for his error in impossible places. He says he will give me five hundred dollars if I get off his balance sheet before the month is out, so I am going to work in earnest on Monday. I must find out now where to go to church to-morrow.

NEW YORK, MONDAY, *June 21, 1836.*

I have spent this entire day over the insurance books, and begin to see daylight. The original error was an uneven sum, and I have found two or three small ones, and am now looking for precisely one hundred thousand dollars. I am sure of finding that, by a regular and systematic examination of all the large accounts, taking them *ab initio.* When I make my next entry here, I shall be able to record my victory. The whole thing is so simplified by my fortunate discovery of the small mistakes, that I feel entirely confident of success to-morrow or on the next day.

WEDNESDAY, *June 23, 1836.*

A good long yarn to spin to-night. I found the error, and gave Mr. Hardy the balance sheet this morning. I have now in my pocket a nice crisp new note for five hundred dollars, which was the more acceptable, because Mr. Hardy seemed to pay it with genuine pleasure. Received a letter from Mother, enclosing a note from Mr. Denham, which I may as well copy here:

BALTIMORE, *June 21, 1836.*

"To Mr. HERBERT HARWOOD, New York.

"*Dear Sir:* Mrs. Allen Harwood has shown me a letter from you, in which you decline my proposition to look over your Father's papers, without fuller information from me as to the object in view. Briefly, I may say, that I expect to obtain such information from these papers as will enable me to secure to you a sum of money, which you would inherit as the son of Allen Harwood, Esq. It is not possible for any one to obtain this money without the information which I alone can give. If I succeed, I shall require your obligation to pay me a percentage of the amount obtained; and I shall also require that you put me in possession of certain data, which I am sure will be found among the papers left by Mr. Allen Harwood. These data will, no doubt, have to be collected from old letters, &c., or other memoranda; and as I cannot specify more explicitly the kind of information I want, I can see no way to arrive at the desired end save by a careful examination of the papers referred to. My address for the present is Barnum's Hotel, Baltimore.

"Very respectfully yours,

"MARK DENHAM."

The writing is identical with that in the letters signed "Signa-ture" and "Nemo," in Ret's packet. I have not yet answered Mr. Denham.

I am at a loss to account for this man's conduct; that he designs to gain possession of the box, left by his stepmother to my grand-mother, I can easily understand. But why should he change his name to Delancy, and how does he know anything about my Father's family? He has been hunting this lead-covered box for more than five years, and this is his first appearance in this lati-tude. He is undoubtedly the same man who volunteered the lie which deceived my father, and prevented a natural intercourse between the cousins, which might have led to the discovery of this property. John Harwood died in the belief that my Father had perished in the Indian Ocean; and my Father died in the belief that his cousin had fallen a victim to some southern fever, in 1812. On one hand, I am forearmed by the knowledge of Den-ham's rascality, and by a tolerably clear insight into his motives and intentions; but, on the other, I feel as though I am fighting in the dark, and with an adversary having cat's eyes. I think I have decided to write to Mother, requesting her to tell Mr. Den-ham that I shall call upon him, if I conclude to entrust the mat-ter to him. If I can evade him until I get back to Louisiana I may be able to spoil all his nice plans.

After I left Mr. Hardy this morning I walked down into Wall street, to hunt up Mr. Carr's correspondent. I found his office at last, on the second floor of a house which seemed to be occupied entirely by stock brokers. Every door had a little tin sign on it, and all the signs bore the word "stock broker," in addition to the names of the occupants of the rooms. Mr. Callahan's office is a dingy looking back room, furnished with two or three chairs, two desks, some files of newspapers, and two spittoons. The office was taking care of itself when I entered. There was a card stick-ing upon the front door, bearing the following inscription:

> *At the Board.*
> *Will return at noon.*
> *Take a seat.*

Supposing the invitation to be addressed to me, I seated myself, and taking one of the files, I found it contained some compara-

tively recent numbers of the London *Times*. I have long had a
curiosity to see this paper, and was buried in one of its editorials,
when I heard a great shuffling of feet on the stairs, and presently
the door opened and Mr. Callahan and another gentleman entered
the office. I laid aside the paper, and rose as they came in, and
Mr. Callahan waved his hand, saying, with a slight Hibernian
twang:

"Keep your seat, sir; I shall be at leisure in a moment."

He and his companion went off instantly into an animated dialogue, which they kept up in an almost unknown tongue. The
broker began by saying: "I took a thousand shares of Pacific
Canal to-day, me boy, at nine and three-eighths. You can have it
or not, as you plaze."

"I'll take it," said the other; "but it was only a quarter yesterday."

"Thrue for you! but there is a corner in it!"

"The deuce!"

"Sure there is thin!" said Mr. Callahan. "It'll be ten, or ten
and a half to-morrow."

"Why didn't you go deeper?" said his companion.

"Oh, I was not fool enough to run it up on meself, ye divil; but
niver mind. It is good enough for you as it is."

"Well, you want the money?"

"Send me your cheque in the mornin'. Let me see, nine and
three-eighths, and the commission—ninety-four hundred and forty-
three, seventy-five. Ye'll not want a statement?"

"I guess I can cypher it out!" drawled the other. What about
the copper?"

"Illegant! but it will not be on for a week or so. I'll let ye
know in time. Good day! Now, sir; if you'll excuse me, I'll draw
me coat. It's hot as blazes!"

He looked quite cool and collected as he sat opposite me in his
shirt sleeves. He had a sharp nose, and a pair of flimsy looking
red whiskers. I handed him his own letter to Mr. Carr, and while
he was reading it I made up my mind, if either of us was to be
taken in, it would not be Mr. Callahan. When he had finished
the letter he refolded it and bowing to me, said:

"You represent Mr. Carr, I presume, sir?"

"Yes, sir; I have that honour," I replied.

"Well, sir; will you favour me with your instructions?"

"Will you oblige me, in the first place," said I, "by letting me understand a little about this stock? Mr. Carr's instructions to me were extremely vague, and I must be guided by my own judgment in the matter. I left Louisiana very unexpectedly, and had no opportunity for much conversation with him on the subject."

"With all the pleasure in life, Mr.——"

"Harwood, sir."

"Happy to meet you, Mr. Harwood. I believe you are Mr. Carr's ward; but we always call him Judge. Isn't he a judge or something of that sort?"

"Not at present. He was parish judge some years ago, but resigned his office. He retains the title, however, almost universally. I am not——"

"Oh, well; divil's the difference! About the stock. Judge Carr was here in the summer—a year ago—and I had just returned from a trip to the copper regions on Lake Superior. While I was there, my travelling companion, who is a geologist and mineralogist of considerable ability, induced me to join him in the purchase of a tract of land, which he thought very promising for mining purposes. We did buy it, and the former owner stipulated for a fourth part of the stock in part payment, when we had formed the company and issued certificates. All this has been done. Mr. Carr proposed taking a fourth interest at the same time. The original cost of the land, with the expenses of getting a charter and other incidentals, amount all together to two thousand dollars. The former owner has received his certificate for twelve thousand five hundred shares. Mr. Ludlow, the mineralogist, has his certificate for a like amount; I have mine, and here is Judge Carr's all complete, except the filling in of his name. The charter establishes the corporation with a capital of fifty thousand dollars, in fifty thousand shares of one dollar each."

"I don't understand," I answered; "I thought you said the cost was only two thousand——"

"Oh, the value fixed to the shares is only nominal; but nobody in the world knows anything about the cost excepting the parties interested. When the stock comes upon the market it will represent a property valued at fifty thousand dollars. You need not laugh, I can sell the whole of it in an hour for very nearly that sum."

"Do you really mean, Mr. Callahan, that you can get for Judge Carr's portion anything like ten thousand dollars?"

"That's precisely what I mean, sir. The stock has never been regularly before the board, but I have had private offers for my interest from several well informed men."

"Well, sir," said I, taking my hat, "I shall decide to-morrow about the matter. You know I am acting for another, and must, therefore, be as prudent as possible."

"Certainly, sir," rejoined Mr. Callahan; "and if you conclude to resign Mr. Carr's interest I will make you a present of five hundred dollars, either now or to-morrow."

I went to Mr. Hardy's office, but he was out, and I am going back there to-morrow to see him and get his advice. Though I don't see how I can hesitate, if a very small percentage of Mr. Callahan's story is true.

THURSDAY, *June* 24, 1836.

Mr. Hardy told me this morning that I ought by all means to take the stock. I did not tell him the original cost, as I thought that was not my secret. But he says it will undoubtedly sell at a dollar a share as soon as it is on the board list. Acting upon this advice I went down into Wall street again, and, it being after noon, I found Mr. Callahan in his office. I had forgotten all about Mr. Carr's commission, when I was with Mr. Bayard on the Mississippi, and not feeling at liberty to use his money, I paid Mr. Callahan my beautiful five hundred dollar note. It cost me a struggle, too, as I had determined to expend a large part of this money in presents for my Mother and sisters. But I knew I was pursuing the proper course, so I swallowed my regrets. Mr. Callahan asked me if I was certain that Mr. Carr's name was Charles, and, as I could not remember positively, he proposed to fill up the certificate in my name. There is a blank form on the back for transfers, and he took my signature (which he pronounced "a beautiful specimen of caligraphy") in the transfer book.

"It would be necessary for me to have Mr. Carr's signature, anyhow," he said, "as I have never seen his writing and could not identify it. It is probable that he will wish to divide his stock, and if so, the directions for transfer must come from you. His letter enclosing the certificate for transfer will be a sufficient voucher."

I put the certificate away in my pocket-book, remarking that I was now one fourth owner of the "Lake Shore Mine."

"That's just it!" replied Mr. Callahan, "and if the Judge should happen to disapprove of your investment, it will be about the luckiest thing that could happen to you."

" It seems very strange, Mr. Callahan," said I, " that so small a sum of money should buy so large and valuable a piece of property."

" Did you ever happen to hear of Wheal Pentland?" said Mr. Callahan.

" Wheal Pentland!" replied I, with a start; " certainly; I have heard of a copper mine of that name in Cornwall."

" That's just it!" said he again, with considerable emphasis. " Do you happen to know the early history of that mine?"

" No, sir," I replied, beginning to be enormously interested.

" Well, then, I'll relate it. About thirty years ago a small party of gentlemen—there were only eight of them—bought the mine, formed a company and got a charter. The par value of the stock was five pounds a share, but there was never more than one pound paid in. Very soon after the company was organized one of the stockholders sold out his interest in small lots at par. He thought he was making a good thing of it, and so he was, considering his original outlay. The other seven, or their heirs, hold the balance of the stock to this day. Here is a late number of the *Times;* will you plaze look at the quotation of Wheal Pentland?"—he handed me the paper, pointing to the column containing the information—" you see it is quoted at twenty-five pounds a share."

" It is true," I answered, somewhat bewildered. " It is set down here just as you say—one pound paid in and quoted at twenty five pounds, offered."

" Just so. There is none for sale, however. When the eighth owner had sold out his proportion the most of it was bought at higher prices by the other stockholders. The last lot that was on the market was sold in small parcels of one hundred shares. It was sold by trustees to close an estate, and it sold up to twenty-five pounds, which has been the standing bid for some three or four years back. It is paying large dividends upon the advanced price."

" Do you expect the Lake Superior mine to do as well as Wheal Pentland?"

" Upon me sowl, I don't, thin!" he answered. " But copper mines are generally remarkably profitable or utterly worthless. I do think the Lake Shore mine will be found in the former category. It has been carefully examined by scientific gentlemen, and the quality of the ores is unusually good, and the quantity is supposed to be inexhaustible. I don't mind telling you, in confidence, that I intend to sell a small portion of my stock when it reaches two dollars a share, and I shall put the balance of it away for my children."

"To go back to Wheal Pentland, sir, allow me to ask you a question or two. My father owned some of this stock, but the certificate was——lost. I have reason to think it still stands in his name. If my surmise is correct, it has stood in this condition for nearly or quite thirty years, and I suppose there is an accumulation of unclaimed dividends. Now, what steps should I take to find out something about it ?"

"How much of the stock did your father own ?"

" A thousand shares."

"What!" exclaimed Mr. Callahan, starting up from his seat; "a thousand shares of Wheal Pentland! Well, by jingo! that bangs the divil! And all the back dividends! Why, by me sowl, you are talking about a hundred and fifty thousand dollars at least!"

"So it seems, sir. I didn't know, until quite recently, that my father owned this stock. *He* never knew it. It was bought for him by his uncle, who hid the certificate somewhere—I don't know where—intending to surprise his nephew with the gift at some subsequent time. But he died before the gift was made, and I am almost positive that the stock still stands in Allen Harwood's name."

"Well, one thing is pretty certain, anyhow," said Mr. Callahan, after rubbing his head in great perplexity, "and that is, that no man in his sinses is going to slape long with such an avalanche of money hanging over his head. Have you taken any steps whatever in the business ?"

"None, sir. I just asked you for advice upon that point."

"Suppose you lave the case in my charge for the present. Give me your name and your father's name here in writing; also the name and residence of your father's uncle, and the date of the purchase, as near as you can remember it."

"It was in 1801."

"Very good. Write it down and lave me your address in Louisiana. You shall hear from me in about sixty days."

I took out my pocket-book, preparing to deposit a fee with Mr. Callahan, when he put a stopper upon the proceeding by saying there would be no expense involved in the mere investigation.

"I have a correspondent in London to whom I am writing anyhow, and it is only the addition of a few lines to my letter. If we get the stock I shall charge you the usual commission when the transfers are made."

"I have only a word more to say, then," I remarked, as I took leave of my new friend; "my father was married in the office of the British Consul at Baltimore, and the certificate in my mother's possession has his official signature and seal——"

"All the better, Mr. Harwood; there will be no difficulty about getting the money beyond some little formalities. Good-bye, sir; I hope to have the pleasure of writing you good news before the year is out."

I shall start for Baltimore to-morrow, D. V. I wrote to Mr. Mark Denham to-night, merely saying that I had no private papers of my Father's which I would allow any stranger to see. I also remarked that the record I had of Mr. Denham's former friendly offices did not encourage me to trouble him with my family matters, which were already in "very, skillful hands." I thought the last remark would settle him.

BALTIMORE, MONDAY, *July* 12, 1836.

Mrs. Leland invited all of us to spend some days with her at her country house. The weather has been hot and the country delightful. We have all been there since I returned from New York. I came into town two or three times a week to attend to business matters, and I am now ready to return to Louisiana. I expect to start to-morrow morning. Dear Mother is up stairs writing a letter to Ret. I don't know what she will say to her, but I am going to take the letter. I can trust Mother.

I saw Captain Delaney Denham get into one of the Frederick cars a week ago. He has started for the South again, no doubt. The servant we left at home says he called twice during our absence, but left no message. I am pretty sure he did not see me. I feel a sort of presentiment that the rascal will work some evil upon me some of these days, and I am half ashamed to say that the thought makes me nervous. I *know* that I am not afraid of him, yet the idea of meeting him again at Carrville makes my heart beat faster. What folly this is! I won't endure it any longer, so I'll quit thinking about him.

CHAPTER XX.

HEARTBROKEN.

CARRVILLE, LOUISIANA, WEDNESDAY, *Aug.* 4, 1836.

OH, I have seen her again! Why should I write any more?
The rest of my life is a blank, for I love her! Yes, yes. All
the story is told in a word. I love her so, that the wildest expres-
sions that come into my mind are tame and meaningless. I love her
without one little spark of hope, but I love her the more, because
I know that the miserable secret must be forever hidden in my
own bosom until it eats away my vitals. All the while I have
been away I have thought of her, dreamed of her, and longed for
her. I thought of the joy with which I should tell her that I
was Allen Harwood's son. I thought I should give her Mother's
letter, and watch her while she read it. Oh, how mad I have
been! Oh, why did I ever awaken from that foolish dream!
While the steamboat was crawling down the long river I counted
the hours that must intervene before I could look upon her fair
face again. I cannot write any more to-night, for I feel that I am
going mad! I am going out—far into the country—into the
woods, and will try to walk myself into weariness. Shall I ever
sleep any more?

MIDNIGHT.

I believe I am sobered again, and may be able to write something like a record of to-day's events. I feel sad enough, Heaven
help me! but I hope I am able to meet whatever Providence may
have in store for me with the front of a man. There is nothing to
say about my journey from Baltimore. All I know about it is
that it continued many long days, and that *she* was at the end of
it. Whether I studiously ignored the fact of the engagement between her and Carr, or whether I had thoughts of entering the lists
against him in spite of it, I don't know. I never said, even to
myself, that I loved her, until to-night. I was in a dream. How
rudely have I been awakened from it!

The steamboat arrived here just after daylight this morning.
After breakfast I walked over to Mr. White's and was warmly
greeted by his household—himself, his wife, and Mr. Hamilton.
I learn, by the way, that the latter is formally installed pastor of
the church in this village. Mr. White offered me his horse, and I

started for Manahio. Before I reached the creek I met Jacobus, and got the following budget of news: Mr. Carr, the Judge, is in Baton Rouge; Miss Harwood and her brother are keeping house at Harwood, having moved over there shortly after my departure for Baltimore. For the last month Miss Ret has had a guest, a relation of her mother's family, Miss Lucy, or Lucille Latour. Mr. Charley spent most of his time at Harwood, and was there that moment.

I wonder now that the truth did not flash upon me while the negro was speaking, for I remember the leer upon his black face when he said "Mars'r Charley pooty nigh live at Harwood now!" But I was only conscious that a half hour more would bring me to the presence of my idol, and, spurring my horse on the road to Harwood, I soon forgot everything else. When I reached the house there were evident signs of habitation about it. The windows were open. There were chairs on the broad verandah. I heard a sweet voice singing a French song, and the piano accompaniment—the sounds issuing from the drawing-room, where I saw her last. While I fastened my horse at the rack, where Charley's was already standing, I heard a man's voice join in the chorus, and recognized Carr's magnificent bass. I walked up the steps, and into the room through one of the French windows, and was clasped around the waist in a moment by Herbert, who exclaimed:

"Oh, Ret! here's Cousin Harry!"

The music suddenly stopped, and Ret came forward, holding her hand out to me. I took it an instant and dropped it, for I was awake at last! When I entered the room she and Carr were standing at the piano, his arm around her waist, and the bright smile upon his handsome face told me how happy he was. I hardly looked at Miss Latour when Carr introduced me, for I was watching Miss Harwood, and noticing the embarrassment of her manner. Women know things by intuition, and I suppose she knew that *I* knew how matters stood between her and Charley. We talked a little about my absence and about the changes that had occurred while I was away, until I asked for a renewal of the music.

"Come, Cousin Lucy," said Herbert, "come, sing that song once more."

"Yes, come on Lucille," said Charley, "there is another stanza. Listen, Harry, to the sweetest music you ever heard. I mean the bass part, of course!" They went to the piano again and Ret remained upon the sofa.

"You were singing when I came in," I said to her; "I hope you will allow me to hear you once more."   .

"I was not singing; I do not sing," she answered.

The song commenced again and we were silent. When it was finished, I selected an English song and asked Miss Latour to sing that. She complied with a great deal of grace, and sang it charmingly, her little accent making it only more piquant. She speaks one language about as fluently as the other, though I judge she prefers her native tongue.

"I owe you a drubbing, Master Harry," said Charley, when we were all out on the verandah, "for going away without seeing me, and I intend to give it to you now. Herbert, go get your foils and masks."

"Oh, that will be charming!" said Miss Latour. "Here, you shall fight on the lawn, and I will crown the victor;" so saying, she began to collect some flowers, which were growing luxuriantly all around the verandah, and with nimble fingers twined them into a wreath.

"Well, I know whose temples that wreath will adorn," said Charley, grasping his foil. "Come on Harry, and meet your fate!"

"I have already met it!" I answered, as I followed him. As I passed Ret I caught her eye. She had heard me and was looking at me earnestly and sadly. Oh, Ret! does she know how miserable I am?

I went through the salutations mechanically, and there were two or three introductory passes before I gave my attention to the business on hand. She was sitting there looking at me, and suddenly I determined to conquer. Carr was fencing with his accustomed skill and confidence, but I attacked him vigorously, and at last touched him slightly on the breast.

"Hit, by Jove!" he said, dropping his point.

"Not quite, not quite!" exclaimed Miss Latour, dropping her hands. "Try again."

"Yes," I said, "we won't count that. Come on."

We struggled five minutes longer, and Carr's hand raised suddenly, and I knew he was going to give me his favourite thrust, *en seconde*. If I had not caught it so frequently before in our various encounters he would have had me, but I parried the thrust and disarmed him the next instant. I bowed to him, and taking off my mask, I knelt at the little French lady's feet, while she placed the wreath on my head.

" How pale you are," she said, as I rose.

" Am I pale ?" and I felt the blood rushing back to my face.

" No, not now. Charles, *mon ami*," she added in French, " what a handsome fellow your friend is ?"

" Very," said Charley in the same language, " and he also understands French !"

Miss Latour blushed scarlet, and everybody else laughed. She made some slight attempt at explanation and apology, and as Carr continued to laugh, she ran into the house. During the morning Miss Harwood made two or three attempts to entertain me, but I could perceive the restraint which she tried to hide. If it were not for the ever present dread that she also knows that I love her, I think I could better endure my own sorrow. But the thought that she has penetrated my secret, and *pities* me, drives me mad! I would have pleaded business in town and left; but my horse was put away, and I had not energy enough to make the effort. I knew that Carr would oppose, and I did not wish to contend with him. He was so obstreperously happy and jolly that my long face must have offered a fine contrast. Herbert hung about me, and asked several times " what the dickens was the matter with me ?" After dinner Charley and I lighted our cigars and walked out on the lawn. I had put my arm through the wreath and it attracted his attention as we started for our walk.

" Look here, Harry," he said, " I am going to fight you again for that wreath."

" I'll give it to you," I said, " that is if you won't tell Miss Latour."

" I'd rather fight for it," he said.

" Well, here are the foils. Let's have it out at once."

" With this understanding," said Carr, " I am to hit you once, to make us even, and then I am to hit you again for the wreath."

" Agreed." He was very eager, and in a few minutes he had the prize on his arm. Why should I grudge him this poor triumph ?

" You did not fence half so well this time," said Charley, doubtfully.

" Indeed, I did my best. The ladies were not looking at us this time, and I missed the inspiration."

" By Jupiter! I believe I lost this morning because *she* was looking on," said Carr. " Hubbard, my friend, I am going to tell you a secret."

" Let us sit down here," I said. Now, I thought, if there is enough manhood in me to endure the formal recital of all that I had seen, it will be put to the test. We sat down in the shadow of a fig tree on the lawn, and he was too much interested in his own happiness to notice me very closely.

" I am going to be married——"

" So I supposed," I answered calmly. "Come now, skip all about your happiness and her sweetness. I will take all that for granted."

" Well, I thought while Herbert was getting the foils and we four were standing together on the gallery, that we would make two very passable looking couples to stand up before the parson."

"No doubt about the beauty of the ladies anyhow," I replied, " and the less we say about their partners the better."

" I am sure *your* beauty is established upon the very best authority. Poor Lucille! She never dreamed of your understanding French. You see we have been talking about you during your absence, for I had set my heart upon having you for groomsman, and Lucille has been anxiously waiting to inspect you, to see if you would do."

"Have you consulted Miss Harwood on the subject?" I asked. I was holding myself in an iron grasp, trampling upon a thousand thoughts, as they arose in my mind.

" Undoubtedly. She approves of my choice entirely. Dear Ret gives you credit for first knocking the foundations from under my free-thinking theories. I told her of our conversation on the subject, just before I went to New Orleans. You know I am no longer an infidel."

" I am heartily glad to hear it, dear Carr," I replied, shaking his offered hand. " And now, dear friend, will you do me a kindness, a *real* kindness?"

"Why, Harry! what ails you?" answered Carr, in amazement at my excitement. " I will do anything you ask me."

" Then do not talk to me any more about your marriage until the time arrives." He gazed with wondering eyes at me as I continued. "Dear Charley, since I saw you last something has happened. I know you will not ask me what it is, but I tell you this much—something has occurred to me since we parted, or has been revealed to me at least, that has inflicted a wound which no time can heal. I look for nothing in this life but grace to endure. Alas! I am not the lighthearted boy to whom you were so kind, and who learned to love you so soon. I am a man, old in sorrow and in self-denial. Do not look at me with those sorrowful eyes, or I shall break down."

"I suspect I know, or guess, Harry. It was in Baltimore, was it?"

"No. Don't ask me any questions," and I stamped violently. "I only wish to say to you that while the wound is so sore any talk of marriage maddens me. Will you bear with me a little while?"

"Surely. If you would rather not be groomsman——"

"But I am not going to allow you to recall that invitation. I hope I am equal to the emergency. My new manhood is hardening day by day, and I shall be placid enough soon."

"And happy, Harry, I hope."

"Nevermore," I said, pressing his hand. "When are you to be made happy?"

"Next month, I hope. She says October. I wanted to be married sooner. But she vows she won't be married this summer."

Her last words to me were that she would not be married this summer!

"It is all settled then," I said, as we walked toward the house. "I will be ready when you want me."

The ladies and Herbert were seated on the verandah. The boy had a handsome cane in his hand which he brought to me, saying bashfully:

"I wanted to make a nice speech, dear cousin Harry, when I gave you this. Please take it with my love. I got Charley to buy it for me while he was in New Orleans, but you went away before he got back. I wrote to him the day after you and I were *swimming.*"

"I thank you, cousin, for your beautiful present, and I shall value it very highly for your sake. Why, it is a sword cane!"

"Yes, pull it out," said Herbert. The blade is broad and strong, and as long as the cane. It is truly a formidable weapon.

"I walked down Chartres street," said Carr, "after I received Herbert's letter, and I met Captain Delaney in one of the stores. He was buying a cane exactly like this, and I thought I could trust his judgment. You see it is not at all like the ordinary blades you find in sword canes. It is a regular sword blade, and if you can manage it as well as you did the foil this morning, you need not be——"

"But you have got the crown," said Lucille.

"Yes, ma belle. We fought for it fairly. I hit him twice, plump and fair, and he was obliged to relinquish it."

I came away at dark. After I got to town I tried to write a brief account of the day's proceedings, but I had been subjected to severe tension all day, and there was a reaction. I feel wonderfully calm now, and wonderfully miserable too.

After I had tried in vain to record in my diary all that I have now written, I started out for a walk. I suppose it was nearly or quite ten o'clock. I walked out on the Baton Rouge road, and noticed nothing until I arrived at the bank of the Manahio. I wanted to go to the Laurels. I don't know why, but I was first conscious of this desire when I found the creek rippling between me and the trees. The obstacle only served to interest me a little, but did not cause me to alter my intention for a moment. I slipped off my boots and trousers and waded across at the usual ford, and then sat down on the soft grass and dressed. I had enough sense left to remember that there might be snakes in the long grass, and to replace my boots. I then walked into the grove and sat down at the root of one of the big trees. I heard nothing but the chirp of ten millions of insects in the trees, the croak of frogs in the distant bayou, and the murmur of the stream. I thought of the affectionate boy whose life I had saved at that spot, and tried to resolve that I would exert the influence I might have over him to do him good, not only for his sake, but also for the sake of another who loved him. I tried not to think of her, but it was so recently that she sat there just before me, while her horse pawed the ground impatiently. Then I thought of the legend which had peopled this locality with horrors, and I rose to my feet involuntarily and glanced round the grove. Why should I deny that I felt my heart thumping painfully against my ribs as I descried a figure slowly and noiselessly advancing into the area? There was a cloud over the moon and I could only see the outlines of a tall form, which seemed to be human, but which moved without a sound. I had my new cane in my hand, and instinctively drew the sword, and advanced a step from the shadow of the tree. As I drew near I thought I recognized Misty, and a moment after he spoke.

"Young chief come back? Welcome! Shake hand!"

I slipped the sword back into the sheath, and cordially greeted my old friend. He was very much changed in appearance. He still wore his hunting shirt, but the leggings were gone. He had a tomahawk and knife in a broad belt, which also bore a bullet pouch. His powder horn was suspended under his left arm by a thong, and he carried his rifle in his hand. On his head was a cap made of raccoon skin, with several feathers stuck in it. There was no sign of intoxication about him. Altogether he looked like a warrior. He noticed my surprise, and spoke again.

"Misteono hunter no longer. Warrior again. Let the young chief go to Indian's wigwam, and get the skin of the tiger cat. Misteono dressed it for young brother."

"You don't mean to-night, my friend?"

"No, no!" he answered. "Bime-by. Brother find the skin and take it. Misteono going away."

"Where are you going, chief?" I asked.

"Yes, chief again! Misteono's tribe is on war path. Chief going to lead them!"

"When are you going, Misteono?"

"Soon go. Want one scalp to take back to my tribe. Get it bimeby."

At this instant I heard voices and the tramp of horses' hoofs. The Indian held up his finger to enjoin silence, and listened intently. The sounds came nearer, and I heard some one say,

"Not to-night, d——n it. I don't half like this neighbourhood after dark!"

"Pooh! don't be a fool!" said the other. "Come on, I want to look at these trees." I thought I recognized this voice, and almost as he spoke the two came into view, through the bushes. They saw us, just as I recognized Captain Delaney and Becket. The latter wrenched his horse round, saying,

"There *are* the Densons, I swear!" and he galloped off, followed by Delaney. The moon was shining on their faces, and I could detect the look of horror which sprang into them as they caught sight of us in the shade of the trees. In a few minutes we lost the sound of their horses' hoofs.

"Cap'n brave warrior," said the Indian, "he not come back to-night. Young chief going back? Misteono go to wigwam. Good night."

This was a queer adventure, and it has set me to thinking. I will overhaul those letters again to-morrow. I have an idea! I am happy to say that I am weary at last, and I believe I shall sleep a little.

CHAPTER XXI.

RECOGNITION.

THURSDAY, *August* 5, 1836.

I HAVE read a little of yesterday's record to-night, and I am half ashamed of myself. I am twenty to-day, and ought to be man enough to endure the rubs of this life. I have been going about to-day, and feel much more like my old self. Perhaps I may be able to look back upon these trials when the wounds heal up, and see how they have done me good. If this wedding were only over, and the whole thing finally settled!

Mr. Gowrie keeps a store here, and ships cotton for the neighbouring planters. He is a thorough Scot, with high cheek bones and sandy hair and whiskers. He takes snuff, and it is a treat to see him helping his little turned-up nose to its refreshment. He is snappish and cross-grained, but is honest and intelligent. I think he is rather a favourite with his clients. I walked down to his establishment this morning, as I saw Becket there, and wanted to hear if he was telling his adventure of last night, but he was not. He and Gowrie had been disputing about the shipment of some cotton, and as I stepped upon Gowrie's gallery I heard him say,

"I'll no do it, Maister Becket. I wadna alter my books for the whole Harwood plantation."

"I might as well talk to a stone as to you," replied the overseer. "Good morning, Mr. Hubbard. By-the-bye, you are from Maryland. Did you ever go down to the mouth of the Chesapeake in one of those pungy schooners that do the turtle fishing?"

"No, sir."

"Well, *I* have. I'll tell you how they manage the beasts. After they get them on deck, they just head them off till the turtle gets his foolish head against the mast. Then they are safe. They will keep butting away at that mast while the voyage lasts. We always called them *Scotchmen*, because they were so darned obstinate and stupid. Good morning," and he rode off.

"Ay, ay," said Mr. Gowrie, "walk in, sir. So yon chap is a countryman of yours?"

"I don't know, sir. I am a Marylander, but I never saw him until I came here. May I ask what the difficulty is between you?"

"Oh, just nothing. I have always shipped the Harwood cotton, and I believe the young leddy has been investigating Mr. Becket's accounts. Anyway, he wanted me to give him a statement of shipments under false dates, but I would not do it. That's all."

"You were perfectly right, sir," said I.

"Why, one might as well tell a lie with his tongue as with his pen, ye know. I am too auld to begin that business."

"I am sure you would never violate the truth, Mr. Gowrie.

'Lord of the Isles, my trust in thee
Is strong as Ailsa rock.'"

"Ay, ay," replied the Scot dryly. "But I wadna quot at all, if I were you, unless I could quot correctly."

"Do you mean, sir," said I, half amused and half offended, "that I have misquoted Sir Walter."

"Just so. Sir Walter never wrote the lines as you quot'd them."

"I would be willing to lay a small wager that you are mistaken, Mr. Gowrie. I read Sir Walter very constantly, and the passage from the Lord of the Isles I read only to-day."

"Weel, it is a puir cause that has to be bolstered up by a bet," and Mr. Gowrie walked into an inner room and returned with a well thumbed volume. "Here is the book, and ye can satisfy yourself."

I soon found the passage, and sure enough I had changed a word. "It is '*firm*' as Ailsa rock, Mr. Gowrie. I acknowledge my error."

"It is no guid to be too positive, ye see," said Mr. Gowrie, with a grin of satisfaction. "I was sure of the case, because I know the pome almaist by heart; besides, I am weel acquaint with the locality, having seen Ailsa Craig more than once, when I lived in Glasgow."

"Are you from Glasgow?" I inquired, with sudden interest.

"Yes, I was born near the city, and lived there a gude mony years."

"Did you ever know or hear of Hector Macailan, of Linmuir?"

"Macailan!" and he stared at me with astonishment. "And where did you hear that name?"

"I have seen the name in some family papers in my possession. If you know anything about this laird, I should like to ask you a question or two."

"Ye may ask the questions, and I'll tell you no lies if I am not able to give you the information you want."

"Did you know Mr. Macailan, of Linmuir ?"

"Yes, I knew such a mon."

"Did you ever see a Mr. Denham, who visited Mr. Macailan thirty years ago ?"

"It is just possible that I did. I'd rather ye wad not be so particular about names, ye see."

"Well, then, please answer me one more question. Have you ever seen here, in Carrville, anybody that knew Macailan, or that you knew in Glasgow ?"

"Come into the back room, Mr. Hubbard. Jamie! Jamie!" A small likeness of Mr. Gowrie answered the summons and came forward. "Keep a look out a wee bit, laddie. I am gaun into the counting room. Call me if anybody comes." So saying, he led the way into his counting room, at the back of the building. He handed me a chair, and then perched himself upon a high stool that stood at the desk.

"Ye seem to be a respectable young mon, Mr. Hubbard. I have seen you twice at the church, and ye listened to the minister instead of gaping round the church, as most young men do. I think the better of you, too, because ye can read Walter Scott. I'll find ye plenty of young men in this town that can quot' 'Don Juan' for you by the yard;—but not many that ever heard of 'The Lord of the Isles.' "

"Walter Scott is a great favourite of mine, sir; though he is rather hard upon Presbyterians sometimes."

"Weel, let him have his fling! What was it you were wanting to ask ? Ye need not just call people by their names. I can understand you without that."

"I have reason to think that a man is sometimes in Carrville, under a different name, who once visited Mr. Macailan in Scotland. It concerns me very much to be certain of the fact, as I might be able to thwart some evil intentions of his."

"It is vera curious—but John Harwood said vera much the same thing to me the night before he died."

"He probably had the same reasons." Mr. Gowrie looked at me very curiously. "I'll tell you in confidence, Mr. Gowrie—that I am related to the Harwoods, though they do not know it, and I do not wish them to know it at present. You need not hesitate to trust me. I hope I shall do whatever I do in the fear of God."

"I'll no deny," said Mr. Gowrie after a pause, "that I have seen a person here, and also in Pensacola, who vera much resembles a friend of Macailan's. He is an aulder man than he was thirty years ago, but he looks vera much the same." Here Jamie called his father, who slid down from his stool. "Ye need na' refer to me as having given ye any information," he added, cautiously, as we left the office—"ye know that I am only positive about a resemblance after all!"

I am going to Harwood again to-morrow.

FRIDAY, *August* 6, 1836.

This has been an eventful day. I spent most of the morning in a revision of Ret's bundle of letters, and I came to the conclusion that the lead-covered box is hidden somewhere in the Haunted Laurels. The three trees stand in a triangle—almost a right angle. I have seen them again to-day, and have decided just where the probable spot is, namely, on a line between the two trees most remote from each other—because that line is the hypothenuse of the triangle—and nine feet from the tree that stands on the margin of the creek. I had noticed several times the relative position of these trees, and the other night when I was there I remember that the well known problem about the "sum of the squares of the base and perpendicular being equal to the square of the hypothenuse," kept coming into my mind. That, joined to the fact that Delaney—who has somehow got some information on the subject—had the hardihood to visit the spot near midnight, occurred to me while I was writing in my journal, after I had returned to town on Wednesday night. I am going to make a thorough investigation to-morrow.

After dinner, when I had the pleasure of seeing the spruce captain—who however did not pay any attention to me—I got Mr. White's horse and went to Harwood. I stopped at the Laurels only long enough to notice the exact localities a little more particularly. I am hastening to record my interview with Ret, which is to me the most interesting of the events of the day.

The doors and windows were all open when I reached the house, but no one was visible. I rang the bell, and Phany came immediately. I asked for Miss Ret, and learning that she was at home I walked into the drawing room, while Phany went to announce me. When she came I was startled to see that she wore a white dress—though there were black ribbons about her person. She looked so different—but oh, so lovely! There was also something in her manner betokening her constant consciousness of her approaching happiness—a nervous and hurried manner of speaking. Heaven forgive me!—I cannot help *feeling* that she does not love Charley Carr as much as she thinks she does! But I have promised myself to bury that subject out of sight.

"Lucille has gone with Charles and Herbert to Mr. Maltby's," she said, after a few commonplaces about the weather. "Lucille wished to ride Midnight, and I have been left to my own resources all day."

"I am glad it has so happened," I answered, "as I want to talk to you a little. Carr has asked me to assist at a certain ceremony——"

"Yes, yes!" she said hurriedly, "he told me. Are those the letters you got from me?"

"Yes;" and I gave her the packet. She touched a bell on the table, and Phany appeared.

"Phany, go bring the black box from my room. You have done with the letters?" she said inquiringly.

"For the present—yes. Though I have something to say to you about them."

"That will do, Phany," said she, as she took the box. The boy vanished, and she replaced the packet in the closet in the chimney jamb. She then resumed her seat, and looked at me, waiting with apparent anxiety for the next word.

"When you gave me the letters I presume you thought your cousins in Baltimore were Barnard Harwood's widow and children; is it not so?"

"Certainly."

"They are not. Mrs. Harwood is the widow of Allen Harwood, who was supposed——" She had leaned forward, covering her face with her hands, and I saw the tears coming through her fingers. I never could endure the sight of a grown woman shedding tears, and I was greatly shocked.

"Miss Harwood! Ret! shall I ring the bell? You are ill!"

"No, no!" she said, without looking up. "Go on."

"I have a letter here which Mr. Harwood left for his son. I thought you perhaps would like to read it, and have brought it with me."

"Oh yes!" she said, taking my father's letter. "Will you excuse me a little while? There are some books on the table. I will return presently."

I waited a long time—it seemed hours—but she did not return. I opened the books—but I don't know what they were about. Then I went to the piano, and ran my fingers over the keys. There is a composition of Beethoven's which I learned long ago— I forget the name of it—and I began to play it. As I went on with it I grew calmer and sadder. While I was playing she came back. She stood by the piano, and I thought the melancholy strains of the music affected her, for her eyes were still moist.

"You seem to play with great feeling," she said, when I left the instrument. "You don't look as happy as you should be."

"Who? I? I am not happy. Are you pleased to know that your relations are not the family of Barnard?"

"I have been in my room," she answered, gravely and solemnly —"trying to thank my beneficent Father for the unspeakable joy this letter has brought to me;" and she gave me back my letter. "I cannot understand why you should feel differently."

"I was intrusted with another letter," I said, and I gave her my Mother's; "if you will read it now, I will go back to Beethoven;" and I went through the piece again. I looked round at her once or twice while I was playing, and I saw her brush the tears from her eyes as she refolded the letter, though her face was like sunshine.

"Do you know the contents of my letter?" she asked.

"Not one word of it."

"I will perhaps let you see it at another time," she said, putting the letter in her key box; "I want to read it again before I decide upon that point. And now please to tell me why you are not happy."

"Do not ask me, Miss Harwood."

"You called me 'Ret' just now!"

"Did I? Pardon me, I did not know it until it was too late."

"You wished me to call you cousin Harry two months ago. Have you changed your mind since then?"

"No indeed! I wish——"

"You wish what?"

"I wish I might venture to call you cousin Ret," I said.

"Well, you may, cousin Harry. You see I set you the example. Didn't you risk your life to save Herbert's?" she said impetuously, the tears springing to her dear eyes again.

I took her hand and kissed it. Oh how near I was to an insane confession of everything—my relationship, and my love! I don't

11

know what restrained me. I walked away to the window, and stood there, with my back to her, resolutely choking down every thought and impulse while I reflected that I must tell her before long that I was her cousin, as I was not willing to wait upon her bridegroom under an assumed name.

"You will not allow me to offer you any consolation because you will not tell me why you require it. Something has occurred since you left Louisiana, which you have not told me?"

"You are so much changed since I first saw you," I replied, avoiding her look. "Then you were composed and self-possessed—though you were sad;—now you are nervous and impetuous—yet I do not believe you are much less melancholy. By-the-bye, I will bring Burton out to you to read."

"You also are changed since you saved Herbert's life. Before, you were cheerful and apparently contented;—now, you are moody and restless and—mysterious."

"I cannot tell you the cause of my unhappiness—because I know your kind heart would—— Oh cousin! there is an impending calamity ever before my eyes! I cannot escape it—do what I will. And I am trying to fortify myself in advance—trying to see clearly the path of duty and honour, and trying to banish every selfish consideration that might lead me astray. It is a dire struggle—but *you* cannot help me. I must go through this trial alone."

"You have told me nothing about my cousin Alice and her children," she said suddenly; "are they well?"

"Quite well—all of them."

"Are you sure?"

"Yes. I saw them the day I left Baltimore. They are all well and happy."

"I shall ask you no more questions, but I intend to unravel this mystery in my own way. Have you seen Captain Delaney?"

"Yes," I replied, with a start; "it was about him that I wished to talk to you. I saw him at midnight on Wednesday at the Laurels."

"What were you doing at the Laurels at midnight?"

"I—— nothing. I was not well and could not sleep, so I walked out there and stayed an hour. Never mind me, but listen to what I have to tell you."

"Stop a moment!" she said, while the blood rushed into her face. "You were here on Wednesday. Did Charles say anything—do anything that displeased or troubled you? Answer me, if you please."

"Nothing—nothing! Carr has been my constant friend, and has never given me a moment's pain—at least not intentionally." She looked steadily at me while I spoke.

"What were you saying under the fig tree yonder? I saw you from my window, and I saw that you were violently agitated."

"You must have fancied that. Carr was telling me about his ——marriage"—I got the word out with an effort—"and we talked about very little else."

"What did he say about me?" she asked, quietly.

"Nothing—except that you did not object to my participation in the ceremony." As I looked into her bright eyes and upon her burning cheeks I almost gave way again, but I did not. "If you don't want to drive me mad please talk about something else."

"I am satisfied. Now for Captain Delaney!"

"In the first place, then, he has written a letter which he signed 'Mark Denham.' I saw it, and I saw him in Baltimore. The writing is precisely like that in those letters signed 'Nemo' in your packet. If you remember Allen Harwood's letter to his son you will recollect that a Mr. Denham informed him of your father's death fifteen or twenty years before it occurred. I believe Captain Delaney was the author of that epistle, also."

"Do you think he is Mark Denham?"

"I do. While I think of it, I wish to say that he is very intimate with your overseer—Becket. I have seen them frequently together. Becket was with him at the Laurels the other night. They saw me and the Indian half hidden in the shade of the trees and took us for ghosts of the Densons. They were frightened and galloped away. Now, this Denham is capable of any villany, and I think you should watch your overseer."

"He is going to leave Harwood next week. I have reason to think—indeed I know that he is not strictly honest. Herbert has undertaken the management of the plantation himself."

"I advise you to keep watch in the meantime. Do not think me foolish; but I am labouring under a constant presentiment of evil to come from the hands of this bad man. Will you ask Herbert to invite me to stay here at night for three or four nights to come? Don't look at me so reproachfully! If the evil that I dread threatens you I would be here to guard you."

"I am sorry you think a formal invitation necessary. While

Herbert lives and while I live you will be more than welcome at Harwood, at any hour, day or night, for all time to come."

"I thank you, and I regret that I asked for an invitation. I will *happen* to be here then. Now, please understand the case. I don't want to say anything to Charley, because I don't want to alarm him, and I don't want him to know all that we know. It would seem to be more proper for him to stay here——"

"It would be very improper," she said, her cheeks burning again. "Your arrangement is the best."

"Well, let Herbert ride a little way with me this evening on the near road to town. If I once see the road I shall know it hereafter. I want to walk out here after dark and return early in the morning. I want to *happen* to visit you ladies and Herbert for two or three evenings consecutively. I will bring my violin and some music, and if I am so forgetful as to remain until late you will offer me the hospitality of Harwood. Is it agreed?" She bowed her head. "Well, now about the lead-covered box. I believe it is buried in the Laurel Grove, and I believe Denham thinks so, too. I have been jumping at conclusions female fashion lately——"

"Female fashion! what do you mean, sir?"

"I mean, by the exercise of that rare faculty of intuition by which women arrive at facts without the trouble of logical deduction. You need not frown," I continued, laughing, "it is a much higher faculty than any possessed by men. Do not suppose, I implore you, that I am so base as to think or speak slightingly of women. I have a Mother and two sisters."

"Yes; I know you have," she answered, composedly.

"Indeed! and where did you get the information?"

"From various sources. From Mr. Hamilton, after you went away, and from yourself before that, and from other testimony since you returned."

A light suddenly dawned upon me. What a blind ninny I have been!

"Oh, Ret," I said, "do you indeed know that I am your cousin?"

"How could you doubt it, cousin Herbert! how could you otherwise account for my behaviour! Do you think Mr. Hubbard, with all his fascinations, could have arrived at the present stage of intimacy with my Father's daughter!"

I suppose I looked as bewildered as I felt, for she threw herself back in her chair and laughed heartily.

"When you have done laughing," I said pettishly, "I should like to ask you a question."

"I am sober again, cousin," she answered, wiping her eyes; "but you looked so comical just now that I could not help it," and here she went off again.

"I suppose you and Carr have amused yourselves enormously at my expense," said I, beginning to get in a rage.

"Come, sir, that is unkind and impolite," she replied, gravely; "no one knows your secret. I don't know why you changed your name, but I have never felt at liberty to tell even Herbert. I don't know when I first began to suspect you, but you sealed the packet of letters when you returned them the first time with that seal on your watch chain, I suppose. Let me see it. Yes! it is the Harwood arms and motto, *'Che sará sará.'* I thought you were Barnard's son, and I have had many a good, quiet cry since you went away, thinking over those fatal letters."

"Please keep the secret a little longer, dear cousin. I want to circumvent Mr. Denham, and I am stronger while he is ignorant of my true name. But I did not change my name," and I told her all the story, just as it occurred.

"You are remarkably bashful, indeed, sir," said Ret, when I had concluded; "but I can understand how you allowed the mistake to pass at first and how the peculiarity of the position embarrassed you with each addition to the number of acquaintances. Pray, how do you intend to enlighten everybody when you resume your own more euphonious name?"

"I don't intend to trouble myself about that," I answered indifferently; "so that my friends understand the case I care nothing about *vox populi.*"

"If you will allow me to say so, cousin, I think this is a defect in your character. I have seen it manifested more than once. You owe it to yourself and to society to maintain a spotless reputation in all things. I do not mean that public opinion should have the slightest influence upon you where any principle may be involved, but you are bound to see that your influence over men is not damaged by your indifference. Your influence is a talent for which you are responsible to God, who gave it."

"If I had you for my mentor, dear cousin," I answered sadly, "my life might be made to accord with the perfect law—so far as poor humanity can attain to perfection."

"You have been blessed with a far better mentor," she said,

blushing a little; "here is your Mother's letter. You may read it now." As the letter is not long I will copy it here:

BALTIMORE, *July* 12, 1836.

My dear Cousin :—Herbert's intelligence of his new found kindred in Louisiana has filled me with gratitude to God for His goodness, and wonder and adoration for His special providence. All that I know of you, my dear, I know from reading my son's journal, and as I know that he has written nothing but the truth, I have learned to love you though I have not seen you. I have left him to select his own time to reveal himself, under the name he bears, to every one in that far-off country who has been deceived by his careless indifference. He thinks you have not penetrated his secret, but I can see that you know him. As I am well acquainted with all the circumstances attending the early life of my dear husband, I know that the children of his cousin John would have been peculiarly dear to him if he had lived to see them. And I can also understand how easily you were led into the supposition that I and my children were the family of Barnard Harwood. If we had heard of your existence in the same way we should have arrived at the same conclusion concerning you. I feel that I shall see you some day and will love you the more—the more I know you. Herbert does not know what I have written. He has not asked to see this letter. Write to me, my dear child, and believe me   Your loving cousin,   ALICE HARWOOD.

"And now, sir," said Ret, imperatively, as I gave her back the letter, "I want to see your journal, if you please."

"Not for a million worlds!" I exclaimed, starting up in horror.

"I desire to know, sir," continued she, without noticing my exclamation, "what you have written about *me.*"

"That is precisely what you must not know," I replied. "Mother is a wonderfully wise woman, but she don't know *everything.*" She was silenced. No doubt she conjectured some part of the truth. I'll be hanged if I don't believe she would discuss the matter of my loving her with every drop of my blood, with every breath I draw, and with every impulse of my life, in as cool and business-like a manner as possible. She would demonstrate the folly of my passion, and show me how the straight path of duty must be pursued through a life of self-denial and usefulness. It is all true, but these reflections do not restore to my heart its former vigorous and cheerful pulses.

I came away just as Carr and his companions returned. Herbert came all the way to town with me, and took my violin and music out with him. I have promised him to walk out to-night after mail duties are over.

HARWOOD.—MIDNIGHT.

When I had finished with the mail, I walked over to the hotel and went into the playing room. Judge Carr was there, playing euchre with Captain Delaney. I was seated at one of the tables near them, and overheard Delaney say "game!" Mr. Carr looked anxious and excited. They whispered a while, and then Delaney said, loud enough for me to hear, as he was shuffling the cards, "the whole debt now against the mortgage. Cut!" I walked over to their table and held out my hand to Mr. Carr, as I had not seen him before since my return. He shook hands with me and was very affable.

"Will you please let me say a few words to you, sir," I said. "I must get some information from you before the mail closes."

He rose from his seat, and I led the way out of the room. He followed down stairs and stopped when I reached the street.

"Where are you going, Mr. Hubbard?" he said.

"Only to the post-office, sir. Please walk down there with me. I will not detain you long."

I let myself into the office, and then went through the door into the store-room, and admitted him. I lighted a candle, and we sat down for a talk.

"I bought the Copper stock for you, sir."

"Good Heavens! Did you not receive my letter?"

"No, sir. I got no letter from you. Mr. Callahan did not know your Christian name, and he has filled up the certificate in my name. There is a form of transfer on the back, and I will fill it up at once, if you will tell me your initials.

"I am not able to pay for this stock, sir," said Mr. Carr, in great excitement. "I wrote to you immediately after you left, directing my letter to the Hudson Hotel, as you told me. I have drawn all the money my crop will bring, and more too."

"That is a matter of no consequence, my dear sir. I paid for the stock with my own money, and you can repay me whenever it suits your convenience. The stock is enormously valuable, and you can sell it to-day at twenty times its cost."

"If this is true, Mr. Hubbard," replied he, absently, "why should you not take the stock yourself?"

"I should be very glad to have it, Mr. Carr; but, of course, I shall do no such thing. I do not need the money, and if you don't wish to retain this stock, I will order Mr. Callahan to sell it at once for your account. You will receive enough to replace the value of your crop for this year at least."

"Please let the matter stand, then, as it is," he said, rising; "I will see you again to-morrow. I must go back to Delaney. He will be impatient."

"Mr. Carr." He stopped. "I did not bring you here, sir, merely to talk about the stock. I implore you to get your horse, and go home without seeing Delaney again. I *know* that he is a great scoundrel, and I know that he is cheating you."

"By what right and upon what evidence do you dare to say so?" said Mr. Carr in astonishment. "Do you know that your life would not be worth an hour's purchase if I repeated to Delaney what you have just said?"

"I will save you the trouble of repeating it, sir," I answered coolly; "if you go back to the playing room I shall go with you, and say it to Delaney myself."

"Are you mad, Mr. Hubbard? Delaney would shoot you with as little compunction as——"

"I do not fear to incur the risk, sir. I happen to know some portion of his former history, and I know he is a villain. If you wish to hear what evidence I have of his present rascality, I will tell you that I saw his handkerchief spread over his knees just now, and saw the knaves of hearts and diamonds lying upon it. He intends to play them at the proper moment, and get possession of *the mortgage.*" He started as I said this, and I went on. "If you will get your horse and go home it will be the best course. I will walk with you as far as Harwood. If you decide to go back and lose the mortgage, and thus leave Charley penniless—for I know how much you are involved—I swear to you that I will prevent it, by charging Delaney with his thieving before all the people in the room. If I cannot otherwise prevail upon you to quit playing with him, at once and forever, I will try this last step. In honour you do not owe him one cent, so your debt to him is nothing. Be persuaded, sir, to go with me to-night, and think over the matter. You can ruin yourself as well to-morrow."

He was vanquished. We went back together to the hotel, and looking into the playing room we saw Delaney engaged in a four-hand game.

"You must excuse me to-night, Delaney," said the Judge, "I have to go home at once."

Delaney nodded to him, glanced darkly at me for an instant, and we left. I walked beside Mr. Carr's horse as far as this house, and when we parted he grasped my hand with great fervor.

"You have awakened me, my young friend, to a sense of duty to myself and my son." Here he held up his right hand and continued solemnly: "I swear, before God, that I will never gamble again." After a little pause he went on. "I have also decided finally about the Lake Shore stock. Unless you *lose* by your kindness in attending to this business for me, I shall never take the stock. It is yours to sell or retain, as you please."

"My dear sir, you do not believe what I tell you. The stock is worth ten or twelve thousand dollars."

"So much the better for you. I have thought over the matter, and shall not change my determination. It is yours. Good night, and God bless you."

He thinks he has settled the matter, but I also have decided. I shall sell the stock, take out my five hundred dollars, and give the balance to Charley.

We had a lively time in the drawing room. Lucille, who is a darling little woman, played accompaniments for me. After playing an hour she called Ret to take her place, and she and Carr walked out on the verandah. I have a composition called "Echoes from the Mountains," which is more of a duett than any of my other pieces. Lucille refused to attempt it without preliminary practice, and Ret asked for it at once. I set the piano part up before her, and she played it without hesitation. She seemed to catch the ideas of the composer, and we went through it delightfully. Herbert looked on with astonished eyes, as I went through the *gymnastical* part of the performance, playing high up on the finger board, and dealing largely in harmonics. The listeners made us repeat the performance, and were loud in their applause. Ret plays wonderfully. Oh, how sweet would have been my life if I had been permitted to win her for my life's companion! It was quite late when Carr left, and Herbert brought me up here to "my room," as he calls it. "It is your room always, cousin Harry; nobody else shall ever sleep in it. Ret says so."

Since he left me the house has become quiet, and I have been sitting here writing ever so long. It is time I was seeking "tired nature's sweet——"

CHAPTER XXII.

THE CRISIS.

HARWOOD, SATURDAY NIGHT, *August* 7, 1836.

I WAS interrupted last night. There was a tap at my door, and when I opened it there stood Ret and Herbert in the hall.

"Somebody is trying to get into my room, cousin," said Ret. I knew you had not retired, as I saw your light and heard your pen going." She spoke with perfect composure, while Herbert, who had his gun, was full of excitement.

"Where is your room?" said I.

"Here across the hall. The window opens on the verandah roof. Some one is on the roof cutting the shutter."

"Is there a light in your room?"

"No."

"Cousin Harry," said Herbert in a whisper, "let me go down on the lawn while you go to Ret's window. Maybe I'll get a pop at him when he tries to get off."

I stepped softly into the room and listened. I heard the knife cutting into the shutter in the thin part of the panel. Herbert had gone down stairs. I had my sword cane but no firearms. I put out my hand to open the shutter, when some one touched me. It was Ret.

"Do not incur any needless risk by your rashness, cousin," she said with a tremulous voice. Before I could answer some one on the lawn said, in a loud whisper,

"Come down! They are awake!" and I heard Herbert's gun go off with a bang. I dashed the shutter open and caught a man by the collar as he was retreating from the window. His face was covered with black crape. He had a large knife in his hand, which he dropped in the short struggle. In a moment I was thrust back into the room and the robber gained the edge of the roof. He seemed to hesitate about leaping down, and while he paused I slipped through the window, sword in hand. Before I reached him he leaped, and I heard Herbert's second barrel. I took the sword blade in my mouth, and feeling for the spout with my hand, I let myself down from the roof, and was on the lawn in an instant. But it was dark as a wolf's throat, and nothing was visible. Presently I heard voices in subdued whispers at a little distance, and calling out to Herbert to follow, I ran toward the sound. There was a momentary shuffling of feet, and then I heard the hoof strokes of horses as the marauders galloped off. Ret and Herbert were on the verandah when I went back.

"Are you hurt?" said the former, anxiously.

"Not a bit; but the rascals are off. What did you shoot at, Herbert?"

"At a man on the lawn. I heard him whispering, though I could not see him. I hit him though, for I heard him swear when I fired."

"And your second shot?"

"Was at a fellow who tumbled off the roof. I missed him, I know."

"Well, we may all sleep in safety now. They will not be back to-night," said I, as we reëntered the house. "Cousin Ret, where will you sleep?"

"In my own room," she replied.

"If you would feel safer, Herbert and I will sit up and play chess all night."

"No, you shall not; I am not afraid. You may come and see how much damage is done to my shutter."

There was not much harm done; the fellow had marked out a square place in the panel just over the bolt, and had chipped away a little of the wood. If he had succeeded in getting the piece out, he could have put his fingers in through the hole, and drawn the bolt back. As we refastened the shutter I saw her black key box on the table near the window.

"Ah, here was the attraction!" I said. "Do you keep the box here usually?"

"Always."

"Good night then, Cousin Ret; do not hesitate to call me if you are alarmed again; but you will not be disturbed again to-night."

"My debt to you is getting larger," she said, as I left the room.

"Pshaw! Go to sleep and forget it, then;" and so I left her. Herbert declared he would stay; but she sent him out after me. He reloaded his gun, and slipping back into bed, vowed he would "keep awake any how." I told him I would read awhile then, and in a few minutes he was sound asleep. I put out his candle and came back here to "my" room.

We agreed this morning that we would say nothing about the

night alarm. Lucille had not been awakened, and the servants did not appear to have heard the shots. Ret sent Herbert to see if Mr. Becket was on the plantation; but he came back with the information that he had ridden to town the evening before and had not returned. He is to leave on Monday. He says he is going to Florida to take charge of a plantation there. I asked Ret this morning, as she and I promenaded the verandah before breakfast, if Becket could possibly know where she kept her keys. She said he doubtless did, as she had sent Phany or Chloe for the box several times when he was at the house. He also knew that the box contained the key of the iron closet, as he had seen her open it recently, when she was settling his account.

"I have concluded," said I, still reasoning female fashion, "that the robbers last night were Becket and Denham. I saw them together in the gambling room at the hotel."

"Are you in the habit of spending your leisure time in that intellectual amusement?"

"I? I never gamble, Cousin."

"What were you doing in the room last night?"

"I went there after Mr.—— a gentleman I wished to see."

"Was it Uncle? I won't insist upon an answer," she said, as I was silent; "but I am sure it was he."

"It was; but he will go there no more. He solemnly promised, when he left me last night—here at your gate—that he would never gamble again."

"Tell me all about it—every word!" and she stamped her foot impatiently.

"Come sit down here then, you tyrant. I pity your future husband." She looked at me with an indescribable expression, and I told her all about it.

"Please don't say anything to Charley. I would not have told you, or any one else, if I could help it. I ought not to tell you, as it is none of my business."

"What are you going to do with your stock?" she asked. "I won't tell anybody anything you tell me."

"I have no stock. If you mean this Lake Shore mine, I am going to send it to the broker to sell, and I am going to give the proceeds to Charley."

"Let us go in to breakfast," she said, rising.

We played "Echoes" once or twice afterwards, and then I took my cane and walked down to the Laurels.

I crossed the creek dry shod, at a narrow place half a mile above the ford, where there was a large tree fallen across the water. I then walked down the Manahio road to the haunted grove. It was about nine o'clock, and the morning was lovely. I had walked briskly, and had got pretty warm; so I took off my gloves, coat and vest. When I reached the Laurels, and pushed my way through the bushes, I saw a man in his shirt sleeves, with a spade in his hand, kneeling over the spot I had selected as the probable locality of the lead-covered box. He had a tape measure in his hand, and was ascertaining the distance from that spot to the near tree. It was Captain Delaney.

"What the devil are you sneaking about here for, sir!" he said fiercely, starting to his feet. "Begone while your skin is whole!"

This temperate and soothing salutation had the natural effect upon me. I kept down my rising passion, but I felt in every bone of my body that the hour had come for my struggle with that rascal.

"You forget yourself very strangely, sir!" replied I, haughtily. "As I have not the honour of your acquaintance, I should like to know by what right you address me at all."

"It is just possible," he said, after looking steadily into my eyes, and finding that I returned his stare without flinching—"it is barely possible that you may have brains enough to take your slim body away from this neighbourhood before I knock them out of your head."

"And it is also barely possible that you may find out that I am not to be scared by the mouthing of so poor a bully as you are. There is nothing very terrific to me about Captain Delaney or Mr. Mark Denham."

He stooped down and picked up the spade, and then took a step toward me. I dropped my coat and vest, and drew the sword from my cane.

"So!" he said, pausing, "you would prefer a hole in your lank body, instead of a crack on the crown? I give you one more chance, if only because you have had pluck enough to brave me thus far. Will you apologise for your insolence—and go, and be d——d to you!"

"It does not require any particular amount of pluck to brave a gentleman of your calibre, Mr. Denham. I have no apologies to make, and I am not going away until I get a certain lead-covered box for which you are searching."

He threw the spade into the bushes, gathered up the tape-line, and took his cane, which was leaning against the tree. It was precisely like my own. He drew the blade out and threw the scabbard down at the foot of the tree, with the tape-line. He then saluted gracefully, and, advancing a step, crossed his blade with mine. While we fenced, he talked:

"It is almost a pity to put so promising a youth out of his misery," he said; "but your knowledge is so extensive, that it is dangerous to society for you to be at large any longer."

All this time he was trying my skill, changing his parades with great celerity, and keeping me tolerably busy in parrying his thrusts. Captain Joli's "principles" stood me in stead rarely to-day.

"I thought the same of you last night, sir, when I spoiled your little adventure at Harwood;" he winced a little, but kept on fighting; "and I intend to see that you are not allowed to cheat poor old men out of their inheritance, or to rob defenceless women, hereafter. Your *role* in this locality is about over, sir." I was trying to get him into a passion, but he was cool as ice.

"You might have got off with the loss of your ears," he replied, "if you had not made that last remark. I am surprised to find that you should be bold enough to aim so high in your regards as to the lovely Miss Harwood. Her estimate of you is probably much lower than you suppose."

"I also had the pleasure of making your journey to Baltimore of no avail; as I revealed the secret of your identity with the charming Captain Delaney, and also with the correspondent of your friends, who took leave of society about this locality five years ago." He sprang back a step or two, and stood gazing at me with an astonishment which he did not try to conceal. I watched him narrowly, expecting him to dart suddenly upon me. "I am not fighting a duel with you, Mr. Denham. If you will go quietly away, and leave Carrville never to return, I will not interfere with you. I know you to be a great scoundrel, and I can satisfy anybody that knows you, that you are not entitled to the name of gentleman; but if you will go, I will be silent on the subject, and leave you in the hands of God."

"Who the devil are you?" he said at length.

"No matter. I *am* a gentleman, and I will keep my word. Will you go?"

"Not until I kill you. No man ever braved me thus and lived!

You will be dead in five minutes !" and he advanced again to the centre of the area and assaulted me.

As I look back upon that final encounter I remember that I thought the man's muscles must be made of steel. He evidently meant to kill me, and I was beginning to think I would have to kill him to save my own life. I had depended upon cowing him by the revelations I made, but I had calculated upon encountering a man of different metal. I could feel the vigour of his strong arm at the very point of his weapon, and once or twice his sword glanced past my throat almost grazing it. He did not strike at my body at all. The advantage with me was solely in that I was defending myself—not attacking him. But I soon found that he calculated upon this forbearance and pressed me more fiercely. He had not touched me, when I took advantage of an opening, and slipped my blade into the fleshy part of his arm, just above the elbow. I saw the shirt sleeve become crimson in a moment, but he only ground his teeth and fought with a little more caution. I was cooler than I am now while I write about it. Neither of us uttered a word, and there was no sound except the stamp of our feet as we traversed the little area, and the continued rasping of steel against steel. I think we fought full fifteen minutes in this way. At last he struck at my breast with a fierce lunge *en tierce*, and, as he recovered, I thrust my sword through his wrist. I saw the point as it came out through his arm, and he dropped his weapon as I withdrew my own. In another moment he was upon me—my sword again passing through his shoulder—and gripping my throat with his left hand, he bore me to the ground, and knelt upon my body. I was virtually disarmed, as my blade was still in his shoulder, and I saw him feeling in his bosom for the knife, which he at last drew out with his wounded hand. I mentally offered a brief prayer—for I thought my hour had come—when I heard the crack of a rifle, and my enemy rolled over on the grass.

I thought he was dead, as I sat there beside his body, trying to get back the breath he had nearly choked out of mine, but a convulsive twitching of his limbs showed me that he still lived. I then kneeled over him, and saw that the bullet had entered his right breast. There was not much blood issuing from the wound, though his right sleeve was red from the shoulder to the wrist. While I stood irresolute, trying to decide what ought to be done, I heard a horse splashing through the water at the ford. I ran out of the grove and met Doctor Markham as he rode up the bank.

"Oh, doctor! God must have sent you here!" I exclaimed. "Come quickly! there is a man dying here in the grove!"

"The deuce!" answered the doctor, "and what may be the nature of his disease, Burton?"

"Oh, come, doctor! he will bleed to death!"

"Bleed!" and the doctor dismounted and followed me—"why didn't you say he was hurt? Hitch my horse, please. Why it's Delaney, by all the gods!"

"Yes, sir, and I am afraid he is killed." The doctor opened his shirt bosom and looked at the wound; then he told me to get his saddle bags. When I got them he opened one end and took out a case of cruel looking instruments, and, selecting a probe, he passed it carefully into the wound. Delaney groaned.

"I am afraid you won't groan very long," said the doctor, rising. "Burton, we must get him to some house. It is too far to town. I wonder if we might take him to Harwood?"

"Is it too far to Maltby's?"

"Yes," answered the doctor, decidedly. "His only chance is to get him to some place with as little motion as possible. Jump on my horse and ride over to Harwood, and ask Ret if I may take him there; and if yes, bring four niggers back with you, with a door and a pillow."

"A door?"

"Yes; take some door off its hinges to carry him on. Have you lost what little sense you used to have? Be off!"

I picked up my sword, wiped the blade on the grass, and replaced it in the scabbard, and unfastening the doctor's horse, I galloped back to Harwood. When I arrived I rode up to the verandah and called Herbert out of the parlor.

"Send your sister here, dear Herbert. I want to see her alone, just a moment." She heard me, and came out as her brother retired, his eyes dilated somewhat beyond their usual dimensions.

"What has happened?" she said, pale and tremulous; "there is blood on your hands and face!"

"It is Denham's. I am afraid he is dying, or dead! Some one shot him near The Laurels, and Doctor Markham has sent me to tell you that his life depends upon prompt treatment, which can be given no place but here. He will die, Markham says, if we attempt to carry him to town or to Maltby's."

"What shall I say? Do you decide the question," she answered.

"He will die, anyhow, I believe. He is shot in the breast."

"Did you do it?" she asked, coming a step nearer and speaking in a lower tone.

"No, thank God! Yet he would have killed me in another minute. I was in his power, and his knife was almost at my throat. I will tell you hereafter. Herbert! Captain Delaney has been severely wounded down on the creek, and Dr. Markham thinks he had better be brought here. What do you say?"

"By all means—hey, Ret? You know uncle is his friend. We can put him in the spare room on this floor."

"Go back, then, cousin," said she—"take some men with you. Herbert, brother, go attend to it. I will have the room prepared."

Herbert got his horse, and we were soon on our way back to The Laurels with four stout negroes, who bore a stable door and a pillow. When we arrived we found Denham was conscious. The doctor had bound up the wounds on his arm, and was giving him water from the creek. He was placed carefully on the door, the pillow under his head, and Herbert started with his negroes, crossing the creek at the ford. I walked beside the doctor's horse as we followed them.

"Are you going to tell me what your share of this business is?" asked the doctor. "What did your bloody sword mean, and who has been making the holes in Delaney's arm, cutting two arteries, and doing other mischief?"

"I believe I gave him all the wounds except the shot, doctor," replied I. "He first insulted me very grossly, and then assaulted me. I met him by accident, and when he attacked me I was obliged to defend myself. I stabbed him in the arm on purpose, as I did not wish to kill him."

"If I had not arrived when I did he would have bled to death. You severed two arteries, one of them a large one. Who shot him?"

"I don't know. He had me down and was about to cut my throat when I heard the shot, and he tumbled over."

"What the deuce set you to quarrelling? I thought you were a peaceable young man."

"So I am. I tell you he swore at me, and at last attacked me with his sword. I was compelled to fight or run, and——"

"Well?"

"I had never learned to run."

"I cannot imagine where the bullet came from," said the doctor, after we had gone a half mile in silence. "It is out of reach—probably in the lung. The man will die, Burton, I think."

"The shot came from this side of the creek, doctor. No one could have seen us from any other quarter. Besides, I remember that I was lying with my head towards the stream, and he was kneeling on my breast. My sword was sticking in his right shoulder, and I could not draw it out, pinned as I was to the ground. I tried to get it out, as I wished to put it through his body, and I must have hurt him horribly in the effort."

"His shoulder is very much lacerated, and the artery is divided, I think," answered the doctor. "I could not decide positively without a more thorough examination. But the wound in the wrist is a dangerous one also."

"I had to give him that to get his sword from him. He fought like a devil, as he is. Why, sir, he did not make one thrust at me, except the last, that was not addressed to my jugular. I have been within half an inch of death twenty times this morning."

"You are not to blame, Burton," said Dr. Markham, after musing a little, "but here we are. The room is on the ground floor you say?"

CHAPTER XXIII.

BARNARD HARWOOD.

WE followed the negroes with their unconscious burden, and they entered a room from the verandah. It is built in an angle of the side wall of the house, and communicates with the main building through a side passage which separates the library from the breakfast room. The doctor directed the arrangement of the door, so that he could operate on both sides of it, and dismissing the negroes, who very willingly vanished when Markham opened his surgical case, he asked Herbert if he would like to assist him, while he looked for the ball. I know the boy is brave as a lion, but with white lips he begged to be excused. The doctor laughed and let him go.

"Now, Burton," he said, taking off his coat, and preparing coolly for his work of butchery. "I know *you* are not afraid to help me a little—hey?"

" If you want me, doctor," I answered—" my stomach feels a little weak, though—what shall I have to do ?"

" Take this saw and saw one of his legs off," and he handed me the murderous little instrument. " Come, don't be an ass now! Reflect, that we are trying to save this man's life, and that *he* will not suffer much, as he is nearly unconscious. I shall only require a few minutes. Take off your coat, and then cut his sleeve open without moving his arm. I want to get his shirt off." I took one of the knives from his case. " Not with that, you whelp! You are a beautiful operator to ruin the edge of your knives by cutting cloth with them ! Take your penknife."

While I was cutting away the shirt from Denham's arm and breast the doctor went on talking. He seemed to enjoy the prospect very much.

" I have been quite lucky to-day, Burton. I was called up at two o'clock this morning to pick half a dozen buckshot out of Becket's body. He was carrying his gun carelessly, like a fool as he is, and it went off and sprinkled his legs beautifully. One shot was within a hair's breadth of the femoral artery. He'll be laid up for a month. By-the-bye, I promised to ask Herbert to send his traps to him to the hotel. Please to remind me of it."

" Yes, sir. When did the accident happen to Becket ?"

" About one o'clock, I believe. Delaney came after me. They were preparing to go on a pan hunt, as they call it. Have you got the shirt off ? Now, help me to turn him gently on his left side."

Delaney groaned a little as we moved him.

" Now, Burton," said the doctor, " just hold him steady. I am going to find the bullet somewhere under the arm. You may shut your eyes if you don't like to see a little cutting done; but hold him still! I shan't be long."

He felt along the back with his fingers, then taking a keen little knife, he cut away as coolly as if he were whittling a stick. In a minute he had the ball in his hand.

" I thought I felt it," he said. " So! that part is done. Now we have to secure the brachial artery, and then we can put him to bed." He took the bandage off his shoulder, and in a few minutes more he had tied the artery. My sword had cut it in two.

" I tied this round stone up in my handkerchief, and made a sort of tourniquet out at the creek," observed the doctor. " He would have been dead in a few minutes. I have been uneasy ever since, fearing it would begin to spout again ; but he is safe enough now. All we want is a stitch or two ”

He revived a little as we laid him on the bed, and asked for water. I handed him a drink, giving it to him with a spoon. I began to feel as anxious to save him now as I had been to kill him a little while ago.

“ Where am I ?” he said.

“ Never mind,” answered the doctor. “ You are as well off as you can be. Keep quiet and we’ll try to get you well.”

He closed his eyes again, then opened them suddenly and looked at me earnestly and intently.

“ Is that Allen ?” he asked. “ I thought I killed him as well as John !”

“ Will you please to be quiet ?” said the doctor. “ Nobody wants to hear about your killing people, Captain Delaney.”

“ I’m not Captain Delaney ; I am Barnard Harwood,” said the wounded man.

“ He’s out of his head,” said the doctor, feeling his pulse. “ It looks bad to find his mind wandering in this way.”

“ Don’t be a fool, doctor,” said Delaney, quietly. “ I am not out of my head. Let that youngster stay here with me and I’ll be quiet.”

The doctor looked at me, and I nodded my head in acquiescence. I understood everything now. Markham got some medicines from his saddle bags and left me, directing me what to do if the patient became restless.

“ I am going to Manahio. Judge Carr is ill, the boy said. I was on my way there when you met me at the ford. Delaney need not die from his wounds, with careful nursing, but I think he *will* die, notwithstanding. It looks unpromising for him to be talking nonsense so early. He has no fever. I suppose he knew he was at Harwood, and has got to wandering in his mind.”

“ I don’t think he is wandering, doctor. His real name is Barnard Harwood, no doubt.”

All this was spoken in whispers on the verandah. Markham stared at me, as though he suspected me of some slight tendency to insanity.

“ I’ll tell you about it when I have opportunity, doctor. I think you ought to know that he is in his senses. I am perfectly certain that his name is Barnard Harwood. There are some family secrets that I have recently learned, and this is one of them.”

" Do you know what he meant by ' killing John,' then ? And do you know what he meant by calling you ' Allen ?'" The doctor thought this was what he calls " a stumper."

" Yes. My father's name was Allen, and I am said to resemble him in his young days."

" And this man knew him ? Oh, well, I'll ride over to Carr's now, and will return this way," and the doctor rode off.

When I went back into the room the wounded man had his eyes open, regarding me intently. .

"Come nearer," he said in a low tone. "You belong to my race, young gentleman. You are Allen's son ?"

"I am. But don't talk now, cousin. I will tell you all you wish to know when you are better. I thought you were Mark Denham. Try to go to sleep, and I will nurse you as carefully as I can. I won't talk to you now," I added, as he tried to speak. The doctor says you *must* be quiet. I will not leave you without your permission, and while you are weak and helpless you shall have all the kindness I can show to my nearest kinsman."

" I don't want to die until I can tell you some things that you ought to know," he murmured.

"You won't die, the doctor says, if you will only keep quiet and calm," and I pressed his hand. " Shall I read to you ?"

"Yes, Allen. Let me call you Allen. I know your name is Herbert."

" Very well, cousin. Now, what shall I read ?"

" Anything you please," and he closed his eyes again.

There was only one book in the room, and that was the best of books. I read from the Psalms, then from the Gospels, concluding with the wonderful story of the Prodigal Son. He was breathing quietly, and I thought he was asleep. I looked at the strong man, lying there in pain and weakness, and all my hatred for his person and character gave place to compassion and strong interest. He is my kinsman, and he may live to amend his life !

I stole quietly from the room, and walking round to the front verandah I found Ret and Herbert there. I put my arm through Herbert's, and walked with him near enough to his sister for her to hear our conversation.

"Herbert, my cousin, I am going to tell you a secret, which you must keep a little while. My name is the same as yours."

" Are you my real cousin ?" said he, astounded.

" Yes, I am Herbert Harwood, the son of your father's own cousin Allen !"

"Does Ret know? Oh, sister, ain't that jolly? But I'm not going to love you any better, because I can't, you know."

"Your sister will tell you how my name was changed. I am able to see now that it was a kind Providence that so ordered it. Do you so regard it, cousin Ret?"

"Yes, it is a case in which one is allowed to *see* that one's steps are directed by a higher Power. Many things have occurred which, perhaps, would not have happened if you had borne your true name at first. It is not probable that we should have known each other to-day."

"I have undertaken to nurse this wounded man, and the doctor says he may recover, if he is carefully watched."

"I have sent word to Mrs. Maltby that Captain Delaney is here, ill," she answered, "and I think she will probably come here this afternoon."

"He is not related to Mrs. Maltby——"

"I know; but he has always been intimate with the Maltbys, and he has no other friends in this parish. I thought I ought to send her word."

"You were right, cousin." Herbert had gone into the house. I fancy that he half expected Miss Lucy Maltby to drive over here with her mamma, and he went to change his dress.

"It is Barnard Harwood, cousin," I said, when we were alone. "He recognized me since the doctor extracted the ball. He calls me Allen." She was looking at me with astonishment. "He has done both of us much evil. I have forgiven him. Can you forgive him also?"

"I had forgiven him," she answered, "before you brought him here this morning. I had my struggle. Perhaps I have more to forgive than you think I have."

"What do you mean? Did you hear anything——"

"No. I won't tell you what I mean now. It is a mere suspicion. I have read those letters over and over again, until the various writers have become like people with whom I have daily intercourse; and I have unconsciously filled up the vacancies in the story with motives and actions, which may, after all, be the mere product of my own imagination. I think Barnard has been a wicked man all his life, but, for some reason that I do not fully comprehend, I have come to think that he is, perhaps, not so much to blame as would appear from the letters."

"Allen!" The voice came from Barnard's room. I hastened back to him. He was awake.

" I thought you said you would not leave me," he said crossly.

" I have only been on the gallery. What will you have ?"

" Water. More, more !" he said, impatiently, as I gave him a drink. " Can't you devise some better way than that ? I cannot abide a spoon !"

" The doctor says I must not lift your head up. He will be back presently."

" Will you tell me where I am ? The atmosphere of this house stifles me !" I did not answer him. I thought he would be more excited if he knew he was at Harwood. " How did you escape me ?" he resumed. " I thought I cut your throat."

" Some one shot you just in time to save me."

" Ha ! do you know who shot me ? It is here in the breast. Is the ball out ?"

" The ball is out. I don't know who shot you. Never mind now. I'll read to you again, shall I ?"

" Not at present. What did you read that old fable to me for ? Do you think I am fool enough to believe in forgiving fathers or in returning prodigals ? Fathers don't forgive, boy, nor do prodigals return !"

" Yes they do, cousin. I know they do !" replied I, gently.

" That is, priests have told you so. You should not say ' you know.' One of Allen Harwood's most prominent weaknesses was his strict adherence to the truth. When he said ' I know,' you might safely swear to the truth of his assertion."

" You are not strong enough to argue now," I answered; " when you get better I will have it out with you. I hear the doctor's voice."

The doctor came in, felt his pulse, glanced at the bandages, examined his eyes, and said he was " getting along."

" How long am I going to live, doctor ?" asked Barnard, quietly.

" Who said you were going to die ?" answered the doctor, roughly.

" *I* say so; I am not a girl; you need not be afraid of alarming me. I want to see Maltby."

" You are not going to see anybody for a few days, except one person to nurse you. Maltby may do that if you will keep quiet.

" I am going to nurse him, doctor. Please stop at the post-office and tell Mr. White."

" Why the devil can't you answer me," interrupted Barnard. " You know I shall have fever presently, and will probably die. I want to see Mr. Maltby half an hour while I keep my senses."

" He is coming," answered Markham. " I passed his carriage on the road. If you will not get excited you may see him a little while."

"Can't you prop me up a little ? I don't want to drink out of that damned spoon any longer. You might put two or three pillows under my shoulders and head."

" Very well; wait till Maltby comes. Do you feel any pain in your breast ?"

" Not a bit. I have no pain anywhere." He listened a moment and then added, " I hear wheels. Maltby is coming. Go get some paper and ink, Allen, and do you and the doctor take yourselves off when Maltby comes."

We got his head and shoulders a little elevated with Maltby's assistance, and then left them together. Dr. Markham and I walked out on the lawn.

" He is going to die, Burton !" said the doctor. " I thought this morning he might get over it. I wonder how old he is ?"

" Over fifty."

" He looks much younger. You might as well let him talk if he wants to talk. It won't make much difference."

" Is it the rifle shot that kills him, doctor ?" I asked, anxiously.

" Certainly. The wounds in his arm are nothing. They would get well in time. But his lung is torn to rags. He will die to-night or to-morrow. There are two or three fatal symptoms about him."

When we went into the house Ret said to me, " I have given orders to have Midnight ready for you whenever you wish to ride. Order her when you want her."

I thanked her with a look. Mrs. Maltby and Miss Latour were discussing the propriety of the latter lady's taking the vacant seat in her carriage and spending some days at Highlands. Lucille wished to go, but was doubtful about the propriety of leaving Miss Harwood. Ret settled the point by saying, in her decided manner, that " Lucille could drive over to Harwood daily to see her." The current impression seems to be that I found Delaney wounded on the Baton Rouge road and got the doctor to bind up his wounds, while I came here after the negroes to carry him. No one but Ret and the doctor knows anything about my fight. There is no reason why I should tell any one else.

" Mr. Maltby says," remarked his wife, " that Delaney has had a quarrel with somebody at the gambling room in town, and that they had a fight when they met on the road. All the men carry pistols, you know."

" I don't !" said Herbert, " and I never will, I think."

" Charley don't," said Ret.

" I don't, either," said I.

" Neither do I," said the doctor; " if I get maltreated I have no weapons but pills."

" If you carry those knives I saw on Captain Delancy's bed just now," said Herbert, " I think you are pretty well armed. They are a great deal worse than pistols. You've got a saw, too," he added, with a shudder. " I saw it !"

" You saw the saw !" said the doctor, laughing.

" Yes, *sir !*" answered Herbert, " and I don't want to *saw* it any more."

I went round to Barnard's room and found Maltby busy writing. I asked the sick man if I might ride to town and return in an hour.

" No !" he answered, decidedly; " to-morrow you can ride where you please; *I* want you to-day."

" Can you sign, Delancy ?" asked Maltby; " your hand is so bundled up——"

" I've got two hands," rejoined Barnard, " and I can write equally well with either. Let me see what you have written. Tell the doctor to come in again before he goes, boy. In five minutes."

In less time than he had specified Mr. Maltby came into the drawing room and sent the doctor and me to the patient. Markham felt his wrist and looked grave.

" Pooh, doctor !" said Barnard, coolly, " I don't want you to give me hope of recovery. You and I both know better. How long shall I be able to talk ? Give me a candid answer."

" From six to twelve hours," answered Markham. " I wish I could cure you."

" But you can't. Here, doctor," and he handed him a bank note, " please attend to that poor devil, Becket, and tell him I have paid his bill. It was my fault that he was hurt. Good-bye, doctor;" there was a momentary gleam of emotion on his smooth face as he spoke; " you have been kind, and I thank you."

" Would you like to see——any one ? I have a——friend in town—Mr. Hamilton—who will be too happy to come if you wish——"

"I thank you again, doctor, but my time is limited. · I don't wish to see any one to-day, except my nurse here." The doctor pressed his hand and went out of the sick room. "Go after him, Allen; I shall sleep a little, I think. Keep within reach of my voice."

An hour later they had all gone. Lucille went with Mrs. Maltby, after we had had luncheon in the breakfast room. Mrs. Maltby did not propose seeing the dying man after her arrival. There was a gloom upon us all, and I think it was a relief to Miss Latour and the Maltbys to get out of the neighbourhood. I was sitting in the library conversing in a low tone with my cousins when Barnard called me.

"Come, sit close to me," he said; "I want to talk to you while I can." His voice was slightly tremulous and his face haggard.

"Oh, cousin," and I knelt by his bedside and took his hand, "let me talk to you about the dread realities upon which you are entering!"

"Presently. Listen to me now. How much of my history do you know?"

"All of it—up to the time of your marriage and departure for America."

"I have but little to tell you, then. My wife and I embarked for Baltimore, but the vessel was driven out of her course by a long storm, and put into Pensacola. We were the only passengers. My Alice died in a few weeks after we landed, and she is buried in the cemetery at Pensacola. Lay me beside her—will you?"

"I will. Don't talk, if it distresses you."

"It does me good. Mark Denham and his son found me at Mobile five or six years ago. They were hunting your box which contains the Lacy diamonds. Denham had some information and I had more. Let me say here that my wife died in happy ignorance of everything but my idolatrous love for her. She thought my uncle gave me the money I had, and although she gave me much information about the lead covered box, she never suspected me of any ulterior designs. My uncle and his wife were accustomed to converse with perfect freedom in her presence, and it was from their conversation that she learned that the box was buried in a grove of three remarkable trees on the edge of John Harwood's estate. My visit to Baltimore was to find out the exact spot. If your father's papers revealed that, you baffled me, and I came back no wiser. It was then that Becket gave me the exact locality, though he did not know it. He had opened a drawer in this house and found a bundle of letters, and, stumbling on the right one, he read and remembered a memorandum referring to the box."

"On the hypothenuse of the angle, nine feet from its junction with the base," I said.

"Precisely. Go there to-morrow and get it. To resume: I did not rely entirely upon Becket, and determined to see the papers myself. It was only to get a bunch of keys and open a door. I have done more difficult things. But you thwarted me again. This morning I provided myself with the needful implements, and would have found the box, but you interfered the third and last time. You are a brave boy, Herbert! I have never been met as you met me to-day, except by your father and John Harwood. You have the rash courage of one and the calm self-reliance of the other.

"I must go back again now. Denham had got entangled in some visionary conspiracy, and, in spite of my cautions, he was caught and hanged—he and his son——"

"The Densons!" I said.

"Yes. He changed his name when he started on his insane crusade. There is some legend current about his threatening to haunt the grove. You will think I am unsettled in my intellect when I tell you that I *saw* something——Pshaw! it was some infernal delusion——"

"*I* was at The Laurels the other night, cousin, and the Indian, Misty. We saw you and Becket."

"You relieve me very much. I believe I was frightened, though the sensation was new to me. I have faced real dangers more than once in my life and have ever borne me as became a man of our race. But no matter. Go ask the girl if she will come now and hear how her father died!"

"I dare not!" I answered, shuddering.

"Repeat what I have said. If she shows the slightest sign of repugnance I shall not press it. But I have watched her in vain for three or four years if she does not come."

I found her alone in the library. When I delivered my message she rose at once, pale and calm, and followed me. I resumed my old position, kneeling by the side of his bed, and she stood near his pillow.

"Have you divined that I killed your father?" he said, looking into her calm and pitying eyes. She bowed her head without speaking.

"Hear how it was done. I am not a murderer. I think John suspected me from our first interview—or perhaps he had a hint from the Scotchman yonder—Gowrie—who knew me. He was cold and distant always when we met. Twenty years had changed us both in appearance, and he had not seen me since I was a mere boy. I had ridden from Baton Rouge one night, late, and was going to Maltby's. I went out of my way to look at those Laurels, and to see if they were haunted by anything worse than myself. There had been some foolish stories afloat—I think Carr was the author—and something had been seen there—I never could learn what—but everybody avoided the road after nightfall. I rode in among those trees and met John there. He had doubtless come on the same errand. In my surprise I called him by name, 'John!'—and he answered, 'Barnard!' I cannot remember all that passed. We had always quarrelled when we were young, and now he struck the last blow by referring to my dead wife as the partner in my infamy. I answered so as to exasperate him more and more, and when he was nearly beside himself with rage, I suddenly drew my pistol, and said, 'You are armed, so am I. Count ten aloud and fire!' Our pistols exploded together. The scar from his bullet is still on my neck. As he fell from his horse he said, 'God protect my children!' and all was over. Now girl, curse me before I die!"

"May God forgive you, cousin, as freely as I forgive you," she answered, as she knelt by me.

"So!" he paused a moment, then went on—"I rode directly back to Baton Rouge. I have heard John's dying words every night since that night; and I think if I had had a human heart I might have been softened a little. I did set myself to get from Carr the mortgage he holds on the Harwood estate, and I would have cheated him to gain it. I thought if I could burn that mortgage I should hear those words no more! If I had won it I should have given back to Carr all my other winnings from him. I tried to buy it from him, but he would never sell; and to-day I have directed Maltby to pay it—and to pay Carr everything else he has lost to me. I never cheated, and I was probably clumsy in my first attempt. He quit playing before I accomplished my design. And, children, I did not try to kill John. Even while he was counting, I changed my mind, and when he called out ' TEN !' my hand acted without my will. God knows—if there *is* a God —that I am innocent of the intention !"

A change, rapid and appalling, was stealing over his features.

"Oh, cousin," I said, eagerly, "do not doubt that there is a God —infinite, eternal and unchangeable in mercy. Oh, if you could feel as the poor sinner felt, of whom I read to you to-day—the man who went to the temple to pray——"

"Is that you, my Alice ?" he said, looking at Ret, "with sad and tearful eyes! Look, love, at this beautiful land! We will live here in peace, and I will try to find the religion you speak of. If it is made for sinners, surely I can meet the conditions! And you, Allen! fie, fie! what have men of our name to do with tears! Are you weeping for me, boy ? The Indian shot me! I saw him! It was just, for I shot him long ago. I was sorry when it was too late. Let him go free!" He closed his eyes a few minutes, and when he looked at me again the terrible expression had passed from his face, and he looked more like himself. "Say it again, boy," he murmured,—and the sweet voice of Ret answered :

"It is a faithful saying, and worthy of all acceptation, that Christ Jesus came into the world to save sinners, of whom I am chief !"

"It is Alice! No, it is my young cousin. Your tears are a comfort to me, children! What did you read, Herbert ? ' He saw him afar off!' God be merciful to me—THE sinner!"

He was dead !

Mr. Maltby came this afternoon, and has undertaken every-thing. I am going to start for Pensacola with the body to-mor-row. Since I have been here in my room writing the shadows have grown longer, and now the sun has gone. I have been the more sorrowful because I wounded him to-day—though my reason tells me that I could not do otherwise. But when I think of his arm, and the bandages upon it, my heart sinks and my eyes over-flow. I could bear all the rest! I have avoided the society of every one. Herbert was here an hour ago with a message from her. I sent him away, saying I would see her to-morrow. It has occupied me, and perhaps comforted me, to write all the after-noon. And now the sad story is all told.

CHAPTER XXIV.

A Year Later.

HARWOOD, *Sunday, August* 8, 1836.

IN an hour I am to begin my journey to Pensacola. All will be prepared, and I have only to hail the first boat for New Orleans, and get the coffin on board. Maltby has given me a well filled pocketbook, acting, as he says, under Barnard's instructions. I hope to be back in two or three weeks. Charley was here for a few minutes this morning; he did not dismount. His father is ill, and he hastened back to him. I have hardly exchanged words with my cousins to-day. They are going to Carrville, and there are other carriages gathering about the grounds to swell the funeral procession. I cannot get up the least excitement, in view of the trip to Florida, but am longing for the melancholy duty to be finished. Mr. Hamilton is here, and there will be religious services in the house. It is nearly time to begin them, and I must go down stairs. I leave my portfolio here until I return.

HARWOOD, *Monday, August* 30, 1836.

Since I got back from Florida I have been occupied with various matters, and this is the first night I have had access to my diary. To-morrow I once more start for my home, and probably shall go to Europe before I return to Carrville—if I ever return. I found a letter from Mr. Callahan here, on my arrival from Pensacola, in which he invited me to join him at once in New York. And I received a second letter to-day enclosing a note from Mr. Alfred Parchment of London, recommending me to go to that city without delay. There has been so great a change in my circumstances since I wrote the last record here that my whole life seems to be beginning anew. I will try to recount events in order.

In the cemetery at Pensacola I found Barnard's vault without difficulty. There was a single word carved on the marble front— "Alice." I caused his name "Barnard" to be added—and saw his body placed beside his wife's. One day was afterwards occupied in attending to some instructions of Maltby's regarding the sale of Barnard's property in the beautiful little city. It was at last given into the hands of Captain Delaney's lawyer—who has since remitted the proceeds to Maltby. He has paid the mortgage on Harwood, and has also paid Judge Carr's estate (the Judge died during my absence) a large sum of money, which my cousin said he owed Judge Carr. Herbert has received for himself and his sister fifty thousand dollars in stocks, bonds, and money—and I have inherited the remainder of Barnard's estate. Already Maltby has paid me one hundred thousand dollars in money, and he says there is valuable property still unsold in New Orleans and Mobile. Barnard's instructions were full and explicit, and, with the exceptions I have mentioned, all of my poor cousin's wealth is left to "his beloved cousin, Herbert Harwood, son of Allen Har-, wood, formerly of Harwood House, Essex." There has been no dispute about the will. Maltby is a lawyer, and has observed all requisite forms, and no one has appeared to contest it.

Three weeks ago to-day—that is, the day after I left here—Ret and Herbert drove down to The Laurels and dug up the box. It is now in the iron closet, and we are going to open it to-night. Barnard directed Maltby to give me his pocketbook after his death, and I found a memorandum in it which I will copy here and then destroy. It is as follows:

"Facts about the ———.

"Sir H. had determined to purchase for A. the plantation adjoining J. It is undoubtedly the one now owned by C., and separated from the other by the stream. A. declined, reason not known. Sir H. had brought the —— to this country to surprise A. with the gift, when he took possession of his plantation. There was some danger of robbery, as Sir H. had incautiously revealed the value of the —— to one or two suspicious characters. He therefore decided to bury it, instead of taking it back by way of the city. It is in a grove of remarkable trees. All these are facts, and no other facts are known."

Herbert says they took none of the servants with them, because they did not wish it known that anything so valuable was in the house. Herbert found the spade in the bushes, and the box was near the surface. When they reached the house, on their return, he carried it unobserved into the drawing room, and locked it in the closet. We three know its history, and no one besides.

I met in New Orleans an old acquaintance from Baltimore, who was in search of employment. He and Mr. Bayard are now in Carrville, unpacking the goods which have arrived. I have been aiding them for several days, though I have no longer any business connection with the establishment. The people received the intelligence of my good fortune and of my changed name with a great deal of interest. The belief is current that my name, Harwood, has been assumed under instructions in the will. My intimates know the truth, but they do not talk much about it, I suppose. Mr. Hamilton, who has been always kind and friendly, is more kind than ever. He has always some new question to ask me about my Mother and sisters. I think he listens most intently when I talk of Alice.

I must go down now and open the box. Oh, shall I ever spend another night at this house? I forgot to say that Carr's marriage is postponed on account of his father's death. He was here to-day, but went home shortly after dark. He looks melancholy, poor fellow. He and Ret had a long talk on the verandah, while I beat Herbert two games of chess. Miss Latour has gone home. Not one word has been spoken about the marriage by any of us. Mr. Hamilton told me of the postponement.

MIDNIGHT.

We have opened the box and examined the contents. The certificate of the Wheal Pentland stock is now in my pocketbook. It is transferable only on the books of the corporation, by Allen Harwood, gentleman, his heirs, administrators, executors or assigns. The probable amount of money it may represent does not appear so enormous to me now as it did a month ago. The coins, about two hundred, are mostly gold and silver, and none of us have ever seen any like them. There is a sort of pedigree of several of them—fully fifty, I suppose—in a little manuscript volume we found in the box. I hardly know what to say about the diamonds. There are several other brilliant jewels, emeralds, rubies, and amethysts, but the diamonds are in a separate box, and the name "Lacy" is on the cover, both inside and out. There are finger rings, earrings and bracelets, and one brooch and one necklace. It is the last mentioned that is the most magnificent. I have not the slightest idea of the value of these jewels, and Ret, who is a better judge, said her estimate would sound fabulous, and that she would not name it. There is an inventory of jewels and coins, but no value set down. Most of the coins are marked "unique" on the schedule. By-the-bye, the inventory professes to be a "list of the Lacy coins;" and then a "list of the Lacy minor jewels," and finally, a "list of the Lacy diamonds." As we sat there, looking at the blazing gems, I thought how poor and contemptible they were in comparison with one kind glance from her calm eyes. I am glad that I am going away. I cannot endure her presence any longer. When she looks at me I feel my heart bound, and the blood rushing to my face. She seems to know all that I think; and once or twice to-night I caught her looking composedly at me, while I was allowing my foolish imagination to picture a future, in which she reigned queen of my life; and each time the conviction flashed upon me that she knew my thoughts.

Who were the Lacys, I wonder?

On the night that Barnard died the Indian was here. He left the panther skin with Herbert, who saw him, saying it belonged to "young chief Hubbard." Since that night he has never been seen. His wigwam is empty, and the Indian has gone—somewhere. Mr. Maltby says he is a Seminole, and no doubt has returned to Florida, to join the tribes now in arms against the whites. If I could feel that it was an entirely just warfare waged against these savages, I think I should volunteer; but there may be some fighting to be done in Texas, and I have a longing for the wild, rough life of a frontier soldier, and very little shrinking from the possible fate of such a warrior. If it were not for Mother and my sisters, I might——

But I will not indulge these thoughts. I am going to walk into town early. They made different arrangements down stairs; but I will have no leave-taking. I have written on a card "good-bye, dear cousins;" and I shall leave it on my portfolio, in which I once more lock up this melancholy diary. When shall I open it again?

HARWOOD, MONDAY, *August* 31, 1837.

A whole year ago! I have returned in the nick of time. Charley is to be married to-morrow! I thought it would have been all over, or I should have delayed my arrival.

I have brought back with me a pair of magnificent whiskers. They were in embryo when I left America last September; they have matured in Italy, and Greece, and Egypt. Many days have I lingered in many a famous capital. I also imported an entirely new manner. I have acquired from observation and long practice that charming air of indifference, and indolence, and superiority which distinguishes travelled men. Alas! I have not had

13

the opportunity to display this last acquirement. Old memories haunt me in this locality; and if I were boy enough to turn back a leaf or two I should lose my manhood, as I recalled the events I last recorded. *Allons!*

When I reached Baltimore, a year ago, I learned that Mr. Callahan had been there to see my Mother; and he had taken certain depositions from her and others; got various certificates from the British Consul; and left a message for me, instructing me to get my Mother's marriage certificate, and a certified copy of the registers of my birth and the birth of Alice and Grace, and to present myself with these documents at his office in New York as soon as possible. I complied with all these instructions, and two days after my arrival in New York I sailed for Liverpool. I might say a great deal about the voyage—the people I met on shipboard and in England—but I don't feel in the mood to-night. Hereafter, I may think it worth my while to recount some of my adventures. I went to London; found Mr. Alfred Parchment, and was escorted by that gentleman to Lavington, Lord Morton's residence in Devonshire. Here I found my only surviving English kinsmen, namely, Lord Morton, and Sir Allen Harwood, my father's first cousin. His brother, Sir Charles, had died before he attained his majority. These gentlemen received me with cordial kindness, and my entire European life was spent in their society. It was at the instance of Allen, my beloved cousin, that Mr. Parchment had written for me. In a day we were "Allen" and "Herbert," and while he lived, the intercourse between us two was peculiarly close and intimate. I told him all my dearest secrets; and I believe he opened his whole heart freely to me. His health was then very much impaired, and his physicians had ordered him to the south of France for the winter. Lord Morton was to accompany him, and it required very little persuasion to induce me to join their party. Before we left England the formal transfer of the Wheal Pentland stock was made to me, and as Lord Morton vehemently opposed the sale of it, I still own it. I intend to pay my Mother and sisters their proportion of its value, according to their inheritance under American law; or I will transfer their proportion of the stock itself, whichever they may prefer. I had no trouble whatever in the business. Mr. Parchment had charge of Lord Morton's legal business, as well as Sir Allen's; and as Mr. Callahan had obtained all the certificates that were requisite, under Mr. Parchment's instructions, the matter was speedily settled.

On the banks of the beautiful Garonne, Lord Morton found a chateau, occupied only by an old housekeeper, and we spent the winter there. Allen talked to me about his boyish days; his college life; his early friends; his sickly brother, who was so kind and loving always; and, finally, one glorious night, when the moon was bright in a cloudless sky, he told me about his love—Mary Lacy. "You seem like a dear brother, Herbert," he said, "and I am telling you what no mortal has heard before." During his school-days, he spent his vacations at Lavington, with his guardian, and he met her there while they were mere children. Then in later years he encountered her in London society, when she was in her first season. Then he learned that she was going to marry his friend and her brother's friend, and the rest of his short life was spent in rooting out the affection that had brightened that life from his boyhood. He told me his story like a man, and spoke hopefully of a time to come when he might love her without sin. She was a happy wife now, and never knew the throne she occupied in his heart. Then I told him of Ret, and the brave gentleman, who had laid bare his wounds to me with calm courage, was overcome by the recital of my sorrows. "It is a luxury to sympathize with you, Herbert, because you are healthy and strong, and will have to endure through life what I shall soon escape. You don't know how thankful I felt when the doctor said the climate here *might* do me good, as I understood him to mean that he had no such expectation."

We went to Italy in the early spring; then to the Nile, and spent the summer—or the most of it—in Greece. He came home a month ago, to die. "*Che sará, sará.*"

I wrote to Mother from Paris, saying that I would go home by way of New Orleans. I wanted to look once more into those dark eyes, so calm and quiet; but *I* have seen them flashing with girlish merriment; I have seen them kindle at the recital of some heroic deed, and I have seen them sparkling in teardrops. And, now, that I have seen her, I am disappointed. She is not sad any longer; she is not gay, but she is quietly happy—brimfull, running over with happiness. Oh, Ret! what a dog I would be if I could wish you otherwise!

When I landed this morning, I got a horse and rode out here, like a crazy man. I had only time to remember that I must be on my good behaviour, when I walked into the house. I saw a white dress, then the wearer of it rushed upon me, with an embrace and a little hysterical scream, half laugh and half sob. It was Grace! then Alice, and then my Mother! No ordinary man could maintain his gravity under such circumstances. My good behaviour was forgotten in my bewilderment, while half a dozen were kissing me and pulling me to pieces among them. Herbert's salutation was characteristic. First he hugged me, then he stood off a yard surveying me, and then the scoundrel said—

"Oh, golly! just look at his whiskers, Ret! Ain't they prime?"

He is a very trying young man to encounter, when one is endeavouring to maintain one's self-possession. I gave up at once, and behaved naturally all the evening.

Ret looks so superlatively happy. She and Lucille have had an overwhelming quantity of private business to transact. I have seen her only by snatches all day. Mother and the girls are also in full feather. They seem to have some terrible secret among them, which they are keeping from me. They are here, in answer to an invitation from Ret, which Mother says "she could not withstand." I wrote to Herbert two or three months ago, telling him that I would come to Louisiana first, and Ret wrote upon that text. Mother received my letter, announcing the same intention, a day or two after Ret's invitation reached her, and she answered the letter in person. I evaded her twice to-day, when she had nearly cornered me for a talk; but she followed me into my room to-night, and putting her arms round my neck, she whispered—

"Do you still love Ret, Herbert?"

"Yes, Mother."

"She is a lovely woman, my son!" I did not answer, and she handed me a box, marked "Lacy." "Here are your diamonds, Herbert."

"They are yours, Mother. I never dreamed——"

"Well, I give them to you. They are yours now."

"I can't wear necklaces and bracelets, Mother, and you surely don't want me to sell them?"

"Do what you like with them, Herbert. Good night, my dear boy," and so she left me.

I thought I would give them to Alice and Grace, but I have changed my mind. Wait until to-morrow.

Tuesday, September 1, 1837.

How much gratitude is due to God for creating so beautiful a world! I have been blind hitherto! I have looked with transient admiration upon lovely scenes in both hemispheres, but never until to-day have I seen the marvellous beauty of the earth. I have just come in from a ramble in the woods, all the way to The Laurels, and have brought back with me a handful of wild flowers, mostly inodorous, but surpassingly lovely. I must arrange them presently and take them to——.

I had come to a definite conclusion about the diamonds this morning, and, after breakfast, I went into the library with them to wait for an opportunity. I read a book—read like a man stuffing for an examination—but I don't know what book it was. At last I saw her passing through the little hall, and I called her.

"Ret, cousin, please come here a moment."

"Please don't keep me long," she answered, as she came in. "I have *so* many things to do."

"I know you have. Here, sit down. I want to ask a great favour of you," and I shut the door. She looked surprised, blushed, and then grew pale as I produced the jewel case.

"I want you to accept these and to wear them to-day."

"I won't!" she answered, and she moved towards the door. I slipped round the table, and backed up against the door.

"You don't get out, madam, until you explain yourself," I said, decidedly. "Pray why won't you take the diamonds?"

"They belong to cousin Alice. What right have you to dispose of her property?"

"She gave them to me last night. Find some other reason."

"It would be indecorous to receive a present of such value."

"Oh, Ret, I am going away soon. I am going back to England, and I want to leave these with you. Don't talk about values. I do not consider them worth one kind look from you."

"When are you going?" and again the blood was in her cheeks and forehead.

"Soon. To-morrow, maybe. Will you take them?" and I held the box out to her. "I want you to wear them to-day——"

"I cannot. It would be highly indecorous. It would be insulting to Lucille! I'm ashamed of you!" and her eyes were sparkling and her face burning.

"Will you please explain why?" I asked, in wonder.

"Yes, if you will let me out," she answered, desperately. I moved away from the door, and she said with great composure:

"Because the bridesmaid should not wear diamonds when the bride has none to wear. It would be in horrid taste, to say the least."

"The bridesmaid! Oh, Ret! go now if you dare! Do you mean to tell me it is Lucille who will be married to-day?"

" Yes, I believe she has some such intention."

"And you knew that I thought—— Come back here!" and I stamped my foot violently. "I swear that I will set the house on fire if you leave me!"

She came back trembling, half laughing and half crying.

" Cousin Alice told me the other day that you had fallen into a mistake. You never asked *me.* How could I know?" I had her in my arms then, and her face was hidden on my breast.

"What must I say to you, Ret, my beloved? You know all I wish to say. It will take a lifetime to tell you how I love you."

"I know. You need not say anything. You *have* been telling me a year and a half!" She extricated herself from my arms and sat down on the sofa, motioning me to a seat beside her.

"Ah, Ret!" I answered, " I have spent all these dreary months in trying to hide my love from you! How could I tell you?"

"Do you remember the day you saved Herbert? Do you remember how you held my hand, and how you said with your eyes, with your hand, with every tone of your voice, 'I love you! I love you! I love you!' Oh, my darling, I have been happier since that day than ever before, since my father died! Do you remember when I gave you the letters, in the drawing room yonder, and how you flamed with rage when I said the Baltimore Harwoods were false? Then I knew you were my cousin, and I thought you were Barnard's son, and I thought I must never marry Barnard's son, because my father's letter, leaving me free in all else, forbade all intercourse with that unhappy man and his family. And then"—and the tears filled her gentle eyes—"and then I tried to find excuses for Barnard, and I thought I saw the possibility of some other explanation of his dark story; and when I learned your true relationship—do you remember? it was on the 6th of August last year!—oh, happy day!——" And once more she hid her eyes upon my breast.

" Ret, have you been loving me all this time? And oh, cruel! keeping me in ignorance when you knew I was dying for a word or a look——"

"You foolish boy, I have been telling you all the time! Be quiet, sir! or I'll run away. Everybody else knew it—Charley, Lucille, cousin Alice, your sisters. Why, the first words your Mother said, when she kissed me, were, 'My daughter!'——"

"Oh, I'll be in a towering rage presently," I said. "I am too happy now. How could I be such a mole? I have avoided you! stayed in Europe, trying to kill my love by absence——"

"I don't think you have avoided me much, sir!" said she, maliciously. "I don't believe you stayed an hour longer in Europe than was necessary. I think you came to New Orleans instead of New York, you undutiful boy! to see *me* before you saw your Mother. I think you have been with me every minute when you were not obliged to be elsewhere. Oh, such work as I have had with Charley and your dear Mother, to keep them quiet!——"

"How *could* you torture me, Ret?——"

"Come, sir, you have only been here a day, and the torture did not last very long. Did you wish me to run up to you and say, 'Please to marry me, sir!'"

"I have a great mind to vow that I'll never marry you until you ask me."

"Try it! How dare you! you great rude monster! Let me go! I'll tell your Mother!" and she tore from me, pausing a moment at the door to throw me one loving look, and then, covering her glowing face with white hands, sped away.

WEDNESDAY, *September* 2, 1837.

It seems to me that I am nearly done with journal writing. Indeed, I do not know any sort of writing that will express my present emotions. How can I write coherently, while Ret sits there, only a few yards from me? She pretends to be engrossed in a whispered dialogue with Mother. I wish I could make a picture of those two! My Mother is seated in the great armchair, and my Ret is on a lower seat at her knee, and Mother's slender fingers are tangling Ret's brown curls. I am jealous of both of them by this light! They love each other more than——. Ret shot a sly look at me and stopped that atrocious slander. My love! my love!

The wedding was a great success last night. There were forty dashing beaux here. Some from the neighbourhood, sons of planters, one or two from New Orleans, quondam admirers of the bride, no doubt. Several from Baton Rouge, army officers and embryo lawyers. Unfortunately, the first bridesmaid, Miss Harwood, did not dance, but she was kind enough to play for the dancers, and I, who was too bashful to dance, turned over the music for her. Probably some of the beaux thought I was a regular muff, and probably they were right in their judgment. It was midnight before they were all gone. Charley and his bride went to his home in the state carriage—followed by a cavalcade of squires and dames, returning to their domiciles. Mr. Maltby's carriage took his family and the city gentlemen; and my Mother and sisters, Mr. Hamilton, the doctor and I, were the only guests who remained at Harwood. We spent a quiet hour before we separated for the night in the lovely moonlight, on the broad verandah. Somehow, we fell into couples—Alice and Mr. Hamilton, Grace and the doctor, while Mother and Herbert courted each other with unblushing effrontery. Ret and I had several small dialogues—about five seconds long. She was intent on hospitable cares, and took fiendish delight in tantalizing me by flying off to attend to some needful household duty a dozen times in the hour. But to-day I have had a glorious time. Mother wanted to see The Laurels, and, escorted by Herbert, she riding Midnight, while he bestrode Dick, his rascally pony—they went. Ret and I walked. It is only a mile or two, and the morning was charming. The girls had letters to write to Baltimore friends, and we four formed the party. We stayed an hour in the shade of the famous trees, Herbert recounting the story of the bathing adventure, when he was "drownded," to eager listeners, and I was forced to fight my terrible duel over again in detail. They would not relinquish a solitary word, and kept me longer in telling the story than the time occupied in the combat. They imperiously demanded each phase of my changing emotions from slight anger to cool ferocity in the concluding passages.

On the return journey the equestrians soon distanced us, and we lingered a little to admire the lovely glimpses of the bright stream as it came into view through the glades of the forest. And the darling tyrant steadfastly persisted in her inquisition until I had told her all my thoughts on that terrible midnight, when I walked out to the haunted grove alone. She seemed to gloat over the recital of my misery, though she clutched my arm, and looked at me with tearful eyes, while her face was bright with smiles. In turn I propounded sundry questions, and will now proceed to note down the substance of her replies. Much that has been mysterious in the past record is cleared up by the dialogue that enlivened that lovely walk.

The "engagement" betwixt Charley and Ret was a veritable engagement, in so far as the tacit agreement of all parties interested was concerned. Both of them had been taught from early childhood that they should be man and wife when they were of age. There had not been much talk betwixt them on the subject, as Ret instinctively avoided it, and Charley was not a very eager wooer. After I appeared upon the scene, and especially after Herbert's rescue and our subsequent intercourse (while Charley was in New Orleans), she dismissed forever all idea of fulfilling this *quasi* engagement. When he returned I was on my way to Baltimore, and the dear girl says I took her heart with me. She was certain that I was the son of her father's life-long enemy, and many sorrowful days were spent in the struggle between her old devotion to her father and her new affection for me. But she quietly gave Carr to understand that there would be no marriage. He expostulated a little- and then yielded, confessing that he did not love her as he ought to love his wife, but certainly, as a dear sister, whom he had known familiarly from infancy. Curiously enough he did not ask her any questions about her own affections, but readily promised to say nothing about the sundering of the old compact. " Charley was very useful," she said, " in keeping other young gentlemen away." But he had met Lucille while in New Orleans, and as soon as it was settled that he was free from the old tie, he began to discover that he did like Miss Latour amazingly. Accordingly another trip to New Orleans soon after my departure brought matters to a crisis, and Ret moved to Harwood to play hostess to Charley's *fiancée*. When I returned, and Carr announced his approaching marriage, it was nothing but my repugnance to talk upon the subject prevented a full explanation twenty times a day. The truth is, Charley was snubbed whenever he approached the topic, and at last Ret discovered that I was in unblissful ignorance of the true condition of affairs, and supposing the truth would inevitably be revealed almost immediately, she rather enjoyed my discomfort. Then events crowded rapidly upon us. The attempt to rob, and then the conflict at The Laurels, then Barnard's death, and my departure to Pensacola. When I returned I found many changes had occurred. Mr. Carr was dead, the marriage postponed, Lucille gone, and I was summoned to New York and thence to Europe. I wrote regularly to Herbert and sometimes to Carr, but never asked a question about his marriage. Indeed, I *could not.* I received only two letters from Charley, and he imitated me in avoiding that subject. Herbert's letters were carefully examined by Miss Ret, and therefore

I was not enlightened by him. "I could not endure the thought," she says, "that any one else should tell you. I had not decided how to tell you, when you called me yesterday into the library, but I knew the time had come *then !*"

"If it had not been for the diamonds, Ret——"

"I knew all about the diamonds. Cousin Alice told me the night before. Indeed, she made me promise to tell you at the first opportunity, saying she would not allow her boy to be kept in misery any longer. She says I am a 'hardened wretch !'"

"Mother always tells the truth, Ret."

"Does she? She has told me many things about you, sir! I know the larger part of your history, up to your arrival in Carrville, and now I mean to know the rest! I want that journal, sir !"

"You shall have it when you take me! Oh, Ret! consider how long I have waited for you! I can't live another week without you——"

"You are certainly stark crazy! I don't intend to think of matrimony for ever so long——"

"Let us make a bargain, Ret," I said, desperately. "Will you let Mother fix the day? I promise to say nothing if you will promise to be guided by her. Is it a compact?"

"I don't know—I'll see about it—there's the house, so behave circumspectly, sir."

"Ret," I said, stopping suddenly, "if you don't promise to settle this point this very day I will burn the journal before I sleep !"

"What a cold-blooded tyrant! Come on, sir. I will promise to talk to her if she asks me."

And they are talking about it this blessed minute. I can tell by Ret's shy glances and by Mother's happy face.

Ret has suddenly demanded this book. She stands here by my side while I trace these final lines. Shall I ever be allowed to see it again? I cannot refuse to give——

HARWOOD, Christmas, 1837.

By special favour I have the privilege of writing a little more in this journal. For one solid month I have been the merest slave. I no longer have liberties, preferences, opinions or property. On Thursday, November 26th, I was taken into legal custody by a remorseless female tyrant, who has never ceased to domineer over and hector me since that day. She sits just opposite to me now in this dear library. Everybody else has gone to Manahio, and we are to follow presently. We are to dine with Carr to-day. Maltby, wife and daughter, Mr. Hamilton and Doctor Markham are in the party. On this day week we are to have them all here —Herbert doing the honours. Ret and I are guests of Mr. Herbert Harwood, and we have an invitation to "stay here and live all over the house for forty years." I have engaged to kill two wild turkeys, and Carr has promised another deer. We killed one two days ago. I am now the ostensible owner of Midnight— with an encumbrance. Ret wore the diamonds a month ago, and she has locked them up since, vowing that she will wear them no' more. There are other articles that once belonged to me which she wears—— There! she says I must stop "scribbling," give her back "her" book, and get ready to start. To hear is to obey!

NEW YEAR'S DAY, 1838.

I shall have a quiet hour or two. Ret is superintending the cooking arrangements and I got her keys and have stolen my diary. I am writing in her room and am tolerably safe from interruption. My darling says I write such "horrid nonsense" that she is not willing to trust "her book" in my hands. Oh, how happy I am! But I have promised to write nothing "horrid" this time.

There was a rich scene in the library this morning. Dr. Markham called early, pretending he had patients in the neighbourhood; but he came to see Grace. I was in the breakfast room and Grace was in the library. The doors were open and I heard what I now relate. I must say, by way of preface, that Markham has been extremely attentive to my little sister, and that she evidently admires him. He went into the library, hunting for her, and did not observe me as he passed the door.

"Good morning, Miss Grace," said the medico.

"Good morning, doctor. Take a seat; I have just been reading about you."

"About me! I did not know my fame was so extended. Do you mean in that big book?"

"Yes. Sit down and I'll read it to you."

"Hey? I don't know. Is it long?"

"I shan't read it now, sir!" and I heard the book slap as she closed it; "it is a beautiful day."

"Yes; rather. But you've no business with those thin shoes on! Have you been out?"

"Certainly. Alice and I walked a mile at least this morning."

"In those shoes?"

"Not both of us. She had her own shoes," answered Grace.

"Humph! you have been taking lessons from Burton! Well, read the book."

"You will have to ask a little more politely, and also to manifest a little more anxiety to hear it first."

"Hey?" and the doctor meditated. "Well," he said at length, "tell me what you want me to say and I'll say it."

I heard Grace turning over the leaves and presently she began to read: "The country people use kitchen physic, and common experience tells us they live freest from all manner of infirmities that make least use of apothecaries' physic. Many are overthrown by preposterous use of it, and thereby get their bane, that might otherwise have escaped. Some think physicians kill as many as they save, and who can tell ('Here's some Latin,' said Grace, in parenthesis, 'and I am afraid to try to read that; besides, I don't know what it means') how many murders they make in a year (more Latin), that may freely kill folks and have a reward for it? and according to the Dutch proverb—a new physician must have a new churchyard; and who observes it not?" Here Grace went off into a violent fit of laughing.

"What the dev—— I mean, what book are you reading, Miss Grace?"

"Wait, wait!" she answered, "there's more of it, and it gets better and better." She resumed: "Many that did ill under physicians' hands have happily escaped when they have been given over by them—left to God, and nature, and themselves. 'Twas Pliny's dilemma of old: every disease is either curable or incurable. A man recovers of it or is killed by it; both ways, physic is to be rejected." Another long laugh, in which the doctor joined. Then Grace went on: "If it be deadly it cannot be cured; if it may be helped it requires no physician—Nature will expel it of itself. Plato made it a great sign of an intemperate and corrupt commonwealth where lawyers and physicians did abound; and the Romans detested them so much that they were often banished out of their city, as Pliny and Celsus relate—for 600 years not admitted. It is no art at all, as some hold, no, not worthy the name of a liberal science (nor law neither), as Pet. And. Canonherius, a patrician of Rome and a great doctor himself, proves by sixteen arguments, because it is mercenary as now used—base, and, as fiddlers play, for a reward."

"Oh, doctor," said Grace, "it is prime! as cousin Herbert says—it is positively jolly!"

"What book is that?" said the doctor. "Burton, by all the gods! I thought so! Where did you get this book, Miss Grace?"

"It is my brother's," she answered.

"Did he select this delectable passage for you?"

"Oh, no; I stumbled on it by accident just before you came."

"Young ladies have a wonderful faculty for stumbling upon forbidden fruit. However, there is a great deal of truth in it. Old Burton don't make many mistakes. Do you like to read him?"

"Not much. There is so much Latin, and besides, he is so prosy."

"I suppose you prefer the stuff you call poetry?" said the doctor.

"Poetry is not 'stuff,' sir—at least it is not so bad as 'doctor's stuff,' according to Burton. He says a little lower down that the——old gentleman was the first inventor of physic."

"If I was not so old," said the doctor, deliberately, "I should——"

"Old!" interrupted Grace.

"Well, I mean if you were not so young——"

"Young! I'm nineteen!"

"The d—euce you are! Hey! I was going to say I should like to ask you if I might fall in love with you? But it would be a horrid shame to ask so charming a young lady to marry an old devil of a doctor. There! you need not run. I'm not going to say another word. I am going to dine here to-day, ain't I? Well, I must go see Carr's sick negro. Good bye, Miss Burton!"

"Don't call me Miss Burton, if you please."

"Hey? I should like to call you Mrs. Markham. There! I am going! Suppose I were to brush my hair nice and smooth and let my whiskers grow?"

"Do go, doctor. Your patient will die—*felo de se* instead of *felo de medico*."

"I thought you did not know Latin? Grace, I am in earnest; would you think me insane if I——"

"There, doctor, you have carried this joke far enough," said Grace.

"Joke! I tell you I love you, you little vixen!" and here I

sneaked out of the breakfast room, as the business appeared to be growing serious.

The mail has just arrived. My lady has brought me a letter with the London post mark. It is addressed to " Sir Herbert Harwood, Bart," and is from Mr. Parchment. It contains but a few lines, informing me of the removal of all technical obstacles, and inviting me to " take possession of my estate in Essex."

*   *   *   *   *   *   *

HARWOOD HOUSE, ESSEX, *November 26,* 1847.

My lady gave me my old book to-day, which has but one blank leaf left. She must know it by heart, as I have caught her reading it many times in the past ten years. What can I say on this final page? My darling will have it back when I complete the record, and she has forbidden me to write anything about her. But I have nothing else to write about and I have no thoughts in which she has not a place—my Ret!

I erred in the above statement. I have four things to write about, to wit: John Harwood, aged eight, a young rascal of fiery impulses and tender heart. Herbert, aged six, who promises to be gentle and good, exhibiting a certain calm determination in surmounting difficulties. Allen, my baby boy, claiming the allegiance of my household, although manifesting no " moral qualities" to mention.

But the fourth—— I have kept the best for the last. She stands here at my knee, tugging at my watch chain. Imperious and wilful, with three years' experience of life, and thirty years of wisdom in her clear, calm eyes. Her mother's eyes! and her name is Ret. Not Henrietta, but RET! There is no name like that!